Praise for *Shadows of Ladenbrooke Manor*

"*Shadows of Ladenbrooke Manor* by Melanie Dobson is a beautiful and touching novel filled with family drama, mystery, and romance. You'll be swept away to the English countryside as you follow the interwoven stories of three women in one family who discover the healing power of love and forgiveness. Engaging from beginning to end!"

—Carrie Turansky, award-winning author of *The Daughter of Highland Hall* and *A Refuge at Highland Hall*

"An old, cherished house is like the human heart: we keep treasures safely tucked within—some conquests we proudly display; some treasures we put behind glass; and some secrets we hide from sight, our own and others'. In *Shadows of Ladenbrook Manor*, Ms. Dobson skillfully plaits the complex strands of life: golden and dark, truth and deception, love and loss into an engaging, multigenerational story of heartache and ultimate, unexpected redemption. Any reader might both lose and find herself between the covers of this compelling novel."

—Sandra Byrd, author of *Mist of Midnight*

"Melanie Dobson's new book skillfully weaves together past and present as she takes the reader on a fascinating journey to a shocking secret held for generations. A book about choices, consequences, and ultimately redemption, this beautiful story highlights the love of family, and the sacrifices we make and secrets we keep for better or for worse."

—Jennifer Shaw, Telly Award–winning speaker, author, songwriter, and fivetime Top 40 Billboard artist

SHADOWS *of* LADENBROOKE MANOR

A Novel

MELANIE DOBSON

HOWARD BOOKS
An Imprint of Simon & Schuster, Inc.
New York Nashville London Toronto Sydney New Delhi

Howard Books
An Imprint of Simon & Schuster, Inc.
1230 Avenue of the Americas
New York, NY 10020

This book is a work of fiction. Any references to historical events, real people, or real places are used fictitiously. Other names, characters, places, and events are products of the author's imagination, and any resemblance to actual events or places or persons, living or dead, is entirely coincidental.

First Howard Books trade paperback edition June 2015

Interior design by Davina Mock-Maniscalco
Interior map by Jeffrey Ward

Manufactured in the United States of America

10 9 8 7 6 5 4 3 2 1

Library of Congress Cataloging-in-Publication Data

Dobson, Melanie B.
Shadows of Ladenbrooke Manor / Melanie Dobson.—First Howard Books trade paperback edition.
pages; cm
1. Family secrets—Fiction.
2. England—Fiction. I. Title.
PS3604.O25S53 2015
813'.6—dc23
201403968

ISBN 978-1-4767-4614-2
ISBN 978-1-4767-4615-9 (ebook)

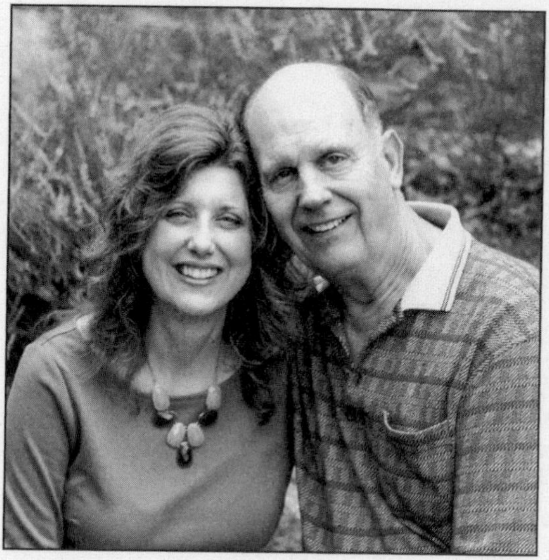

JODI STILP PHOTOGRAPHY

For James Beroth

My Dad

THE COTSWOLDS *and* ENVIRONS

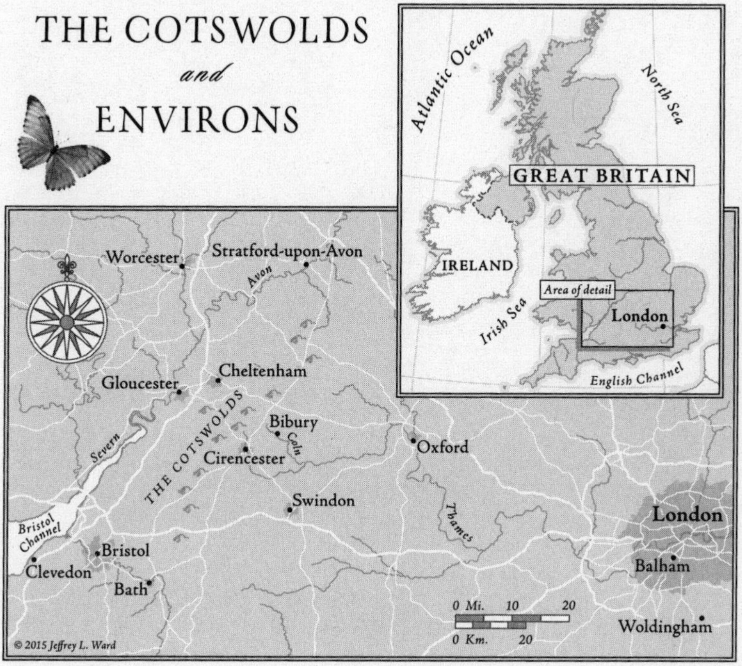
Atlantic Ocean
North Sea
GREAT BRITAIN
IRELAND
Irish Sea
Area of detail
London
English Channel
Worcester
Stratford-upon-Avon
Avon
Cheltenham
Gloucester
THE COTSWOLDS
Bibury
Coln
Severn
Cirencester
Oxford
Swindon
Thames
Bristol Channel
Bristol
Clevedon
Bath
London
Balham
Woldingham
0 Mi. 10 20
0 Km. 20
© 2015 Jeffrey L. Ward

Libby's Book of Butterflies

Autumn Dancer flutters among the flowers, chasing the last rays of sunlight until her haven is swallowed up by the night. Her sisters are asleep now, hidden under the fronds, but she doesn't care. She dances alone in the twilight, embracing the warmth of the golden hour, her wings sweeping past silky petals of the late summer blooms. In the safe cocoon of her garden, she dares believe that no harm will ever enter the gates. This is her world of beauty and peace, of sweet nectar and life, completely unspoiled by the footsteps of danger or the silent mockery of time.

PART ONE

The papers liked to call it "the storm of the century." It blew into England sixty years ago, the winter of '54, but I remember it like it was yesterday. The overturned boats. Wooden shutters smashing glass. The collapse of the pavilion on the pier.

The gale swept up the Bristol Channel that night like a band of pirates ready to pillage our little town. Brackish water poured over the promenade, stealing bits and pieces from the streets of Clevedon and sweeping it back out to bury in the depths of the sea.

I didn't know it that day, but the winter storm of '54 was the storm of the century in my life as well. Or at least it will be if I live another fifteen years.

Much later I discovered that a tidal wave had crashed into the seawall of my soul that January night, cracking the foundation, leaving hairline fractures in its wake. What I thought was strong, secure, had been weakened from its violent blow, and though I didn't know it yet, a slow leak had begun to seep into those places of my core that should never have been exposed, acid burning me from the inside out.

But I'm getting ahead of myself.

That stormy evening marked the best day of my life until the day my daughter was born. Unfortunately, life got all muddled after Libby's birth.

I've spent the last years of my life trying to sort it out. Pride, the Good Book says, goes before destruction and a haughty spirit before a fall, but I've no place left to fall now.

That night in '54 changed my life.

If only I could restore the plunder of time and mend the broken places. Blow those terrible winds away.

If only . . .

I

JANUARY 1954, CLEVEDON, ENGLAND

Moored fishing boats sagged in the harbor's waves as the lights on Clevedon's wooden pier flickered in the wind. A storm was brewing over the swollen waters that separated England from Wales, the dark clouds bulging with rain, but Maggie Emerson didn't move from her bench along the wide promenade.

She pulled her knees up to her chest and wrapped her warm, woolen skirt over her stockings. In the summer, day-trippers paraded up and down this promenade, gawking at the sailing boats and the Welsh mountains across the estuary. They clambered over the rocks along the shoreline and paid two pennies each to stroll onto the famous pier that stretched over the water. But few people visited Clevedon this time of year, and on stormy nights like this, most of the town's residents hunkered down in the safety of their homes.

Maggie knew she should return home too, but even when the clock tower chimed five o'clock, she didn't stand. Her gaze remained fixed in the distance where salty water from the Bristol Channel collided with the River Severn.

Every evening, after she finished her work at the library, she sat on this bench and watched for a certain yacht to appear. But for the past two months all she'd done was sit alone, watching the fishing boats sway. Aunt Priscilla had warned that the yachtsmen who stopped here wanted only one thing, and then they'd be gone. Maggie hadn't understood what her aunt meant at the time, but now she knew exactly what Elliot wanted when he'd sailed into their town.

Last summer, when Aunt Priscilla found out about Elliot, she'd threatened to pack Maggie's suitcase and drive her to the station for the next train headed to London. But Maggie had sworn that she'd never see him again, and she'd kept her promise . . . until Elliot sailed back in October.

Another wave smashed into the seawall of the promenade, and the pier lights flickered one more time before darkness fell over her.

Elliot had said he would return by Christmas and spend the rest of the winter in Clevedon with her. He said they would marry, and when the weather turned warm, they would sail far away from here.

But more than two months had passed since she'd seen him and now—

Her hand rolled over her abdomen, her tears mixing with icy raindrops that began to fall from the sky.

Aunt Priscilla and Uncle Timothy—who weren't really her aunt and uncle at all—might wonder why she hadn't returned home yet, especially with the impending storm, but as their three biological children grew older, they'd stopped asking where she went after work. The Frasers had been fostering her since she was five, and recently they'd made it quite clear that it was time for her to either marry or return to London. She had opted for marriage . . . or at least, she thought she had.

She rocked against the bench, her arms wrapped over her chest.

What was she supposed to do?

If the truth of her indiscretion took wings, it would taint the impeccable reputations of her aunt and uncle and destroy all they valued. Everyone in town admired Aunt Priscilla for her charity work and Uncle Timothy for championing the production of penicillin. If Aunt Priscilla found out about the baby, she would insist Maggie hide her shame—their shame—from the entire town, and Maggie couldn't blame her. Though the Frasers had required Maggie to work hard over the years, she knew they'd sacrificed much for her.

The people in Clevedon treated her like she was one of the Frasers' children, but she'd never stopped missing her brother or parents. While she knew her dad and mum would never return, she'd dreamed for years about reuniting with her younger brother, Edmund. He had been evacuated with her in 1940, but after the war ended, the Frasers sent Edmund off to an orphanage. Maggie had begged them to keep her brother, swore she would care for him, but they'd only wanted a girl. Then by the time she was old enough to travel to Swindon to visit him, Edmund was gone.

The conditions at the orphanage hadn't been horrific—not like the stories she'd read about the old workhouses—but the rooms were sterile. Cold. The kind of place that probably killed her brother's spirit before pneumonia took his life.

The wind blew away the tears on her cheeks, her hand cradled over her stomach again. No matter what happened, she would never send this baby away.

Another wave crashed over the pier and smashed into the seawall, shooting thirty feet above her, the frigid spray showering down on her head, soaking her coat and skirt.

Like Edmund, not all orphaned children found homes, but even if her baby were adopted, she would never know if her child was being raised with love or contempt. She didn't want to give up her child and yet the alternative was impossible. No reputable employer would hire an unmarried mother, and she wouldn't be able to support herself and a child with assistance from the government. Even if she were able to get a job working as a skivvy or a laundress in Bristol, there would be no one to care for her baby.

She shivered in her soaked clothing. If she stayed out here much longer, she might catch pneumonia like her brother. She might—

A seed of a thought began to germinate in her mind.

Perhaps an illness wouldn't be such a bad thing. Perhaps an illness would be the answer to her prayers.

She'd already begged God's forgiveness in the chapel, her knees aching as she'd knelt by the altar. She and the baby could escape this world together. Surely God, in His goodness, His mercy, would welcome them home. Into a safe, warm place where her baby would thrive.

A loud crash startled her, and she turned as the storm tore a shutter off a nearby shop. Then she curled her fingers around the edge of the bench, battling to stand in the wind. If she caught pneumonia, her aunt would call the doctor, and the doctor would find out—

She couldn't let the doctor examine her.

Another thought slipped into her mind, a dim beacon in the haze.

Maybe she wouldn't have to succumb to an illness or the questions of doctors trying to cure her. She was terrified of the water, but maybe she should embrace the storm and its fierce lashing. Let the winds blow away her fears. In seconds all would be well again. Her heart would be calm—

As her muddied mind cleared, her heart seemed to numb, sucking away her fear. She reached for the railing that separated the promenade from the harbor and wrapped her hands around it. Stepping onto the bottom rung, she imagined the waves sweeping her body into the depths of the channel, all her fear washed away.

When she didn't return, the villagers would pity her aunt and uncle for their loss. There would be no shame, no remorse for them, only a brief sorrow and perhaps curiosity at her disappearance. No one would ever know about the baby.

She leaned against the wind, her hair whipping her cheeks, sand and water piercing her face. Her mind screamed for her to run, to escape the gale, but she willed herself to push into it. It would be better for the baby. For her aunt and uncle.

For her.

The sea was the only way out.

Another wave smashed into the wall. The surge shot straight up, entangling her, and she lost her grip on the railing. Her body began to teeter over the seawall, toward the bay.

"Maggie!" a man shouted.

At the sound of her name, her numb body wakened. Flailing, she grasped for the wet railing.

But it was too late to stop her fall.

2

JANUARY 1954, CLEVEDON, ENGLAND

The saltwater was supposed to sting Maggie's cheeks, the current pulling her down to the depths of the channel. Instead, strong hands encircled her waist and yanked her back from the railing, away from the angry sea.

Spinning around, she saw Walter Doyle gazing down at her, his hazy blue eyes more intense than she'd ever seen. He released her waist, but one of his hands folded over the sleeve of her blouse as if he was afraid she might blow away.

Anger warred against gratefulness inside her.

"What are you doing?" he demanded, his voice battling the noise of the wind.

How could she tell him she'd wanted to escape into the sea?

But he didn't wait for her answer. Instead he glanced back out at the churning water and quickly led her away from the seawall, back into the corridor of shops, to the portico at St. Andrews. When she began shivering under the awning, he wrapped his coat over her shoulders. With Walter beside her, the promise of freedom slipped away.

"You must be more careful, Maggie," he chided, like he was decades older instead of only twenty-six years to her nineteen.

"I was just—" She hesitated. "I wanted to feel the wind."

"Those waves will swallow you whole."

Frustration raged inside her again. That was exactly what she'd wanted the waves to do.

He reached for her hand, his wet fingers encircling hers. "Let's get you home."

She yanked her hand away. "I can walk by myself."

"I'd never forgive myself if something happened to you."

She wanted to shout at him, *Too late!* Something had already happened, and he'd stopped her from making it right again.

"The storm's only going to get worse," he said, imploring her.

"The worst has passed."

"Maggie—" he paused, and she saw the serious creases that ran like rivulets under his glasses. He was handsome enough with his light blond hair and clean-shaven face, but she'd always thought him dull. Nothing like the daring sailors who came to their town from France and Italy. Nothing like Elliot.

"What is it?" she asked.

He lowered his voice, barely audible in the wind. "I sure wish you'd marry me."

His words slapped her with cold reality, a jarring reminder of all she'd tried to escape. She studied his face, waiting for him to laugh at his joke, but he was in earnest. She shouldn't be surprised. He'd asked her to marry him last summer, when they'd picnicked with friends at the cove, but she had told him no. Back then, she'd wanted to marry for love.

He squeezed her hand. "Maggie?"

She glanced back at the rain drumming the asphalt, his words echoing in her ears. Perhaps there was another way.

She took a deep breath, shivering again as she tugged on the lapels of Walter's borrowed coat, pulling it around her chest. "You are supposed to get on your knee."

His eyes creased again. "What?"

She inched up her chin in a weak attempt to calm the racing in her chest. "It would be indecent for any woman to accept a proposal of marriage when the man is standing before you."

He dropped down to one knee and grasped her hands. "Maggie Emerson, would you give me the pleasure of becoming my wife?"

She nodded. "Right away."

A VEIL SHROUDED MAGGIE'S FACE, and she hoped the lace hid her trepidation from the man standing before her. Walter looked quite dapper in his gray flannel suit and maroon tie, not a bit of fear reflected in his face. Only admiration and excitement. If she kept her secret, he would never find out about Elliot.

She'd always been good at making up stories, but not so much at acting. Aunt Priscilla only had to glance at her face, and she could read every emotion, but Uncle Timothy was so distracted by his work that he never questioned her.

She hoped her husband would be more like her uncle.

Walter's gaze softened as the rector began to read their vows. If only she could bask in his love like the day-trippers from London did with the summer sun . . . but his love would dissipate if he ever discovered what she had done.

It seemed as if the entire population of Clevedon had crowded into the sanctuary to watch the Frasers' foster niece and the local newspaper editor wed. She felt the stares of the congregation on her back, but she couldn't look at Uncle Timothy, Aunt Priscilla, or their three children. Couldn't bear to see the excitement in their eyes—a different kind of excitement than Walter's in that they were finally parting with the evacuee who'd come to them by train almost fifteen years ago and never left.

She smoothed her fingers over the cool satin that hid her stomach, and guilt coursed through her veins again as Walter smiled down at her. When she agreed to marry him, he hadn't wasted any time in helping to arrange the wedding, as if he was afraid she might change her mind.

But now, standing here at the altar, the whirlwind of wedding plans complete, she prayed she hadn't made a mistake. The Germans had taken her family, but she would do her best to make a new one with the man standing before her.

Walter took her hand, and she turned toward the rector, a middle-aged man with graying hair and a white robe that fell to the tile floor.

"The vows you are about to take are to be made in the presence of God, who is judge of all and knows all the secrets of our hearts," he said, his voice heavy with the weight of his words. "Walter and Margaret, if either of you knows a reason why you may not lawfully marry, you must declare it now."

The rector studied Walter's face and then his gaze penetrated the lace of her veil. She wished she could shrink into herself, disappear, but she forced herself to hold steady.

Her lips opened, but words didn't come out, and she felt trapped, her nerves tangled inside her. The baby wasn't Walter's child, but she'd already made a bad choice with Elliot. She didn't want to make another one by turning back now.

The rector had moved into their declarations, and Walter promised before her and God to honor and protect her, to be faithful to her as long as they lived.

Then the rector returned his gaze to her.

"Margaret, will you give yourself to Walter to be his wife: to love him, comfort him, honor and protect him; and, forsaking all others, to be faithful to him so long as you both shall live?"

Maggie glanced back at Mrs. Doyle—Walter's mother—on the front row. She wore an elegant pastel yellow and white dress, and joy radiated from her face as if she were the bride. Walter's dad had died in the war so Mrs. Doyle traveled almost two hundred miles alone by bus to watch her only son marry.

Walter gently squeezed Maggie's hands, bringing her back to the reality that the entire congregation was waiting for her to respond. In that moment, she decided she would do everything possible to honor this man and their marriage. "I will."

Likely no one else heard Walter's sigh of relief, but it pounded like thunder in her heart. Then they began to say their vows.

Over his shoulder, through the clear glass among the stained, the sea called to her. Instead of answering, Maggie silently vowed to remain strong for the baby growing inside her even as she promised Walter to love and cherish him, for better or for worse.

When they finished, the rector pronounced them man and wife, and Walter took her hand, guiding her down the long aisle, past the smiling faces and eyes critiquing the details of her white gown.

She knew all these people, but very few were friends. Her childhood friends had been other war evacuees who'd returned to their families after the bombings stopped in London, and her school friends had either married or left Clevedon for college. She'd wanted to attend a university, but her aunt and uncle felt they'd already done more than society and even God required of them. And she didn't have the income to pay for an education on her own.

She and Walter wouldn't just provide food and a place for their child to sleep, but an environment with love and laughter and an education so her child—and their other children—could go wherever they pleased.

That thought made her smile.

As they emerged into the sunlight outside the church, she blinked. Walter opened the door to the Rolls-Royce he'd borrowed from her uncle, and their chauffeur—a friend of Walter's—pretended to ignore them in the backseat.

"The best day of my life," Walter whispered as he put his arm around her.

"Mine too." A white lie, spit and polished, so it wouldn't hurt either of them.

Then he pulled her close and kissed her. Their first kiss.

There were no fireworks in her heart like when Elliot kissed her. No danger.

She told herself that she wouldn't miss the danger. She was secure now, and she would savor the security.

He took her hand again as the car crawled through the narrow streets in town.

God was the only one who knew her secret, and she hoped He would guard it well.

3

Wheat starch and a few drops of water were all Heather Toulson needed to fix the torn painting of Mount St. Helens. She dabbed the white paste onto the back of the ripped paper and gently edged the pieces of pale-blue sky against the dark fringe of leaves until they were a coherent image again. The watercolors captured the reflection of the volcano in a mountain lake, sixty years before the snow-capped peak erupted and left behind a gaping wound of rock and ash.

The painting wouldn't be worth anything in the art world, but it was invaluable to her client, the tenacious Mrs. Young. And Heather happened to think tenacity was a virtue.

Mrs. Young's mother had painted it in 1922, and after Mrs. Young moved into a retirement village in Southern Oregon, she'd stored her prized painting in her son's basement. Then his washing machine overflowed. Even though the painting was behind glass, the delicate paper had been no match for the moisture. When her son took the glass off, he'd torn a piece of the tree branches that framed the lake and mountain. Mrs. Young had been devastated.

Heather scooted back from the table to admire her handiwork. The spring sunlight filtered through her studio window, illuminating the painting.

She considered herself an expert in devastation. Or at least she was an expert in restoring damaged artwork. *Perseverance*, she'd told Mrs. Young and her son when they'd brought her the picture, *and patience will put the pieces back together again*. If they could be patient, she hoped to fix Mount St. Helens for them.

Mrs. Young and her son left the painting with Heather, at her studio in Portland's Pearl District, and she'd heard them arguing all the way back to their car. The son thought it was a waste of money to fix the painting, but Mrs. Young countered that neither of them could put a price on his grandmother's artwork. He said that if she treasured it so much, she shouldn't have stored it in his basement.

Heather sighed. Treasures from the past kept art restorers like her in business. Fortunately, unlike relationships, very few pieces of artwork were beyond repair.

She lifted the painting and carefully reinforced her patchwork on the verso with Japanese tissue. A restorer was more chemist than artist, imitators who knew how to mimic the greats—and the not-so-greats like Mrs. Young's mother.

Even though the elder Mrs. Young wasn't an exceptional artist, she had left her children and grandchildren an image of beauty from her mind's eye. Anyone willing to expose their heart and mind through art, opening themselves and their work to both praise and critique, was a brave soul.

While Heather didn't snub any type of art, she was clear with prospective clients about the time and expense of restoration. Artwork like this landscape wouldn't have cost much, at least monetarily, to create, but it was very expensive to restore any tears or structural weaknesses. In that, perhaps, art conservation mimicked real life.

She scooted away from her work table, leaving the painting

to dry overnight before she repaired the cockling—rippling of the paper—and did a bit of inpainting to conceal the jagged thread of black where the tree limbs met the sky.

Her cell phone chimed, and she turned toward where she'd stashed it, next to the orchid on her windowsill, but she didn't race to answer it. Ella—her twenty-five-year-old daughter—had selected a head- and heart-pounding drum solo to differentiate her calls from anyone else, and the drum solo calls were the only ones Heather rushed to answer.

Most of her calls were from clients checking on the status of her work or potential clients wanting a proposal for restoration. She waited to return those when she wasn't working on a project, and she didn't plan to take on any new work anyway—not until she returned from her trip to England.

Her newer clients wanted their restoration done quickly. She'd learned to explain that it took decades and sometimes centuries for artwork to decay, so it also took a substantial amount of time to breathe life back into what either time or a disaster had stolen away. Some restorers made grand promises, and a few were actually able to jump over the high bar they'd set. But she was completely honest at the beginning of each new project about her abilities and what she thought she could do. She decided early in her career that she would set the bar rather low. Then she could exceed expectations as much as possible. Some clients moaned about the length of her process, but few ever complained about the quality of her work.

She stepped toward the sink under her window and rinsed the wheat starch out of her brush before reaching for her phone.

The missed call was from Nick Davis, the curator at the Portland Art Museum and a friend who once said he wanted more than friendship from her. She'd been clear that she wasn't interested in navigating the complexities of a relationship. But ever since Ella married earlier this year, Nick had been able to convince her to leave the sanctuary of her studio once or twice a week for dinner or an exhibit at the museum.

She'd just begun to listen to his message when the door to her studio chimed and Nick walked into the small lobby she'd set up for her clients. He moved past the leather chairs where most people waited, straight into her workshop.

Most Portlanders embraced casual attire for work, but Nick wore a tie and dress trousers every day. Today he also carried a portfolio case used to transport artwork.

She held up her phone. "You just called."

"I wanted to see if you were here," he said with a shrug. "I figured you were ignoring me."

"Not ignoring," she retorted, pointing at the light table. "Working."

"You're always working," he said as he put his case onto a table, more admiration than criticism in his words. Whenever he needed restoration work for the museum, he called her—another reason why they couldn't be anything more than friends. "I'd like you to look at this."

He unzipped the nylon case, and inside was a discolored frame that smelled like smoke. A thin layer of soot covered the painting under the glass—a picture of an old manor house. Gothic Victorian. Wisteria climbed the wall near the entrance, the pale-lavender blossoms clinging to the gray stone. The artist had brushed flowers below the windows as well, though those colors had been muted by the smoke damage.

Heather pressed her lips together as she studied it. The stone walls and flowers reminded her of Ladenbrooke, the manor home beside her parents' cottage in England. The place that had mesmerized her as a child.

"Can you fix it?" Nick asked, pointing to the black streaks that rippled down from a garret to the back wheels of a carriage waiting beside the grand entrance.

She reached for her magnifying glass in a drawer and studied the damage. No matter how many hours she spent trying to repair this painting, she'd never be able to restore it to its original state.

Nick leaned closer to her. "Heather?"

She set her magnifying glass on the table. "How did it get damaged?"

"I'm not certain," he said. "It was found in an attic."

She let out a breath. Why did people keep such treasures in an attic? "You think I'm a miracle worker?" she asked.

He straightened his tie. "I do."

"Flattery will get you nowhere," she said, trying to hide her smile.

"Nor will false modesty about your talents," he quipped. "I know you can restore this."

"I can certainly try—when I get back from England."

He sighed. "Can't someone else clean out your parents' place?"

She'd asked herself the same question many times but kept arriving at the same conclusion. She'd spent most of her life cleaning up and restoring other people's artwork. Even though she didn't want to return home, it seemed ludicrous to let someone else rummage through her family's possessions.

She zipped up the case, protecting the artwork in its cocoon until she could begin her restoration. "I'll be back in two weeks."

"Two weeks is too long."

She folded her arms over her chest. "It will be the last time I go to England."

"I'd bet money you'll be back in a week."

She wouldn't bet against him.

After he left, she locked the painting in her fireproof cabinet and escaped to the courtyard outside her studio. Tucked under the maple tree was a fountain, sculpted by a local artist, and she watched the water trickle down it into a small pool.

Her father had passed away in February, and she'd returned home for his memorial service. She'd flown into Heathrow and drove over to the village of Bibury the morning of the service. Then she'd returned to the airport that evening.

Over the years, she'd begged her dad to move to Oregon so she could help care for him, but he'd relocated to a retirement village in Oxford four years ago instead. The last time she'd visited him, the week after his stroke, she'd sat beside his bed and held his hand, suspecting it was good-bye. Still, she'd clung to the hope that one day, before he was gone, their relationship would be reconciled. Restored.

It was much too late for restoration now, but she still had the good memories of both her parents in her childhood home—a stone cottage on the hill above Bibury. Even after her father moved to Oxford, he refused to sell or even let their home out, and she hadn't been able to do it either. But the cottage had sat vacant for long enough now, and a local real estate agent kept contacting her about selling it.

No amount of paste would repair the torn pieces from her past, but she would still return to England and face her ghosts one last time.

4

SPRING 1954, CLEVEDON, ENGLAND

Walter disbanded with all formalities when Maggie told him the news, lifting her off her feet and twirling her around the floor of their sitting room. He startled her at first, but then she laughed along with him.

Just as quickly as he'd lifted her, Walter returned her feet to the woven rug. "I shouldn't have done that," he said, apologizing in earnest.

She straightened the satin headscarf that covered her hair. "You didn't hurt me."

Stepping away, he eyed her stomach as if he could determine whether or not he'd inflicted an injury. "But our baby—"

"You didn't hurt the baby either."

They'd been married two months now, and he'd treated her with utmost care since he found her in the storm, as if he might lose her forever if he didn't watch closely and attend to her needs. His attention overwhelmed her at times, but other times she felt elated at having someone love her so wholly. Someone who would never leave her.

He leaned back against the dark paneling in the room, crossing his arms. "Are you certain you're expecting?"

"Quite." And the growing bulge in her belly didn't lie.

"I didn't think we would start a family so soon—"

Her smile fell. "Are you disappointed?"

"Not in the least." Walter grinned again as he rested one hand on the mantel of their fireplace. "I hope we have five or six children."

She laughed. "Perhaps we should start with two."

He looked around the tiny space as if seeing it for the first time. "We'll need a bigger home," he said, then his eyes clouded with the realization. Even though they were both working, they could barely afford this terrace house they'd rented from her uncle's friend.

"We don't need anything bigger," she assured him.

Walter stepped toward the calendar and flipped the page back to their wedding date.

January 28, 1954

Since their wedding, she kept tightening her girdle, hiding her abdomen under baggy blouses and her spring jumper. She wouldn't be showing if she was only three or four weeks along, but Walter didn't seem to know the difference. Nor would he ever find out. She wouldn't deny him the happiness of fathering a child he thought to be his own or deny her baby the security of having a father.

Even when the baby came, five or so months from now, she could feign an early birth. Like one of her friends from school had done when she gave birth six months after her wedding day.

When Maggie had visited Sally, the midwife in Clevedon, the elderly woman hadn't bought her spiel about being newly pregnant. Sally thought she and Walter—

Her husband reached for her, wrapped his arms around her. "You will be the most beautiful mum in all of Great Britain."

"And you will be the most doting father."

He grinned again, pulling her close. "I will be counting down the days until October."

She tilted her head up. "Perhaps our baby will come a bit early."

His smile turned into worry. "Not too early."

"You're a good man, Walter Doyle," she said before he kissed her.

THE FIERCE STORMS THAT CHURNED the estuary all winter turned placid by late spring. By the middle of May, the water gently loped against Clevedon's beaches and seawall, but another kind of storm was brewing in the town. This one much more covert but in Maggie's mind, just as dangerous.

Maggie knew the moment Aunt Priscilla realized she was expecting. She broke away from her circle of friends at church to greet her and Walter, but her gaze didn't linger for long on Maggie's face or even on the new tweed jacket and skirt that Walter purchased for her at Debenhams. Instead it fell to Maggie's stomach and the swell she could no longer hide, even with her girdle.

Walter telephoned his mother back in March, and she was thrilled with the news. Her first grandchild. Once the baby was born, she would know the timing was off, but now that they were married, everything was in order. Maggie only hoped her mother-in-law would believe the child was Walter's.

But Aunt Priscilla wasn't so easily fooled.

She arrived at Maggie's doorstep the morning after church for a private visit, after Walter left for the newspaper office. Maggie boiled water for tea, pretending to be gay while Aunt Priscilla watched her from the kitchen chair, her arms crossed. "Is Walter pleased about the baby?"

"He's thrilled about being a father."

Her aunt leaned closer. "And what about your sailor?"

Maggie shrugged, willing her heart to beat at a normal pace again. "What about him?"

"What will you tell him when he finds out?"

"He won't find out," she said, the familiar pain piercing her.

"You don't know that—"

Maggie shook her head, determined. "He came and left, just as you said. He won't inquire after me."

"I wouldn't be so certain," Aunt Priscilla said, twisting her purse in her lap. "And then word will get out—"

Maggie tilted her head. "Word about what?"

"Don't be coy, Margaret," her aunt replied, her voice a sharp whisper. "Walter may be entirely clueless about your conduct, but I'm not daft."

Maggie's hands trembled as she lifted the teapot though she managed to fill her aunt's cup. No matter what Aunt Priscilla said, she wouldn't admit her indiscretion.

"Have you seen one of the midwives?"

She nodded. "Sally."

Aunt Priscilla spooned a lump of sugar into her tea. "What does Sally say?"

"That the baby seems to be healthy."

"Not that," she said, waving her spoon. "What does she say about the timing?"

"The health of the child is her only concern."

"You and Walter must leave here at once," Aunt Priscilla insisted. "No one outside of Devonshire will question you about the dates of your wedding or the child's birth."

"Walter would never leave the newspaper."

"You are his wife," her aunt said, her spoon clinking as she stirred her tea, its ripples colliding with the sides of the cup. "It's your job to compel him to go."

"But how—"

"You're smart, Margaret," she said as she mixed in more sugar. "You've gotten yourself married, and that's probably the best thing you could have done under these circumstances. Now you have to protect Walter and your child."

She didn't say it, but Maggie knew the secret must be kept most of all to protect the Fraser family's reputation.

Aunt Priscilla sipped her tea and then stood. "If Walter really loves you, he'll relinquish his position at the paper."

Maggie stared down at her full cup of tea. Walter loved her—she had no doubt of that. He'd spent more than a year in the steady pursuit of her hand before she agreed to marry him. But how could she ask him to choose between his two loves—his wife and his writing?

Aunt Priscilla excused herself to visit the water closet; when Maggie leaned back in the chair, her gaze traveling out the window to the Bristol Channel in the distance.

Walter wasn't so enamored by the fame of a byline, but he thought information was the key to liberty. Reporting the news was his passion though, not creating it. If anyone else suspected that this baby wasn't Walter's child—the gossip would never compete with the facts that Walter religiously collected, verified, and distributed for his subscribers. No one would bother to verify the child's father and she would never tell. The villagers could talk and whisper all they wanted about her, but Walter's reputation was as stellar as her aunt and uncle's.

She drained her warm tea, but didn't taste it.

Could she really influence Walter to leave Clevedon before the gossipmongers began milling her story?

Walter had been only eleven when Hitler invaded Poland. As the war progressed, many British newspapermen became war correspondents or soldiers so by the time Walter was fourteen, he began filling in the gap, writing for a newspaper in Kent. After the war, he left for London to write for the *Evening Standard* until Harold Bishop hired him as the managing editor for the *Clevedon Mercury*.

Her husband hadn't liked living in a big city where he didn't even know his neighbors, but he loved to write and thrived on every aspect of the newspaper business—collecting the stories, setting the type, even selling the advertising pages and weekly subscriptions. And once he moved to Clevedon, he continued to work as a correspondent, feeding occasional stories from Devonshire back to his old boss at the *Standard*.

She couldn't imagine Walter working in any profession that didn't involve writing in some capacity. He was passionate about his stories and about raising their family here along the coast.

When she heard her aunt's heavy footsteps in the back hall, she stood to clear the teacups.

How was she supposed to convince Walter to leave Clevedon without telling him the truth?

5

JUNE 1954, CLEVEDON, ENGLAND

The baby pressed against Maggie's abdomen as she shelved the last novel in her tall stack of returns. Then she gently placed her hand over the elbow—or perhaps the foot—that bulged under her white blouse.

It wouldn't be long now before she'd be holding this child in her arms.

Before he left for work this morning, Walter said they had 132 days until the baby arrived, but according to her calculations, baby would be here in 41 days. Or less.

The number made her feel faint.

It was still an hour before the library closed, but Mrs. Jenkins, the head librarian, said she could leave early. Somehow she must convince Walter that they had to move right away.

Fog had settled over the village, and she slowly navigated the narrow alleys down the hill, toward the greengrocers to buy fresh produce for Walter's favorite salad—a mixture of shredded cabbage, grated onion, and diced tomatoes.

Her stomach roiled from the smells in the air. Seaweed. Gasoline. Greasy fish and chips.

She hadn't liked the taste of fish, any kind of fish, when she'd been relocated here during the war, and she'd never grown fond of the cod or bass from the channel. Still, she ate it several times a week like most of the people in town, even as she dreamt of beef pie and leg of lamb.

Tonight there would be no fish on their dinner table and nothing would come out of a tin. Lamb chops were more expensive than fish or tinned food, but not so pricey that Walter would fret about her extravagance.

When she stepped into the butcher shop, two women turned toward her. Instead of greeting her, however, one woman tipped toward the other like a teapot preparing to pour out. Maggie held her head up as she proceeded in the queue toward the counter, trying to pretend they weren't whispering about her.

It was becoming increasingly apparent that her pregnancy was much further along than her wedding date allowed. Fortunately, these women didn't know about Elliot, and her husband didn't seem to suspect anything was amiss. The baby was technically due in the middle of July, and she prayed the child would be late by a week or two.

Heaven forbid he or she came early.

She must convince Walter to leave this village before the baby was born so they could start over in a new place, far away from the whispers and gossip. Somehow she had to rescue their little family without explaining her reasons.

Maggie tugged on the hem of her oversized blouse, pulling it over the elastic of her skirt as she waited for her meat. With the brown wrappings around her lamb in one hand, the bag of produce in the other, she brushed past her aunt's friends and hurried back up the hill toward home.

Quickly she shredded the cabbage on the chopping block and tossed it along with the onion and tomatoes in a blue Pyrex bowl. Then she slid the lamb chops, encrusted with fresh rosemary, into the oven.

While the lamb baked, she brushed her hair in the washroom and pinned it back again. Then she zipped on a silk floral dress she'd purchased in Bristol and retrieved her grandmother's rhinestone necklace, one of the few family heirlooms her mother packed for her, to clasp around her neck.

At the foot of the bed was the antique trunk she'd brought from her childhood home in Balham more than a decade ago. Opening the trunk, she removed her wedding album along with her treasured copy of *The Secret Garden* and the tubes of watercolors her father had sent with her and her brother. Her father hoped she would spend time painting on the coast, but Maggie hadn't inherited his talent or passion for art. Sometimes she wondered if Edmund would have become an artist.

Carefully she took out her newest treasures—pieces of crystal she and Walter had received as wedding presents, protected by pages and pages of her husband's newspaper. She unwrapped the crystal and two silver candlesticks, then set them on the white-cloaked dining table. She arranged the candlesticks alongside a small silver bowl filled with mint jelly and a basket with sliced whole-meal bread from the bakery. After placing white, tapered candles into the candlesticks, she lit them and stepped back to admire her handiwork.

Satisfied, she blew them out. Once she heard Walter at the door, she'd quickly relight the candles.

When the timer chimed, she removed the lamb chops and turned off the oven, placing the pan on her stovetop and covering it with foil. She'd learned a lot about housekeeping in the past decade, and now she was determined to learn how to be the best wife to Walter. And a doting mother to their children.

If only she could avoid the whispers from her aunt's friends.

Baby kicked her side again, this time much stronger. Bending over, she steadied herself on the counter.

"I'm here," she said to comfort her child, wishing she knew what to call him or her.

She and Walter had been discussing names for their baby—and she did think of the child as *theirs* now—for three months. If it was a boy, they'd name him Walter. If it was a girl, they weren't certain what to name her.

She'd suggested Eliza or Caroline for a girl's name, but Walter liked Margaret or Priscilla. Maggie told him she didn't like either name. If the baby was female, she prayed their daughter would be nothing like her or her aunt.

As she sat on the davenport, Maggie eyed the clock. Strange. Walter was already a half hour late. Usually he phoned if he didn't leave the office by six, but she hadn't said anything about their special dinner tonight, hadn't wanted him to suspect that she had ulterior motives.

She picked up the telephone and rang the *Clevedon Mercury* office, but no one answered. After replacing the receiver, she propped her pumps up on the coffee table, listening to the front windows rattle from the wind. Even though it was summer, the breeze from the bay cooled their town in the evenings. They had no need for the air-conditioning she'd read about in the magazines.

She kicked off her shoes and reached for the afghan that hung over the arm of the davenport to pull over her dress. The newspaper didn't go to press until Friday. She never would have made this special dinner on a Thursday night, but she thought Wednesday would be safe.

Her mind began rehearsing again what she would say to Walter. How she would coyly suggest, not demand, they leave without playing on his love for her. She was doing this because she cared for him and their baby.

Tired, she began to drift asleep and didn't awaken until the front door banged open. She inched herself up, her lower back aching as she slowly remembered that she'd been waiting for her husband.

The streetlamp colored their sitting room with a hazy, orange glow, and she watched Walter hurry across the room, trying to catch his breath even as he spoke. "I'm sorry I'm late."

She pressed her pinned curls back into place. "What happened?"

"A trawler hit the rocks near Battery Point and tipped over." In his voice, she could hear the mix of sadness at the tragedy along with an underpinning satisfaction, the restrained enthusiasm, over covering a real news story. "I had to interview the survivors."

"How awful," she said, crossing her arms over her chest.

"Two fishermen died." He shook his head as he collapsed onto the davenport beside her. "They were trapped inside the hull."

She rubbed her arms, shuddering at the thought of families who had lost men they loved tonight. "I wish you'd telephoned."

"I ran out of the office so fast . . ." He reached for her hand. "I didn't realize I'd be gone so long."

He leaned closer to her. "Will you forgive me?"

The way he said it was so sweet, the way she'd once imagined Elliot would ask for her forgiveness when he returned.

She smiled at him. "Of course, I will."

He lifted his head, and his eyes widened when he saw the crystal and candlesticks in the street lantern light. "You made us a special dinner."

She shrugged. "They're only lamb chops—"

"I'm famished," he said as he stood up and switched on the lamp. She was hungry as well.

"It will be cold."

"It doesn't matter." He helped her stand, and even though it was almost eleven, she relit the candles and peeled back the foil. Then he held out her chair.

"How was your day?" he asked as he served the meat.

She thought about the endless books she'd checked out for children on their summer holiday. And the stacks she'd had to reshelve. And the conversation with Walter that she'd rehearsed over and over in her mind.

It was hardly as riveting as reporting a shipwreck on the coast, but still it was her story.

"Mrs. Bishop keeps coming by to see if we have John Steinbeck's new novel. I've told her repeatedly that it doesn't release until next month but she thinks I'm being impertinent."

Walter laughed. "That's what happens when you've met the Queen of England."

"Queen Elizabeth wasn't a queen when Mrs. Bishop met her!"

"Don't remind her of that," he said before he took a bite of his salad. Mrs. Bishop was married to Harold Bishop, the man who owned the *Clevedon Mercury*. Mr. Bishop spent much of his time away from home.

"It doesn't matter what I say." Maggie sighed. "The woman doesn't like me."

He tilted his head. "How could anyone not like you?"

She didn't know how she'd managed to fool such an intelligent man about her character. "She thinks I'm intentionally keeping her from the books she wants to read. Like I'm the book Gestapo or something."

Walter wiped his face with his napkin. "She doesn't like me much either."

"What could you have done—"

"She thinks I'm covering up the most important news in Clevedon."

She tilted her head. "And what news would that be?"

"I have no idea, and frankly I don't think she does either."

She sighed again. "Apparently the two of us are conspiring against her happiness."

"That's us, Maggie," he said with another laugh. "Two grand conspirators."

She cringed at his words.

Aunt Priscilla had said it was the predisposition of any woman to redirect the conversation to say what she needed to say. If she didn't ask Walter about moving now, it might be too late.

She reached for her napkin and dabbed it on her lips. "I'm tired of working at the library."

"I meant to tell you—" He glanced back up from his meal. "Anthony Morton says they have been looking for someone to let two rooms in their house."

She picked up her fork to stir the strands of cabbage in her bowl. "We can't live with the Mortons. Baby will be up at night crying the first weeks and I would feel so bad . . ."

"They'll understand. They have two grown children."

Maggie looked over at the exhaustion in her husband's red-rimmed eyes, at his disheveled blond hair, at the smudges on his thin spectacles. The timing might be terrible, but she had to make him understand the dire state of their future here.

"What if—" she began, twirling her fork casually even as she tried to calm the racing in her heart. "Oh, it's an impossible idea."

Even though his eyes were heavy with fatigue, he leaned forward and smiled at her. "But I like your ideas."

"What if—" she started again and then took a deep breath. "What if we moved?"

His smile collapsed into confusion. "But you said you didn't want to live with the Mortons."

"I mean—" She put down her fork. "What if we moved away?"

He searched her face intently as if he thought she might be teasing him. "You want to leave Clevedon?"

"I—" she faltered before slowly nodding her head. "Perhaps you could find a more secure position at another newspaper—"

"My position is secure."

She continued, refusing to be daunted now. "A place where you can earn a higher income."

He flinched. "I will never earn as much money as your uncle."

"I don't expect you to," she said, trying to collect her thoughts even as her words rushed out. "I just thought it might be a good idea for our little family to start over someplace new."

"Start over—" His lips pressed together for a moment before he spoke again. "Why would we want to start over?"

Goose bumps bristled across her arms as her mind raced to devise a more compelling argument.

"I thought you liked it here," he said.

She clenched her fork. This was going all wrong. "Not particularly."

"Why not?" he probed.

Her gaze turned toward the dark window. "I don't like the cold air on the coast, I suppose, or the smell of fish, or the way everyone butts into everyone else's business."

He tossed his napkin onto the table. "You should have told me that before we married."

"Everything happened so fast, Walter. My head was spinning."

"I just assumed—"

"You assumed a lot of things," she blurted, and then covered her mouth, horrified.

He clutched the edge of the table. "What else did I assume?"

Answers to his question pelted her mind like rapid gunfire, but this time she controlled her tongue.

"I didn't say that right," she said, sniffling. "I'm all a mess right now."

He slowly released his grip on the table. "We're both exhausted."

This time she softened her voice, tilting her head slightly again, blinking back her tears. She hadn't asked much of him since their wedding, but she thought he really did love her enough to give her whatever she wanted. All she wanted now was for him to consider a move, at least until she could come up with a more pressing reason for them to leave. "Will you think about it?" she asked.

"I run the local newspaper," he said as if he were fastened to the business by wooden stocks.

"Someone else can manage the paper, just as well as you."

He looked insulted at first, but it turned rapidly into frustration. "I'm sorry, love—" he hesitated again, conflicted, and she hoped he still might change his mind. "But we can't leave."

She crossed her arms, tears flooding her cheeks. Walter couldn't tell her what she would and would not do, like he was her father instead of her husband.

"Thank you for the meal." He stood and picked up both plates before pushing in the chair. "I have to finish writing this story tonight."

She listened to the water running from the faucet in the kitchen. Usually he washed their dishes and she dried, but tonight she didn't move from her chair.

Her aunt said if Walter loved her enough, he would leave Clevedon. Walter might say he loved her, but he didn't really, at least not more than his newspaper.

She never should have listened to her aunt.

In the hours before dawn, as she lay in bed next to Walter, she could hear the deep breathing of his sleep. This riff between them tonight was invisible, nothing like the aftermath of a trawler crashing into the rocks, but she'd felt a tear separating her from her husband.

What would he do if he found out the truth about their baby?

Living on the coast, she knew well that it only took a small leak to sink a ship. And if a ship, no matter how strong, ran aground, everything onboard could be lost.

She didn't know what to do next, but she would do everything she could to keep their little ship intact.

6

Yellow rapeseed fields glittered like stamps of gold leaf among the prim and quite proper plots of green and brown. Her nose pressed against the window, Heather scanned the English countryside as the 757 flew low over the farmland and then Windsor Castle in its approach into Heathrow.

Her daughter was flying from Dulles, and if all went as planned, Ella's plane would touch down about fifteen minutes from now. They planned to pick up their rental car together before driving the two hours over to the vacant cottage in Bibury.

It was the last time she'd ever have to visit the place where everything went awry.

Heather's father had been gone from this world for almost four months now, but it seemed like much longer—decades even—and she missed him. Her parents had sent her to an independent girls' school for her primary and secondary education, but when she was home, she'd loved spending time with her dad. Walter Doyle was a man of honor. A man who stuck to his principles when others let theirs slide. He'd been the postmaster in Bibury for more than thirty years, and as a child, she had been proud of his discipline and reputation in their village and the surrounding towns.

On the summer evenings Mum worked as a hairdresser, earning extra money for Heather's boarding school, he would entertain her with the most wonderful tales. It seemed like he knew a little about everyone's business, but when he told her what he'd heard, he would put wings on the stories and make them bigger. Grander.

The childhood that started idyllically, however, began to sour in the latter part of her secondary school years. And then, after what happened with Christopher—

She'd left to attend a university in London though really she'd been running away—from her parents and Christopher and the big, gaping wound she thought would heal with time. For years the wound stung, the rejection from her first love slashing through her core. Over the years, it left behind an ugly scar, but even now, she sometimes felt as if her wound had never fully healed. The thought of reopening it terrified her.

Her father had never forgiven her for eloping with Jeffery during her second semester of college, and none of her visits back to England had repaired the rift that separated them. Unlike the artwork she restored, there were no paints or paste or tools to mend the ragged gap in their relationship.

Regret and shame haunted Heather during her years with Jeffery. She'd tried to forget the young man she'd loved deeply back in Bibury, but her heart warred inside her. It wasn't her love for Christopher that slowly severed her marriage. It was her anger at Christopher—and anger toward herself.

When Ella was six, Jeffery decided to leave, and he never returned. Heather knew she'd made some lousy choices in her struggle to grow up, but she never once regretted being Ella's mother.

She glanced out the window again at the sprawl of London

that stretched like the threads on a cobweb. As if it wanted to capture her and her heart again.

Heather's mum had been disappointed when Heather told her that she and Jeffery had married . . . and were expecting a child. But during the last three years of her life, Mum had loved her granddaughter dearly. Ella attended the service for her grandmother back in 1992, but she hadn't been back to England since then. She and Matthew had been on their honeymoon the week of her grandfather's memorial service.

Having Ella here now would keep Heather focused on the task at hand. For the next two weeks, she was determined to put her past behind her and honor her father by caring for his things.

And she was determined to avoid Christopher Westcott and his family.

Once she set the cottage in order, she would hand the keys to a real estate agent and return to Portland. In the rhythm of her work back in Oregon, her ordered life, peace would be restored.

The plane's wheels touched down, jolting her back to her reality.

She found Ella by the window in the Terminal 4 lobby, texting her husband even though it was three in the morning Phoenix time. Ella looked like she was still in high school, with her short strawberry blonde hair pushed back behind her sunglasses, not the least bit frazzled after her long flight.

"How is my son-in-law?" Heather asked as she slid into the seat beside her.

Ella turned and squealed before wrapping her arms around her in a giant hug. "He says he's afraid I'll love it so much here that I won't come home."

"I have no doubt you'll love it, but I think you love him a bit more."

"That's what I keep telling him." Ella reached for her backpack and strapped it over her shoulder. "I can't believe we're finally here!"

"Me neither." Heather smiled at her beautiful daughter. "I've sure missed you."

Ella grinned back at her. "The last time I was here, I was like two."

"Actually, like three."

"I don't remember a thing."

Heather stood up. "Then let's see England together."

They rolled their luggage out to the parking garage, and when they found their rental car—a compact Volkswagen—Ella opened the door on the right side and started to climb inside.

Heather leaned against the door behind her, holding up the keys. "You want to try it?"

Ella backed away from the vehicle. "I'm not driving on the wrong side of the road."

"It's not wrong over here."

She hurried to the passenger side of the car and buckled in before Heather insisted she try.

As they cruised slowly out of the airport, Heather regaining her confidence in driving on the opposite side, Ella talked about her new job as an account executive and all the weekend trips she and Matthew had planned for the summer. Heather would never tell Ella, but some days she missed her daughter so much, her heart ached. After Jeffery left, some days—and some months—it had been hard raising a child alone, but she and Ella had leaned into each other like two hearty trees that had sprouted from different roots, their trunks entwined into one. And they'd remained there until Ella began growing her branches. Then the winds of life blew her daughter in a different direction.

It was a strange season, having her daughter married and

off working in another state now. Ella used to say they were *two peas in a pod*, traveling, playing, and even studying together when Heather returned to college to finish her degree. They were still two peas, just no longer in the same pod. Ella had a husband and a career, and Heather treasured these rare mother-daughter moments.

"Tell me everything that's happening at home," Ella said, but when Heather started talking about her latest restoration projects, her daughter yawned.

Some moms sang their children to sleep when they were young. Others read a book or told a story. All Heather had to do was start talking about the details of her work, and her daughter would be asleep in minutes. Ella was as curious as her grandfather about the world, but she had little tolerance for details or order.

For a while, Heather thought none of the efficient, orderly genes from the Doyle side of the family had passed down into her daughter's life, but about five years ago, Ella suddenly realized she needed to develop a somewhat orderly schedule to maintain a job. Fortunately, she didn't need to sit still for long in her position with the marketing firm.

"Surely you've been doing something other than working," Ella said.

"There's not much time for anything else," Heather replied, drumming her fingers as she drove.

Ella eyed the steering wheel. "Are you nervous?"

"No."

"Perhaps there are some friends in Bibury you'll want to see."

"Most everyone has moved away." Glancing over, she saw Ella studying her face. "What?"

"I wonder if one of your old boyfriends still lives here."

Heather managed a grin. Ella, in her four months of marriage, now thought herself an expert on relationships and she was determined to help her mother find love again. But there were no relationships Heather wanted to discuss. As long as Ella didn't find out about Christopher, everything would be fine. "Maybe," she finally said with a shrug.

Ella clapped her hands. "Is he still single?"

"Probably not."

Ella sighed. "Then I guess you'll have no choice but to stick with Nick."

"I'm not sticking with anyone—" She stopped herself, glancing back over at her daughter. "What's wrong with Nick?"

"He's a bit stuffy and . . ."

Her eyebrows climbed. "And what?"

"You need to be with someone who's not like you!"

"You're saying I'm stuffy?" she asked as she pulled down the sun visor.

Ella tilted her head. "A bit."

"You're getting quite bold in your older years."

"Matthew says I need to practice transparency."

"Don't feel compelled to be so transparent with me."

When Ella laughed, Heather's heart flooded with joy. Matthew's tenacity combined with his responsibility and honesty was good for her daughter. And Ella's love of spontaneity, adventure, and all things beautiful was good for him.

They turned off the main highway and drove back through the grassy hills in the Cotswolds. "I only want you to meet someone who will—" Ella started.

"Who will what?"

"Who will make you smile."

"I can smile just fine on my own." Heather flashed her a grin to prove it.

Ella rolled her eyes. "It's so much better to smile with someone else, isn't it?"

Of course it was, but she didn't tell her daughter that.

Ella closed her eyes, her short curly hair forming a sort of halo around her head as she leaned back against the seat. A couple minutes later, her breathing deepened into the steady pace of peaceful slumber.

Heather glanced over at Ella's unblemished skin and button nose. She looked like Mum, but their personalities were different. Maggie Doyle had been wary of most people and their motivations, but Heather adored her, even during her teenage years when it felt as if her mum interrogated her almost every night about where she had been and with whom.

In hindsight, she should have listened more instead of balking—and ultimately all out rebelling—against both her mum and dad.

Ella woke again as they entered the picturesque village of Bibury. A stone bridge arched over the placid River Coln, and Ella craned her neck to watch a swan and its fuzzy, brown cygnets floating alongside beds of watercress and the boggy watermeadow called Rack Isle.

Ella lifted her phone and snapped a picture. "It's like someone cued them."

"I called ahead." They drove past a row of sandstone cottages with colorful gardens, and in the center of town, Heather pointed out the ancient Saxon church. "St. Mary's was on a Christmas stamp a few decades back."

Ella rolled down her window to take another picture. "It's all so—so perfect."

Sometimes it felt a little too perfect, Heather thought, on the outside at least. For better or worse, one thing she liked about Portland was that no one seemed to be afraid of their imperfections.

As they climbed the hill above the village, Heather sped past the large country home on her left, averting her eyes from the Westcott family residence. But she slowed the car as they neared the Croft family property.

Ella took off her sunglasses to examine the massive iron gates and gray stone wall. "What's behind that?"

"An old manor house called Ladenbrooke."

"How far away is our cottage?" Ella asked, her gaze still on the formidable wall.

"Right next door." She hadn't thought about Ladenbrooke in such a long time, not until Nick had brought that painting to her studio.

Ella looked back at her and grinned. "Perhaps we should pay a visit to our neighbors."

She tapped the gas. "The Crofts moved a long time ago, and as far as I know, they've never returned."

"But you haven't been here in eons!"

"No, but—" She slowed again before turning into the driveway for the cottage. "Their son Oliver died the year after I was born, and the family moved over near London. I don't think they ever returned."

Ella unbuckled her seatbelt. "How did he die?"

"He drowned in the River Coln."

"The same river that goes through town?" she asked skeptically.

"The very one," Heather said as their car bumped over the gravel. "The current travels fairly fast down the hill, but I used to wonder as well how a teenage boy could drown in it."

Ella opened her door, but she didn't step outside. "Did you ask your parents?"

She nodded. "I asked my mum, but she said no one can explain a tragedy."

"Surely she knew something—"

Heather shrugged. "She hated talking about sad things like that."

"I'll do a little digging," Ella said, looking past Heather at the stone wall that wrapped around the Ladenbrooke property, separating the cottage from the manor house. "Perhaps we can figure out what happened to Oliver Croft."

"If the answers are still around, I have no doubt you'll find them." Instead of looking toward Ladenbrooke, Heather stared at the old stone cottage ahead of her—the home for Ladenbrooke's gardeners, decades before Oliver died.

For all she knew, someone had bought the Croft house and renovated it. The old manor deserved to be cared for, yet a small part of her also wished they'd leave it alone. The world changed so fast, those close to you were gone sometimes before you were able to say good-bye.

She wanted everything—well, almost everything—in Bibury to remain the same.

7

JULY 1954, CLEVEDON, ENGLAND

Walter held his sleeping daughter in his arms, his eyes intent on her face as if she might fly away if he dared blink. She had blue eyes like Maggie, tiny toes that flailed when she cried, and a nose that reminded him of his mother. With her halo of blonde hair, she was beautiful, the most beautiful girl he'd ever seen, and—in spite of her early birth—she was absolutely perfect.

When the midwife first handed him his daughter, he'd been terrified that he might hurt her. She was so small—only five pounds, eight ounces—but Sally said it was a healthy weight. No need to even call the doctor. While Maggie slept off the pethidine, Sally showed him how to hold the baby properly, and he'd taken great care to follow her instructions with precision.

Now he glanced over at his wife tucked under the sheets of the narrow bed in the maternity home. Asleep. Maggie was still groggy from the medication, but Sally told him not to worry and not to rush in waking her. So he sat in a small chair beside Maggie's bed and tried to feed their daughter from the glass bottle their midwife brought him.

July 27, 1954

The date that would forever be inscribed in his heart.

At first he'd been terrified when Maggie began having contractions, ten weeks before their baby was due. He didn't know much about babies, and he'd spent almost seven hours pacing up and down the block outside the maternity home, praying while his wife labored. Sally had finally given Maggie the pethidine to ease her pain, and after the birth, she said Maggie was recovering well. With that news, he'd breathed deep with relief and thanked the One above for answering his pleas.

He didn't know what he'd do if he lost Maggie or their baby.

Things had been strained between he and Maggie this past month, ever since she'd asked him to leave Clevedon. The morning after their dispute, she'd even said she doubted his love, and her words cut him deeply.

How could she ever doubt his love for her?

The summer he'd met her, two years ago, he wanted to ask her to marry him. She had gone out on a few dates with him, like she had with several other boys in Clevedon, but she hadn't reciprocated any of his interest. Even when he got up the nerve to propose the first time, she kindly but soundly turned him down.

But everything changed that night of the storm, when the wind almost carried Maggie away. She'd later told him that she hadn't been thinking clearly when she'd stepped so close to the railing. Thank God he'd come before it was too late. He couldn't bear to think what might have happened if he hadn't seen her.

Of course, it was almost impossible that he wouldn't see her. Every night for months, whether or not his work was done for the day, he'd taken a walk along the harbor because he knew Maggie would be sitting on that bench. She always looked so intent, her eyes focused on the pier and estuary beyond them. He never spoke with her on his walks, hadn't wanted to intrude.

The night he finally intruded, he discovered that she did love him after all. He understood why she'd waited to reciprocate—

she was almost seven years younger than he was—but he didn't understand why she'd then questioned his love.

He'd wrestled with her words, her accusation that he didn't really love her, for weeks. Now that their baby had come, he was certain Maggie would agree they must stay in Clevedon. How could he give up his newspaper—work he enjoyed—to move away when decent work was so hard to find? The income was nominal, but between the newspaper and his freelance work at the *Standard*, it was enough to provide for his family. Few men in this area actually liked their work, but he thrived when he had a pen and paper in hand.

His daughter stirred, and he picked up the milk again. Nudging the blanket away from her face, he watched her suckle the bottle. It was even more critical now to provide the best he could for his family. Maggie needed to be at home with their baby for as long as possible.

It would be a tall challenge to father well, with all the changes happening in their country, but he wanted to protect both Maggie and their children and give them the gift of hope for their future. He wanted his daughter to look up to him as he had done with his father before he was killed in the war.

Maggie groaned, and he put down the bottle and scooted closer to her side.

"She's stunning," he whispered, pushing back the hair that had stuck to his wife's forehead.

Maggie's eyes fluttered open and then closed again. "Elliot?"

Confused, he nudged her arm. "No, it's Walter."

This time her eyes shot open, and she stared at him before her gaze fell to the white bundle in his arms. He lifted the baby up so she could see her. "It's our daughter."

"Is she well?"

He nodded. "And she looks just like you."

"I hope that's good," she said, her smile creased with concern.

Walter laughed, hoping to ease the worry on her face. "It's very good. I'd hate to think of how she'd look if she took after me."

Still, her smile looked forced.

"You did a splendid job, Maggie." He readjusted the pillow behind her and kissed her forehead. "Sally said she's healthy."

Her gaze remained on the baby. "I'm glad."

She closed her eyes for a moment, and when she reopened them, he gently placed their daughter in her arms. She nuzzled the child with her nose and then leaned back against the pillow again to study her as if she weren't certain the baby was real. "She's so pretty."

"Of course." He eyed their daughter again. "But I think we must find a new name for her."

Worry crept into Maggie's eyes again. "Why?"

"She doesn't look like an Eliza or Caroline." He tapped his foot on the floor, crossing his arms. Maggie still didn't want to name their daughter Margaret so he ticked through the names of past and present relatives, but none of them seemed right.

"Who does she look like?" Maggie asked.

He bit his lip, wishing he had a cigarette.

"What about Liberty?" he finally suggested. He certainly touted liberty enough in his writing, and it made sense to name his baby after what he prized most. "We could call her Libby."

"No—" Maggie's fingers fiddled with the baby blanket. "Why don't we just name her Libby?"

"Libby," he repeated. "Libby Doyle."

His gaze rested again on his daughter, asleep now in Maggie's arms.

Maggie and Libby. Mother and daughter. Two women he would love forever.

His blessings overflowed.

"I like it," he said.

"Libby . . ." Maggie whispered as she began to drift back to sleep.

Walter reached for their daughter and held her close to his chest as he studied his wife, her light-brown curls loose around her forehead, peace softening the lines of worry on her face.

The name of the man she'd asked for—*Elliot*—tossed around in his mind. He didn't know anyone named Elliot, and he'd never heard his wife mention a man by that name before. While he tried to leave his instinct to dig up information at the newspaper office, he couldn't leave this alone. The midwife said Maggie might say strange things on the pethidine, but, still, he needed to know who his wife had asked for instead of him.

"Maggie," he whispered, his fingers resting on her hand.

Her eyes opened slowly, and she focused on him. "What is it?"

He swallowed hard. Instead of answering her question, he asked another. "Who is Elliot?"

Her eyes blinked with alarm. Then another question leapt from her lips, much too fast. "What do you mean?"

He examined Maggie's face as she had examined their daughter's features. Was she trying to deceive him?

His mother would say some of their conflict over the past weeks had to do with Maggie's pregnancy. Or perhaps his distrust stemmed from the past year, after she'd snubbed his first marriage proposal. But maybe it was something else. Someone else—

He silently chided himself for doubting her in the hours after she'd given birth to their daughter. Maggie was his wife—the mother of his child—and he loved her. He must put aside his own doubts, his insecurities as to why she married him. He would lay down his very life for her if necessary. Sure, she had been fond of other men before they married, just as he once thought he'd loved another woman when he was eighteen.

"What is it, Walter?" she asked again, her voice quivering.

There was nothing more for them to argue about. Their daughter was here now, mending the wounds between them. They would put aside the past and walk hand in hand into the future.

He kissed Maggie's forehead. "It's nothing, Love."

Libby would be their hope. Their beacon.

And they would grow as a family, right here in Clevedon.

8

APRIL 1955, CLEVEDON, ENGLAND

Maggie slowly rocked Libby in the morning light, the two of them tucked under a blanket in the sitting room. Walter said their daughter was perfect, and he was absolutely right. She was almost nine months now, and one of her first memories would be of ink-stained hands, stretched out to hold her when Walter came home from the office at night. The smell of cigarette smoke and sweat on her father's clothes.

Libby would have the love of both her parents for the rest of her life.

Maggie looked out the window at the harbor. They hadn't moved in with the Morton family. She'd been honest with Walter—at least in her concerns that Libby's cries might frustrate Mr. and Mrs. Morton. In hindsight, she shouldn't have worried. Libby rarely cried.

Walter found them an apartment over the chemist's office in the town center. Two blocks from the newspaper. The street below was noisy until late at night, but Libby didn't mind the noise. She was quite satisfied watching the colorful mobile Walter found for her at the secondhand store.

Libby liked her mobile and she also liked hearing Maggie

sing. Sometimes Maggie wondered if her daughter understood much more than they imagined.

She gently brushed her hands over Libby's head. Even though she didn't have much hair yet, Maggie could see the tints of copper among the blonde. People might ask about her hair color as she grew older, but Maggie had already concocted another story to combat the inquiries. It was one about an Irish grandparent in her lineage. Walter might ask questions as well, but it wouldn't matter. She'd become quite good at telling her stories.

And after more than a year of marriage, she was perfectly content in this new life of hers in Clevedon. The whispers among the older women were fading, and Aunt Priscilla liked the attention she received whenever she held her new niece, so even she seemed to forget about her insistence that Maggie move away.

"Let's go for a stroll, shall we?" Maggie asked as she stood to change Libby's nappy. Even though the air wasn't terribly cold, she dressed her daughter in her matinee coat and bonnet and then bundled her up in the two afghans Walter's mother—Granny Doyle—knitted for her. She carried Libby downstairs, to the back courtyard where she kept their pram alongside their neighbors' baby carriages and bicycles.

Maggie wrapped a scarf around her hair and began pushing Libby through the center of town, the wheels of the pram bounding along the cobblestone path. The spring had been warm and tulips bloomed in clusters along the streets, the sweet fragrance mixing with the trace of salt in the air.

Libby seemed to like their walks, but she didn't babble or make happy sounds like some of the other babies in Clevedon. The sounds and motion soothed her, though, and after watching the sky and sandpipers, she almost always fell asleep.

In *The Mothercraft Manual,* Mary Lillian Read said babies should sleep seventeen hours a day—and cry for thirty minutes—but not Maggie's daughter. She was much too alert and curious with the world to sleep but fourteen hours. And much too content to cry.

Walter once asked Maggie quietly, as if Libby might overhear them, if she thought something was wrong. He'd heard that some babies born too early had trouble with their mental faculties, and he was worried Libby was slow in the mind. Maggie assured him that Libby was just fine, that Mary Lillian Read said most children have slow mental adjustment until age six. She didn't tell him, of course, that Libby was actually born more than a week late.

The local doctor expressed concern about Libby's "listlessness" and secretly Maggie also wondered if something was wrong. But she didn't want to worry about that now. The fresh sea air was good for both of them, and she sucked it in with gusto.

If Walter hadn't figured out by now that Libby wasn't his, she guessed he never would. Rumors among some of the women might still linger, but they seemed to be as potent as a breeze carried out to sea. Some might hear the whisper of it, but then it would be gone. Walter adored their daughter. Nothing would ever change that.

This town, she'd decided, would be a good place for their family after all.

She sat down on the bench where she used to watch for Elliot's boat *Illimité*. They'd met the first time about three years ago when she'd stopped by the ice cream parlor after work for a strawberry milk shake. Elliot had strutted through the door all confident, like he was James Dean with his dark jeans, V-neck shirt, and slicked-up hair. She suspected that he had been planning to go to the pub with his crew, but when he saw her through the window, he decided on root beer instead of a pint.

Either way, she'd enjoyed flirting with him.

That night he'd invited her to meet him at the cavern on Hangstone Hill, away from the lights in town. She was seventeen at the time, and while other girls were allowed to go out at night, Aunt Priscilla wouldn't permit her to leave their house after dark without a chaperone. So she'd had to sneak out of her window like she was in primary school.

Elliot had been the perfect gentleman that night. He'd roasted monkfish and potatoes over a small fire and spread a blanket over the pebbles in the mouth of the cave. They'd sipped Coca-Colas, smoked cigarettes, and she laughed at the stories of his expeditions. When the fire died down into hot coals, he pointed out the constellations.

She hadn't cared much about the stars, but she enjoyed his attention. On that night, and the nights to follow, she imagined him to be one of the pirates who used to pilfer the coast. A smuggler who was wanted by the local customs men.

He told her he wanted to take her with him one day to see the world. She never told him she was scared of the water, but for him, she thought she could do anything. And she had wanted to be with him and see the places he described—Morocco, Sweden, the Greek Isles, France.

A year passed, and each time Elliot returned to their village, she would meet him by the cavern. By then, she was eighteen and no longer had to sneak out of the house, but she was careful not to be seen with him in town.

Elliot brought her exotic gifts from his travels, though she didn't dare bring any of them home—except the chocolates along with the fountain pen and black leather journal from Spain. As she grew older, Elliot's gifts became more costly even as his gentlemanly manners began to wane. She'd enjoyed kissing him very much in the beginning, but then he began chiding her for her immaturity. She'd refused his advances for months until he said he loved her. That he would marry her. And if she loved him, he said, she would reciprocate his affection.

She'd allowed him to bargain for what should have been priceless, giving him the gift of her heart along with her body. She'd been so foolish. Elliot didn't really love her nor did he want to marry her. He'd gotten exactly what he wanted and then he was gone.

She'd suspected back then—though she hadn't known for certain—where babies came from. Some older women seemed to think ignorance in that area was a blessing. Libby was a blessing, but ignorance was not. She would never allow her daughter to be ignorant about such things.

Reaching down, she tangled Libby's little fingers into hers. Libby was Elliot's last gift—and his best gift—to her.

Walter didn't buy her exotic gifts. He respected and cared for her, even in the months when her body was changing. She'd done nothing to earn his love and yet he gave it freely. She may have lied about Libby, but she hadn't lied about her vows to him. No matter what happened, she would be faithful, as long as they both lived.

A fishing trawler moved past the promenade and cast anchor near the pier. In the distance, she could see the white sails of yachts fluttering between the shores of England and Wales.

She rarely came down to the promenade these days, because whenever she saw a yacht in the harbor, her chest felt as if it might cave in over her heart. What would Elliot do if he found out about Libby? He might get on his boat and sail right back to France, but there was a chance he'd want to keep his daughter. She could never let that happen. . . .

Nor could she allow him the opportunity to shatter her and Walter's future with the truth.

One time she had begged God to bring Elliot back to her, but now she prayed he would never return. Everything would be fine as long as he stayed far away from her family.

9

Nettles clustered together under the dust-coated windows of her parents' stone cottage, like a thorny shield to ward off intruders. The thatch roof glowed an iridescent green from the clinging barnacles of moss, and the beam above the wooden front door sagged precariously.

Beside the door, the name of the house—*Willow Cottage*—was painted on a sign with *The Old Bothy* spelled out underneath. The word *Old* was inconsequential. No description was necessary to explain that the cottage was way past its prime.

When she was a child, Heather didn't think their home was dilapidated. Instead it had been a haven of quiet beauty to her, the stones on the walls harboring stories of the past. Most of her memories were now blurred, but she remembered marveling at the mystery of this place.

Ella stepped up beside her and they surveyed the front of the cottage together. "I remember it."

Heather's eyebrows climbed. "It's been more than twenty years."

"But I still remember." Ella nudged at a loose paver with her toe. "We've aged together."

"You've aged well, my dear, but the house—not so much." She

leaned over and plucked out a tall weed. "Your grandfather used to be meticulous about the upkeep."

Ella pushed her sunglasses up on her head, her curls bunching behind her ears. "Now it's more vintage."

Heather's father had been classic vintage. After a hard day of work, he liked to sit in front of their fireplace, in his overstuffed chair, smoking a pipe and reading one of his many books about philosophy, history, or religion. Long ago she used to crawl onto his lap in the evenings and pretend to read with him. Sometimes she would fall asleep and wake the next morning in her bed.

Ella might have considered him stuffy at first, but Walter Doyle wasn't a snob. He enjoyed people well enough and he was innately curious. Whenever Heather or anyone else asked a question, he searched for the answer.

But her father liked the quiet more than conversation because it gave him an opportunity to think or read one of his treasured books. After a long day of helping people communicate by post, he rarely had energy left for casual communication, though whenever she wanted to talk, he always put down his books to listen. Or tell her a story.

She opened her leather handbag and pulled out the ring of keys the retirement village had mailed to her along with boxes of Dad's books and clothing.

Sometimes the good memories were more difficult to process than the hard ones.

Ella tapped the sign. "What's a *bothy*?"

Heather nodded toward the ivy-draped wall that stood about forty feet to their right. "A century ago, this place housed the gardeners who worked for the Croft family."

Ella stretched up on her toes as if she might be able to see the property on the other side. "They must have had a big garden over there."

"My mum said it was spectacular." She tried two keys on the ring; the second one unlocked the front door.

Ella followed her into the musty-smelling sitting room with its formal couch and two chairs. Heather cranked open a window to let in fresh air and erase some of the remnants of time. A dark wood door to the right of the room looked as if it might lead to a secret cellar, but this house no longer conjured up mystery in her mind like it had when she was a child. Behind the wooden door were steps that led upstairs to two bedrooms where she and Ella would spend the night.

She was tempted to take a nap right now, but that would only prolong her jet lag. She and Ella needed to push through a few more hours, and then they could crash until morning.

Ella collapsed onto one of the stuffed chairs, and dust particles ballooned up around her face. She coughed, waving her hands.

"Oh no you don't," Heather said, reaching for one of her daughter's arms. "You already slept in the car."

"Just another quick nap."

She tugged on Ella's arm. "A *quick* nap will mean you're up all night."

Ella shook her arm free and crossed it over the other one. "Ten minutes."

"I'll take you down to the village right now for a proper pot of English tea."

Her eyes closed, Ella leaned her head back. "I'm too old for you to tell me what to do and much too young to drink proper pots of tea."

Heather rubbed her hands together. "Perhaps I can tempt you with some coffee and a sandwich."

Ella opened up one eye. "A mocha?"

"No promises."

She shut her eyes again. "I'm not getting back in the car."

"We could bike instead."

Ella sat back up. "Where will we get bicycles?"

"From the old stable." At least she hoped the bikes were still there.

Ella stood slowly. "I'll take a nap when we get back."

"We'll both be ready for bed then."

The first key on her ring opened the door of the stable beside the house. The gardeners probably kept equipment instead of horses inside since a much larger stable had been built on the other side of Ladenbrooke. Her parents had turned the building into a bicycle and storage shed.

As she opened the door, sunlight flooded the dark room and the scent of old leather escaped into the light. Rakes, a broom, and a weed trimmer hung on rungs along the wall, and in the center of the floor were rows of plastic boxes, stacked six feet high. At least a hundred of them.

She groaned. Why had her father saved so much stuff?

"Did they keep everything?" Ella asked as she scanned the shed.

"Apparently." On the other side of the boxes, Heather spotted her mother's old bicycle against the far wall, next to the red bicycle she'd loved when she was a teenager.

Together she and Ella inched back between the narrow rows. Each box they passed was marked with an index card and number. The archives at the British Museum in London may be better protected than the Doyle family collection, but they couldn't possibly be more organized.

Some of the boxes had the word *Rubbish* scribbled on the side with a black Sharpie, but Heather wasn't quite ready to throw them away yet. At least not without glancing inside. Lifting one of the lids, she saw a neat row of labeled manila files, each one containing papers and newspaper articles. When she was younger, her father liked to clip out articles from different newspapers and magazines, but she'd never thought to ask what he was collecting.

She rolled her hands over the file tabs.

Walter's Newspaper Articles, 1944

Her dad had been too young to fight as a soldier during World War II, but he'd fought in his own way—with words. Mum told her he'd written for newspapers for more than a decade, but he'd given up his writing when they moved to Bibury.

"This one has your name on it."

Turning, she saw Ella pointing at a box. And she saw her maiden name.

Heather Noelle Doyle, 1969

Her parents named her Heather after the flowers her mum liked and Noelle because she'd been born two days before Christmas. A miracle baby, Mum had said. And a child of the '60s by eight days.

"There are a bunch more boxes with your name," Ella said, lifting one of the lids. "None of them marked for rubbish."

Even if the boxes weren't marked for the landfill, she couldn't keep this stuff if she was going to sell the cottage nor could she bring it all back to Portland with her. Nick would tell her to call a disposal company this afternoon and be done with it. They could haul it all away without her even opening a box. But he would be just as curious as she was to see if there were any treasures hidden here. These boxes were all she had left of her parents and perhaps her understanding of them. They may not have wanted to talk much about the past, but perhaps there were a few answers in what they'd stored.

Ella rapped her knuckles on the top of a box. "We'll never get through this stuff in a week."

Ella was right—it might take her an entire month to sort through it all. "Perhaps I can talk you into staying longer?"

"I can't," Ella replied with a shake of her head. "My boss balked at seven days."

"And I suppose Matthew would have my head if I kept you here for two weeks."

Ella grinned like always at the mention of Matthew's name. He'd already texted his wife dozens of times, it seemed, since she'd landed in England.

Heather remembered well when she and Christopher used to be goofy like that. There hadn't been any texting in the mid-80s, but he would write her notes, telephone her, and sneak over to visit, sometimes way too late at night.

Another wave of regret flushed through her, and she steadied herself on the box.

Ella's smile faded to concern. "You okay?"

"The jet lag is hitting me," she said, rolling her shoulders back. Then she directed Ella through the narrow corridor of boxes, to the two bicycles in the back. As they worked together to widen the path between the boxes, Heather began to hum the teamwork song they used to sing when her daughter was about five.

Ella groaned. "You're insane."

"Only on weekends," she said with a smile.

Together they maneuvered the bikes through the boxes and out the door.

The wicker basket on Mum's bicycle was streaked with mud, the tires flat, and when Ella rang the rusty bell, it sounded more like the muffled croak of a frog. The chain was dangling on the red bicycle but Heather rethreaded it over the sprockets while Ella found the tire pump and inflated all four tires. Then Ella pushed her grandmother's bike onto the driveway.

Heather laughed as she climbed onto her old bicycle and began to pedal.

It had been a long time since she'd laughed. Much too long.

"Race you to the village."

Ella leaned over the handlebars, motivated by the prospect of coffee in her near future. "I'll race you there and back again."

ELLA TOULSON LOOKED JUST LIKE her mother. And her grandmother.

Or at least that's what Mrs. Westcott thought as she watched her and Heather pedal down the lane on the rickety bicycles.

In an instant, her memories flashed back to Heather decades ago, riding in the infant seat behind Maggie. When Heather was old enough to bike on her own, she and Christopher would ride around the village, the two of them laughing together wherever they went.

Mrs. Westcott edged the curtains back a few more inches and watched the two women until they disappeared from sight.

Turning away from the window, she glanced down at the

telephone on the end table. She'd stopped meddling years ago because, in spite of her good intentions, her interference often had unforeseen and sometimes rather unfortunate consequences. Now she only intervened when absolutely necessary.

Before her husband passed away, he made her swear off meddling altogether when it came to their oldest son. Still, she believed Christopher would want to know Heather had returned. It wouldn't be meddling. She'd be more like a messenger, delivering the information. Christopher could decide what to do with it.

Mrs. Westcott began to dial her son's number, but then she stopped and hung the phone back up on the receiver. She collapsed into her favorite chair, looking back out at the street and the flowers on their small front lawn.

It was her fault—hers and Maggie's—that Christopher and Heather were avoiding each other. And with Maggie gone, she was the only one who could remedy it.

Eying her phone again, fresh regret seeped through her. She would honor the memory of her husband by not meddling *per se*. Instead she would try and put a few of the broken pieces back together. If she was careful, perhaps she could even mend some of what she'd helped tear apart. After all this time, she wouldn't point fingers, but there was healing to be had.

The lies had become a foundation for reality, albeit a shaky one, but how could she bring to light the truth without hurting people she loved dearly in the process? There must be some way she could undo the past and still protect those she loved today.

The telephone rang, and it was the husband of one of her patients on the line. His words were muffled, but she understood enough of what he was saying. His wife was about to deliver their baby boy.

She quickly hung up the phone and reached for her black bag of supplies.

There was no more time now to wallow in her regrets. Today she would focus on bringing a new life into the world.

Tomorrow, perhaps, she would remember again a life that was lost.

10

MAY 1955, CLEVEDON, ENGLAND

Maggie blinked twice as she gazed into the window of Severn Jewellers, confused at first and then horrified at the face she saw in the reflection. Elliot was standing across the market street, staring back at her.

Her pulse racing, she pretended to admire a pair of diamond earrings in the display case, as if Elliot might not have seen her, but when she dared a glance over her shoulder, a smile slipped easily across his lips. She tipped back the bulky pram and swiveled it around, her hands trembling as she pushed Libby away from the town center, toward the safety of their new flat. If she hurried, she could be home in five minutes tops.

Her legs felt as if they might collapse under her, but she couldn't allow her fear to cripple her now. If she did, Elliot might find out—

She moved faster.

He could never find out she'd had a baby.

"Mags!" he called out as she turned the corner up Moor Lane.

She ignored him, continuing to goad the pram forward even as she slid the black canopy toward her to hide Libby's face.

Her indifference didn't seem to deter Elliot. He was beside her in seconds, grinning down with his slick smile and all the cockiness that once seemed attractive. "Are you toying with me?"

She glanced back at the busy market street and saw Mrs. Bishop and several ladies from church watching her. Had they heard Elliot shout her name? They would wonder who he was. And why Maggie was trying to ignore him.

"This isn't a game," she whispered.

His gaze fell swiftly to the carriage, and his smile disappeared. "You have a kid?"

"My friend—" she started and then stumbled over her words before trying again. "He's my friend's baby," she said with the slightest of shrugs, but her breath was shallow as she tried to calm her nerves. "I'm watching him this morning."

He stepped closer, leaning down to whisper in her ear. "Meet me at the cavern tonight."

She held her head a bit higher, trying to be confident. Aloof. "I'm no longer fond of caves."

Stepping back, he studied her face with the dark-green eyes that once captivated her. "I've missed you," he said slowly. "I thought you might have been missing me too."

Behind him, Mrs. Bishop and two of her aunt's friends huddled together, glancing toward her and Elliot. Maggie stepped away from him and pointed toward an alleyway between the shops on the opposite side of the street. "We can talk over there," she said. By tonight, perhaps, the women would forget about her brief encounter with a French sailor.

He wrapped his fingers around the handle of the pram as if he would push it for her, but she quickly reclaimed it. "I'll go first," she said quietly but firmly. "Wait three or four minutes before following me."

Her head high, she pushed Libby toward the alley, praying her daughter would fall asleep. No matter what happened, even if

Libby demanded Maggie's attention with her tears, she wouldn't let Elliot see her.

The man didn't wait like she'd asked. He followed her immediately into the alley, and she stepped in front of the pram, a barrier between him and Libby. Her initial shock over his return turned into anger. "Where have you been?" she demanded.

"Traveling the world," he replied, nonchalant. "Norway. Russia. A week in the New York harbor. I brought you the prettiest bracelet—"

She balled her fingers into fists. While her life was falling apart, he'd been touring New York. "You should have written."

"Darling, you know I'm not much for writing."

She tucked her fists under her arms, hugging them close to her chest. "Don't call me darling."

His eyebrows climbed in a way she once thought clever, but it sickened her now.

"You told me you would return by Christmas. You told me . . ." Her voice trailed off. The promises he'd made didn't matter anymore.

He grinned again. "You did miss me, didn't you?"

She slumped back against the brick wall, her gaze on the narrow entrance of the alley behind him, the people passing by as they shopped. All it would take was one person to light the fuse.

Somehow she would have to convince Elliot that there was nothing left between them. And no reason for him to either stay or return. "I didn't think you were coming back."

He rested his hand over her head, against the wall. "I promised you I would."

"More than a year ago . . ."

His face was inches from her, but she refused to look up at him. His clothes smelled like salt water and rotten fish, and she thought she might vomit, both from the stench and the thought of being close to him again. He was no longer a romantic pirate. He was the man who'd abandoned her and then laughed about it.

Her heart screamed a warning, urging her to flee.

Elliot eyed the pram again, as if he wanted to see the baby inside, and she knew well that he was not one to be deterred. If she managed to get around him, back out onto the market street, he would continue following her all the way home.

She glanced at her watch. "I must return to my friend's house before she gets worried."

"Meet me at the cave," he repeated, his voice the same seductive tone that used to entangle her.

"I can't."

He cocked his head. "You've found someone else, haven't you?"

"I have," she said as she smoothed her hand over the canvas top of the pram. "Right after you left."

His breath was on her ear as he backed her toward the carriage. "Just one last time," he whispered. "Then I'll leave for good."

The pram shook when she bumped into it. Libby gurgled, but it was more of a song than a cry. Elliot ignored the child as he reached for Maggie's hand, grasping it in his. Stunned, she looked at his hand and then back up at him with disgust.

Why had she given herself to this man? Instead of waiting for Elliot, she should have accepted Walter's proposal the first time he'd asked.

She tried to pull her hand away from him. "Let me go."

Instead of releasing her, he leered down, his eyes bloated with desire. "We have to say good-bye."

Her stomach clenched at the thought, but perhaps if she agreed to meet him at the cave, he would leave her alone right now. She and Libby could hide in their flat until the *Illmité* left the harbor.

"One last time," she said, the words bitter on her lips.

His smile returned as his fingers caressed her hand.

"Maggie?"

Her stomach clenched again, but this time it wasn't because of Elliot's touch. It was because her husband had stepped into the alleyway.

Walter's eyes were focused on her as he walked up the alley. And his voice was steady—too steady. "Why are you here?"

She yanked her hand away from Elliot's clutch. "I'm trying to get away from this man."

Walter reached for Maggie's trembling hand, and she clung to him. Then he met Elliot's gaze. "Don't touch her again."

Elliot crossed his arms. "Who are you?"

Instead of answering him, Walter looked back at her. "Mrs. Bishop said this man was following you."

Elliot leaned his shoulder against the wall, seeming to enjoy the drama unfolding before him. "Maggie asked me to meet her here."

That much was true, but it didn't sound right. She'd said those words to get rid of him.

Her mind whirled, and she couldn't sort it all out with both men watching her. "I will explain—later."

Elliot smirked. "It seems she has a lot to explain."

"I'm Maggie's husband," Walter said as he stepped between her and Elliot.

Elliot's eyes widened for a split second. Then they narrowed. He looked down at the pram, his arm crossed, before looking back at her. "Funny, you never mentioned you were married."

"You never gave me the opportunity."

Walter released her hand. "You know this man?"

"From a long time ago."

"Not so long—" Elliot insisted.

She tugged at Walter's elbow. "Can we please discuss this at home?"

Her husband ignored her, speaking to the man before him instead. "What's your name?"

"Baron Bonheur," he replied smugly. "But your wife calls me Elliot."

Walter's fist flung out so fast that Maggie gasped. Stunned. Blood streamed from Elliot's lip, and Maggie thought he would surely beat Walter to a pulp, but instead he wiped off the blood with the back of his hand and snickered. Then he winked at her. "Don't worry, Mags. I'll come visit again, next time I'm in Clevedon."

Maggie reached for Walter's hand, holding it steady in hers so he wouldn't hit Elliot a second time.

Elliot strutted back down the alley, whistling as if he hadn't a care. Then she and Walter stood side by side in a dreadful silence. She owed him some sort of explanation, quickly, but she could think of no story to explain away Elliot.

Silently Walter stepped toward the pram and pushed back the canopy. Instead of reaching for Libby, he stared down into her face as if he'd never seen her before. As if she was a venomous snake or one of the blue sharks that trolled out in the channel. Then he backed away from the carriage, recoiling as if the girl he once thought to be his daughter might poison him.

When he looked back up at Maggie, she saw scorn flaring in his eyes. The shattering of his love into a million pieces.

Instead of anger, pain laced his voice. "You said his name."

"What do you mean?"

He raked his fingers through his short hair. "In the maternity home, you asked for Elliot."

She cringed. "I knew him a long time ago, before we married—"

Walter interrupted her. "Why didn't you tell me about him?"

"I didn't want to hurt you."

"You knew him well," he said, more to himself than to her.

She wasn't certain how to respond. "I thought I loved him, but I didn't."

"Before we were married . . ." The anger in his eyes welled again with the realization. "You were expecting before our wedding."

"No—"

This time he didn't listen to her protest. "That's why the baby came early."

"The baby's name is Libby."

He ignored her. "You were never planning to tell me . . ."

She glanced back down at her beautiful girl, resigned to the truth. "It wouldn't have done any good."

"But it would be the truth, Maggie."

She snorted. The man before her might be obsessed with gathering facts, uncovering the truth, but that didn't mean the truth should always be unearthed. This was her story to tell, and she'd known already that the truth didn't always make things better. Sometimes it destroyed things that were good.

With the same hand he'd punched Elliot, Walter slapped the handle of the carriage. And then Maggie watched with dismay as her husband walked away.

II

JUNE 1955, CLEVEDON, ENGLAND

Gray clouds drifted slowly over the estuary as church bells rang out on the hill above Maggie's bench. She and Walter didn't go to church this morning. Instead they sat next to each other, trying to piece back together the fragments of their life.

She gently rocked the pram back and forth to keep her hands busy, trying to calm her heart. Not only had Mrs. Bishop told Walter about her meeting with Elliot, but she'd returned to the scene of the crime and perched herself at the end of the alleyway, listening to everything.

Thanks to Mrs. Bishop and her underlings, the news of Maggie rendezvousing with a French sailor struck Clevedon like the fierce winds of a winter storm. It was the tail of the storm that brought the worst sting though. The whispers about her bastard child.

Walter had only spoken to Maggie when absolutely necessary over the past three weeks. Aunt Priscilla now snubbed both Maggie and Libby. Uncle Timothy tilted his head in greeting when he saw Maggie at church last week, but he didn't dote over Libby like he usually did. Her innocent daughter had become an outcast alongside her.

"We have to move," Walter said, tired but resolute.

Maggie shifted on the bench, her eyes fixed on the calm harbor before them. "I tried to tell you."

"But you didn't tell me why we needed to leave."

"If I told you the truth—" She swallowed. "I didn't want you to hate Libby because of me."

"You didn't want to marry me. You needed a father for your child, and without knowing it, I volunteered." When she looked over at him, she saw tears in his eyes. "After everything, why would you agree to meet that man again?"

"I wasn't going to meet him. I only wanted him to leave Libby and me alone."

He stared at the carriage. "I wish I could believe you."

"Do you want a divorce?" she asked, barely a whisper.

"No—"

"Libby and I will leave Clevedon so you can stay."

Walter shook his head. "I vowed to stay married. For better or worse."

She released the handle and clutched her hands together. "No one expects you to—"

"I promised, Maggie, and I keep my promises."

She glanced out at the bay, at a trawler in the distance, her foot tapping against the cement. She knew the world was big beyond their town, but she had no idea how big. She remembered a bit of London as a girl, the tall spires and the art shop her father had loved. The Frasers weren't people who liked to travel, even after the war, so she never returned to London.

Walter plucked a stone off the pavement and hurled it toward the water. "I don't know where we'll go—"

"Perhaps we don't have to know. Perhaps we can pack up the car and just drive."

Walter didn't move. "At some point we'll have to stop driving."

"I think we'll know exactly when that is."

Libby whimpered, and Maggie glanced over at her husband. She cried so infrequently that he used to jump when she made the slightest noise, rescue her like he was her prince, but he no longer seemed to hear her cries.

Maggie leaned over and lifted their daughter out of the carriage. Libby watched the boats rise and fall with the swell of the waves. She didn't make much noise, but she observed everything.

"Perhaps she'll be a writer like you," Maggie said.

Walter shook his head. "She's nothing like me."

"But she will be," Maggie vowed. "She will want to be just like her father."

Walter turned toward her. "You must stop pretending that everything's fine."

"I'm not pretending—" She started, but then stopped. What was wrong with pretending a little? It was so much better than wallowing.

"It's not fine now," she said, her voice wavering. "But it will be."

Walter stood up and walked away.

Libby grasped one of Maggie's curls and tugged on it. Maggie turned her gaze away from her husband, back down to her daughter. Then she kissed Libby on the forehead.

Before she married Walter, she'd known he was a man of principle, but she'd thought he would leave her and Libby now—he certainly had every right to do so. Instead it seemed he was willing to start a new life with them, and she was immensely relieved.

She prayed he wouldn't stay angry for long. It wasn't Libby's fault that her real father was a fiend.

The only daddy she would ever know was the man who'd rescued them both.

WITH BOXES CRAMMED INTO THE boot of their car, their luggage strapped to the top, Walter drove Maggie and her daughter out of Clevedon at dawn. A few friends had helped them pack last night, but Anthony was the only person who'd come by early this morning to wave good-bye.

The moment Elliot Bonheur said he'd visit Maggie again, Walter knew they'd have to move. Even if his wife had severed her heart from that man, he couldn't risk staying near the coast—for his sake or for hers. The speculating about Bonheur while he was at work, wondering if the man had returned, would drive him mad.

It felt as if everything he'd worked for, everything he desired, had been obliterated back in that alleyway.

As they crested the hill, he glanced into the rearview mirror for one last look at Clevedon. He'd arrived here when he was twenty-two to work at the paper, and in months, Mr. Bishop had handed over the reins of the *Clevedon Mercury* to him. The war had stolen his father's life, but he'd wanted to continue his father's legacy as a newspaperman along with the strong legacy of loving and caring well for his family.

The war had taken Maggie's parents as well, and Walter once thought she wanted to build a family with him. Instead she had started a family with someone else.

She should have told him the truth about Bonheur before they married. About Libby. It would have been painful, but he would have had a choice in whether or not he wanted to raise another man's child.

How could he ever trust his wife again? And how could he love Libby when he despised her father?

Libby slept on Maggie's lap as they traveled east through the rain, the windshield blades sweeping drops of water back and forth across the glass. When Walter told Mr. Bishop he couldn't stay at the newspaper, the man gave him an extra week's pay to help tide them over. He'd thought about going to Kent to live for a short time with his mother and stepfather, just until he found work, but he didn't think his mother's new husband would want them staying there. He prayed he would find a position soon that involved the written word, but it was more important now for him to provide for his family.

As they drove east, he turned the radio dial so they could listen to the news, but about an hour into their drive, Maggie turned it again, skipping past two music stations until she found a program. *Educating Archie*. Quite possibly the worst show on the radio.

The bad jokes, between a ventriloquist and his dummy, grated on his nerves. Along with the decidedly fake-sounding laughter in the background and the requisite applause.

He squeezed the steering wheel. "Please turn the dial."

Maggie looked over at him as if he'd asked her to jump out of their automobile. "Why would I change it?"

"Because this is absurd."

"It's funny, Walter."

"Not to people who appreciate good humor."

She tucked the blanket over Libby's shoulders. "She seems to like it."

He glanced over. It didn't seem to him that Libby cared one whit what they listened to.

The audience laughed again, and he gritted his teeth. He didn't particularly care to laugh about anything right now.

Maggie shifted Libby in her arms, before leaning her head back on the seat.

He'd promised to honor and protect his wife. And to love her, as long as they both lived.

God help him, he would do the best he could. Perhaps one day he would be able to embrace the future alongside Maggie and her child as well.

12

Christopher Westcott slowly drank his pint of ale at the Bird and Baby, as locals liked to call The Eagle and Child, and basked in the familiar smells—old wood bathed in lemon oil, braised beef, stale beer that spackled the bar. The pub was a popular mecca for those who admired J. R. R. Tolkien, C. S. Lewis, and their entire group of literary giants they called Inklings.

Christopher wasn't even close to being a literary giant nor was he a tourist, but he enjoyed writing and liked to feign himself one of the professors who might have basked in the lively readings and debates of the Inklings instead of just the aromas of this pub.

Personally, he admired the writings of George MacDonald, the man C. S. Lewis considered his mentor. MacDonald was a writer and professor. And he was a frequently unemployed Scottish minister due to his views on God's love and grace. The man could speak the language of theologians at the same time he wrote books for children and readers of all ages whom he described as "child-like, whether they be of five, or fifty, or seventy-five." MacDonald was a man of integrity who believed that God did not punish His children except to amend and heal them. A man who believed God's love and grace was available to all people—a direct affront to the Calvinists in his era.

Christopher admired men from the past like George MacDonald, and he admired more contemporary, clandestine men of integrity like Walter Doyle who had encouraged him to lay down his pride and write about the stirrings in his own soul.

He checked his watch. Tonight he and Adrienne had a table reserved at Brasserie Blanc, and with both of their hectic schedules, neither of them were particularly fond of waiting for the other. Sitting and pondering in the Oxford pub was a poor excuse for his tardiness, but he wanted to at least start his article.

He eyed the iPad screen in front of him, trying to collect the right words to oppose predestination, but they eluded him.

Walter had passed away almost four months ago, but sometimes Christopher forgot that his friend was gone. Every time he drove by Oaken Holt—the country estate that doubled as a retirement community—he pretended Walter was still waiting inside to share a cup of coffee and an hour of conversation. Walter inspired him to not only learn about the facts in the Bible but also to delve into the mysteries of the Scriptures. To pray and think and write down all that churned inside him.

Even though Walter had said years ago that Christopher was much too old to call Walter his mentor, he continued to ask his friend for both advice and to critique his writing. It was their own little Inklings group, in the dining room of the Oaken Holt Care Home.

In his final weeks, Walter no longer seemed to know who Christopher was or why he was there, but he liked to think the elderly man was still encouraged by the friendly face of one of his protégées.

His mobile phone rang, and he saw his mother's number on the screen. She'd rung him four times while he was lecturing this week but never left a message. This time he could actually answer it.

"Hello, Mum."

She didn't say anything for a moment, apparently shocked that he was on the phone.

He and his mum had both lost their spouses to cancer in the past decade. It was a bond neither of them wanted, but one they couldn't escape. In their grief, they'd learned to give each other plenty of grace. His parents had four children, but even though he and Julianna had wanted to be parents, God never gave them a child. They'd been married for only three years when Julianna was diagnosed with cancer.

In the past months, Christopher had been trying to convince his mother to sell their large family home and move into something smaller, but she said she didn't want to live alone in a new place. Perhaps she'd finally changed her mind.

"You should leave a message," he said, scolding her like she'd done so often when he was younger.

"Some things shouldn't be said on voice mail."

He leaned back against the wooden slats in his chair, alarmed. "What is it?"

"Heather has come home, and I thought perhaps—" Thankfully, she stopped herself. "I just thought you'd want to know."

He didn't want or need that information. "Duly noted."

"Are you still coming home this weekend?"

Confound it—he had completely forgotten he was supposed to introduce Adrienne to his family on Friday. He couldn't stay away just because Heather finally decided to return.

"Of course." He stuffed his iPad back into the black case. There was no sense in trying to write now.

"Both your brothers and your sister are coming to meet your friend."

He roped the strap of his case over his shoulder. "Her name is Adrienne, and you have to play nice this time."

"I was nice the last time you brought a girl home."

He groaned. "Lauren was a woman, and you were not nice to her."

His mother made a huffing sound. "How was I supposed to know she couldn't peel potatoes?"

"You were testing her," he said as he walked toward the door. And Lauren had failed the test. They ended up in the Accident & Emergency department to stitch up her thumb. The next day Lauren asked him not to contact her again. "I'm serious, Mum."

She sighed.

"No asking Adrienne to help in the kitchen. And no inviting Heather over for tea while we're home."

"What if your friend offers to help?"

"Tell her that you want her to relax like you do with every other guest."

She mumbled her agreement before he disconnected the call.

Stepping out of the pub onto St. Giles', he turned into a mew that wove along the backs of shops. Ancient trees grew amidst the broken cobblestone of this pathway, and small clusters of students, dressed in their traditional black-and-white subfusc, passed by him. Visitors to Oxford usually stuck to the main thoroughfares, making these passageways between the town's shops and colleges a quiet respite from the crowds.

He'd spent his first years here as a student trying to forget Heather. Then the rest of his adult life, he'd tried to avoid her when she'd returned home.

Guilt still gnawed at him for missing Walter's memorial service. He could have canceled his lecture in Amsterdam—as his mother reminded him several times—but he hadn't wanted to see Walter's daughter.

He went the following week instead—after Heather left—to pay his respects at Walter's grave.

If only he could conjure up a reason to postpone this weekend's visit as well.

A WREN CHATTERED FROM A twig nest in the stable, scolding Heather and Ella for invading his world. Or perhaps he was welcoming their company after being alone for so long. It was sometimes impossible, Heather thought, to tell the difference between affection and irritation.

All morning, they'd kept the door of the stable propped open, and the fresh air stirred the decades of dust and dirt. Sweat coated Heather's forehead, and she tried to wipe it off with her sleeve. When she looked over at Ella, her daughter laughed at her. "You just smeared dirt across your face."

"Do you have a problem with dirt?"

"Not particularly, but I didn't think you were a fan." Ella lifted the lid off another box. "It looks like you were caught in some sort of storm."

Her gaze roamed over the remaining seventy-two containers stacked on the floor, and she felt as if she'd been trapped in the perfect storm. She and Ella had been working hard for five days, cleaning out the closets in the upstairs bedrooms first before tackling the ground floor and then diving into the storage here. After she finished, she still had to sort through her parent's things in the basement.

Ella had been disappointed that they hadn't found anything about Oliver Croft yet, but she kept searching, determined to find out what happened to the young man who'd lived next door.

When her daughter's phone beeped, she pulled it out of her pocket, a smile crossing her face as she read her husband's text.

Nick had texted Heather a handful of times this week, mostly with questions about restoration projects and then frustration that she planned to stay the entire two weeks. He seemed to miss her expertise more than her company though, and if she was honest, she didn't particularly miss his company either.

Ella was right—Nick was stuffy and a bit pompous. But he was also safe. Her daughter didn't understand Heather's need for a safe friendship. Nick Davis might not make her smile, but he would also never break her heart.

While Ella texted Matthew back, Heather lifted out another file and skimmed through a set of her father's articles about the production of penicillin in Clevedon. Her parents rarely talked about their years living in that town, about seventy miles southwest of Bibury, though her mum told her she'd lived with a family in Clevedon after being evacuated from her family's neighborhood in South London during the war. Mum must have been terrified to take the train west by herself at such a young age, but she'd never told Heather about her journey or about her years growing up in the coastal town.

Ella slid her phone into her back pocket and started rummaging through the box in front of her.

Heather glanced at her watch. "Isn't Matthew supposed to be sleeping?"

"He wanted to make sure I was really flying home tomorrow." Ella smiled again. "He said he's about to jump on a plane headed this way."

"Maybe he could help us finish this," Heather quipped.

"He would help us carry it all to the dump."

Heather glanced around at the fifty years' worth of accumulation. There was a towering pile of books by the door to sell or give away and another stack of files with old newspaper articles ranging in topic from the threat of communism to how to make a gelatin salad with green olives and cabbage.

But the rest of the task still felt daunting.

"Finally!" Ella exclaimed, holding a book in her hands.

Heather glanced up. "What is it?"

"Something interesting."

Heather scooted around the boxes until she was at Ella's side. Instead of folders in this box, there was a stack of photo albums. And a manila envelope packed with more pictures.

Ella flipped through the pictures in one of the photo albums, most of them from Heather's years as a child. Heather glanced at the pictures over her daughter's shoulder. It seemed her parents recorded every milestone of hers, great or small, through the lens of their camera. There was a picture of her crawling on the linoleum in their kitchen. Planting flowers in the beds behind the cottage. Picnicking in what Mum had deemed their "secret garden."

It was no wonder that Heather once thought magical things happened in gardens.

Ella opened the envelope and dumped the contents onto the lid of another box before quickly flipping through them. "Is this you?" she asked, lifting up a black-and-white picture of Heather's parents when they were much younger, each holding the hand of a girl wearing a pleated skirt and bolero jacket. The girl's long hair was held back with a wide headband.

"No." Heather studied her parents and then the face of the child. "This was taken before I was born."

"Do you know who the girl is?"

"Her name was Libby," Heather said slowly as she studied the picture. "She was my sister."

Ella glanced up. "You never told me I had an aunt."

"She died when I was a baby."

Ella leaned back against a box. "How did she die?"

"She was sick."

Ella's eyebrows climbed. "Like the measles?"

"I don't know." Heather sat down on one of the boxes. "I asked my mother over and over about Libby growing up, but my questions made her so sad that I finally stopped."

There were more pictures of Libby in the cottage gardens and one behind what looked like Ladenbrooke Manor. Heather studied the photo of Libby on the bench in Mum's secret garden.

Her sister had passed away at the age of fifteen, and she wished her parents had told her more about Libby's childhood. And what took her life.

When she was a girl, Heather had longed for a sibling, and for a season—a very long season—she conjured up a sister named Beatrix after her favorite author. Beatrix was practically perfect unless Heather did something wrong. Then Beatrix was her scapegoat. In hindsight, her parents had been incredibly kind to oblige her whims. Heather maintained Beatrix's presence until she was eleven, and then she pretended for years that Christopher's siblings were her siblings as well.

When Ella was seven, she conjured up a sibling for herself too, and Heather had accommodated her. Every girl, she figured, needed a sister, imagined or not.

Ella began flipping through another photo album and held out a page to Heather, tapping on it. "Who's the guy?"

Heather's stomach plunged as she stared at the picture of her and Christopher at the dance at Henderson Court. August 1988. A week before he'd asked her to marry him.

This was a question she didn't want to answer.

Heather looked up from the picture, forcing a smile on her lips. "It's my date, of course."

"Does this date have a name?"

Part of her wanted to make up a story, but she'd promised herself long ago that she would never lie to her daughter. Dodging the truth, she'd determined, was not the same as deception though. Sometimes omission was the best for everyone.

"His name is Christopher," she said simply. No need for further explanation.

But Ella wouldn't let it go. "Christopher who?"

"Christopher Westcott."

Ella placed the open album on top of another box, examining the picture. "Was he stuffy?"

Heather turned the page and there was a silly picture of Christopher making a face as he pinned a rose on her dress. She laughed again as she had done many years before. "Not a bit."

When she looked up, Ella was searching her face. "Why didn't you marry him?"

"At the time, my parents didn't like him much."

Ella crossed her arms over her chest. "Your parents didn't like Dad either."

"It didn't matter to me or to your father what my parents thought."

Ella glanced back down at the picture. "But it mattered to Christopher—"

"I suppose it did." There was much more, but she didn't want to tell Ella how she thought she would marry Christopher, no matter what her parents said. She'd never had the opportunity to marry him. Instead of fighting for her, he'd broken her heart.

"Whatever happened to Mr. Westcott?" Ella asked.

"He went to one of the colleges in Oxford," Heather said, trying to sound much more casual than she felt.

"So he turned stuffy?"

Heather shrugged. She didn't want to think about Christopher anymore.

When Ella reached for another album, Heather stepped toward the open door. Excusing herself, she walked along the overgrown stone path to the gardens behind the house. Two chairs and a table were on the back patio, protected by mildew-stained covers. She zigzagged among the new weeds and tufts of old flowers, the perennials that somehow survived without her mum's care.

Mum had died twenty-three years ago, not long after Heather moved to the States. She had grieved in this garden while her father grieved in the house. Her mother's presence was deeply rooted in every corner of these beds, in every flower that continued to bloom long after its caregiver was gone.

Memories began to flood back. Dad pushing her in the swing that hung from the giant oak. Mum spreading out a picnic of tomato-and-cheese sandwiches, fresh plums, and bread with blackberry jam. Each of her parents holding one of her hands as she waded in the fractured threads of the river down in the forest. She'd been born to her parents later in their marriage, and they'd poured their love into her.

Even though Ella had been raised in Portland, Heather tried to gift her daughter with the same happy childhood she'd had in England.

A rushed archway cut through the overgrown hedges surrounding her mum's secret garden. Heather pushed away the vines draped over the arch and entered the place that had once been a haven for Mum and for her.

She sat on a stone bench and looked up at a tower above the hedge. It was impossible to see Ladenbrooke Manor from the main road, but from here, she could catch a glimpse of it.

When she was a child, she'd often wondered about the old manor. Some said the place was haunted, but she thought it mysterious. Sometimes when she was a girl, she would wander through the wrought-iron gate along Ladenbrooke's stone wall. The fragrance from flowers on the other side captivated her along with the beauty of the gardens. The butterflies reminded her of the fairies she'd loved as a child and, when she was older, of the fairies dancing through the magical garden in *A Midsummer Night's Dream*.

Shakespeare was born forty miles from here. In Stratford-upon-Avon. Perhaps the gardens in the Cotswolds inspired him as they once inspired her.

When Heather was growing up, her mum told her the Croft family used to allow the community to explore their gardens for one day each summer, but after Oliver died, they'd moved away and never opened their gardens to the public again. As a child, she couldn't understand why anyone would want to keep all of that beauty to themselves, but she understood now as an adult. Oliver's parents were probably trying to preserve their son's legacy.

She also remembered an overgrown maze near the bottom of the gardens at Ladenbrooke, with a brick wall surrounding three sides of it. In the middle was a tower crafted to look like one of the three towers on the manor. When she was a girl, she'd tried to find the path to the garden tower but instead had become lost near the maze. That day, a young woman found her and guided her home.

Or at least, she thought there had been a woman. Sometimes she wondered if it had been only a dream.

The shadows began to crawl across the hedge, toward her bench. As if they were chasing her. Leaning back, she refused to run, basking instead in the trailing rays of sun.

"Mom?" Ella called out.

"I'm back here."

Ella turned the corner around the archway and stepped into the garden. She held up her iPhone and tapped on the screen. "He's a professor of theology at Wycliffe Hall."

Heather held out her arms to soak in the last of the sunlight. "Who are you talking about?"

"Christopher Westcott." Ella sat on the bench next to her. "If he wasn't stuffy before, I guarantee you he is now."

"It doesn't matter to me whether he's stuffy or not."

Ella kept scrolling down on her phone. "He's written a bunch of magazine articles."

Heather already knew Christopher was a professor at one of the colleges in Oxford. A few years ago, she'd searched for him online to find out what happened to him. She'd found his biography and then surfed from one article to the next, reading about his views on everything from ecclesiology to eschatology. Then she'd closed her laptop and vowed never to check up on him again. Curiosity was one thing. Obsession was quite another.

She'd wanted to ask about Christopher when she came to visit her father, but there was no good reason, she figured, to inquire about him. Her father never mentioned Christopher though he'd talked about the Westcotts on occasion, telling her when Christopher's siblings had married or when Mr. and Mrs. Westcott became grandparents.

"There's nothing about a wife or children in this article," Ella said.

"I'm sure he married a long time ago."

Ella slipped her phone back into her pocket. "You should drive to Oxford and see him while you're here. Get a pint together."

"I hate beer."

"Then take tea." Ella tilted her head. "And don't tell me that you hate that as well."

"His wife probably wouldn't appreciate that."

"You don't know he's married—"

"Even so," she said with a sigh. "I'm not stalking a boyfriend I haven't seen in almost thirty years."

"It would be reconnecting, not stalking."

Heather glanced at her watch. "Don't you have to pack?"

"I'm finished. All I have left to do tonight is call Matthew."

Heather smiled. "You do realize you'll be seeing him in two days."

"Yes, but that seems like an eternity."

Heather sighed. "I'm going to miss you."

Ella kissed her cheek. "I'm going to miss you too."

Her daughter had grown up years ago, and yet every time they said good-bye, Heather still had trouble letting her go. But Ella had a home and a husband now, far from Portland. Heather had her studio in Oregon and plenty of peace.

She stood, and they began walking back to the house. Four in the morning would be excruciating, but they had to leave early for Ella's flight.

With her daughter gone, she'd work even harder to finish the daunting task before her. Instead of going to Oxford, she would finish her work at the cottage as soon as possible and then return to Oregon for good.

PART TWO

Looking back over my life, the answers seem so clear, but it's meaningless—perhaps even dangerous—to see the past clearly without using that 20/20 of hindsight to sculpt the future.

Some people, when they discover the terrible things that happened in their past, drape that knowledge around them like a cloak of bitterness. They may even dig deep and wallow in it for a season. Or a lifetime.

Libby wasn't like other children, but I've learned now that no two children are alike. Every child struggles in some way and excels in another. I just didn't appreciate Libby's strengths as much as I criticized what I thought were weaknesses.

I tried to bury my anger when she was young, but it seeped through as bitterness at first; then resigned itself into apathy. I had wanted children, many of them. Instead I was given one child who wasn't my own. One who didn't seem to want me as her father.

I thought I knew all about God back then, but I relied only on myself. And I failed both myself and those I loved miserably. In my misery, I brought others down to wallow with me, and I learned that wallowing can be a messy business.

The ugliness of my anger replaced the beauty in life, and Libby craved beauty more than anything. Beauty and freedom.

Perhaps the past should be used more like the frame of eyeglasses as we look forward, the mirrors of a periscope to help reflect what lies ahead instead of a magnifying glass to analyze every detail behind us. For it's not just what we learn about the past that's important. What we discover changes how we view the past, and then we can choose—quite deliberately—to change our future.

Instead of wallowing, I should have protected Libby. Given her the desires of her heart inside a perimeter of love and care. Like the Father above wants to do with each of His children.

I thought Libby needed me, but really I needed her and the gifts she had to offer our family.

God gave me a daughter, the desire of my heart, but in order to succeed as a father, I had to rely on Him. And show Libby how to rely on Him as well.

Perhaps this is why God often gives us our desires in a different way than we expect. Perhaps it's because He knows exactly what we need.

13

JULY 1959, LADENBROOKE MANOR

Forest stretched from the edge of the gardens behind Ladenbrooke Manor, down to the banks of the swift River Coln. The water rushed over branches and stones as it swept past the boundaries of the Croft property and then plunged down a hill that separated British nobility from the commoners.

On the hillside above the river and trees, Ladenbrooke Manor stood as a grand monument to the prominent Croft family, aristocrats whose bloodline stretched centuries back to the Norman Conquest.

The manor house was built in the eighteenth century, and its walls were a weathered, gray stone with three towers that rose above the slate roof—two towers facing the stone gatehouse in front of the house and one overlooking the terraced gardens in the back. Glass from dozens of windows glimmered in the afternoon sunlight, and the tall windows along the dining hall reflected the fountain on the patio terrace.

A stone curtain enclosed the house and forest, the Croft gardens and fruit orchards, forging a distinct line between Ladenbrooke and the outside world. The main gate into Ladenbrooke was used only by the Crofts and their guests; employees and those delivering packages used the gate along the wall nearest to the village. On the opposite wall, there was a much smaller gate—this one wrought iron and used originally by the team of gardeners employed before the Great War.

There were a dozen buildings on the estate—a stable, nuttery, old kitchen house, dovecote, icehouse, and several follies built among the gardens for decor. Outside the wall the Croft property included farmland, barns, and several cottages where their servants and farmers resided.

The war with Germany had knocked many of the aristocratic families down a notch or two, their grand homes crumbling from neglect and decay, but the Croft family clung to their status and property like the wisteria clung to the stone towers on their house.

The hill between the manor and forest displayed layers of Lady Croft's prized gardens. Paved pathways wove through a formal Italian garden, rose garden, water garden, lily pond, and a tulip garden built around Roman ruins.

Maggie stood beside a statue of the goddess Hemera and a row of yew bushes that had been neatly pruned into a wall to form the perimeter of the Croft family maze. Walter sat nearby on a picnic blanket as she scanned the hillside above the maze to see if she could find Libby's copper-streaked hair among the immaculate gardens and all the people dressed in their finest for this entree into Ladenbrooke's gardens.

The Croft family opened the front gate to the public once each summer. Hundreds of people from around the Cotswolds came to peruse Lady Croft's magnificent displays—the golden heather, purple dahlias, peach lilies floating on the pond. Some of them might hope to catch a glimpse of one of the elusive Croft family members or visit the rooms inside, but the Croft family always fled to their home near London before the locals descended.

Thousands of Londoners visited this area during their summer holiday, but only the people from Bibury and surrounding villages knew about this annual event. It was one of the many secrets the local population kept to themselves. And Maggie had a deep appreciation for people who knew how to keep secrets.

Walter had found work as a postmaster soon after they'd arrived in Bibury, four years ago, and a year later, she'd begun working as a housekeeper at Ladenbrooke. Walter tolerated his work, and her position allowed her to bring Libby to work each day. She doubted Lady Croft would let her bring Libby if she was a lively child, but the Crofts employed a quite capable nanny who watched Libby along with Sarah and Oliver, the Croft's young children.

Libby sat in the nursery with the Croft children on rainy days and quietly colored or cut shapes out of paper; on sunny days, Lady Croft allowed her to play in the gardens. Oliver and his sister fought over toys, and sometimes even fought over who would play with Libby, but according to the nanny, Libby wasn't interested in playing with either child.

On the other side of the yew bushes, children laughed and called to one another as they traversed the winding maze toward one of the follies—a stone tower built to look like one of the towers on the manor house. The head housekeeper at the estate told Maggie the tower was built by a former Lord Croft, an aristocrat back in the 1700s who had more money than sense about him. The current Lord Croft, she said, was particular about his finances and even more particular about his family.

Today dozens of children from the village played in the gardens and trees below the manor house, but neither Sarah nor Oliver Croft were playing among them. Both Lord and Lady Croft thought the children of Bibury might somehow taint their offspring.

A child hung out of one of the windows on the folly, waving to someone on the ground below. Other parents might worry that it was their child dangling over the maze, but Libby wasn't like the other kids.

Her daughter was five now, old enough to attend primary school this autumn, but Maggie was terrified for her. Instead of joining in the games with other children, Libby preferred wandering off on her own to stare at the pages in one of her picture books or creating her own world on the pages of her sketchbook. Her daughter seemed to empathize deeply with the loneliness of a blank page. Color, in her young mind, was the cure for everything.

Maggie didn't particularly care what Libby was passionate about as long as she was passionate about something. In her first years, Libby failed to thrive, and Maggie was concerned that her daughter would never awaken to life. The local doctor said the abnormal growth of her adenoids was causing her lethargy, and he removed them when she was three. The surgery didn't seem to help immediately, but Libby's energy increased in the next two years. Still, she was much more interested in stopping to appreciate beauty than participate in games.

Maggie understood her daughter's need to be alone, but whenever Libby isolated herself from the other kids, Walter insisted she join them. Each time, Libby would balk at his intrusion. She hated the sound of the children squealing even when the noise was laughter—almost as if she couldn't differentiate between the sounds of sadness and glee. And it didn't particularly matter if the children were happy or sad. Both emotions overwhelmed her.

Maggie moved back to the edge of the forest, to the blanket where Walter was sitting with Albert Garland and his wife, Rebecca, a couple he'd met at the post office. Rebecca was nice enough, but Maggie wished she had a good friend in Bibury. A woman who understood why her heart ached.

She sat down beside Walter. "I can't find Libby."

"I'm sure she's playing with the other kids," he said, patting her hand, even though he knew perfectly well that Libby wasn't among them. "Rebecca was asking what it's like to work for Lady Croft."

Maggie tried to focus on the woman in front of her, tried to act as if her daughter was indeed with the other children. "I don't see Lady Croft very often."

"I hear she acts all hoity-toity," Rebecca said. "Like she's royalty or something when she grew up working class."

"She's nice enough," Maggie replied even though Lady Croft had definitely acquired an aristocratic air. Often she reminded Maggie of Mrs. Bishop back in Clevedon—and sometimes Aunt Priscilla—but she would never say that to the Garlands or anyone else. The work at Ladenbrooke was hard, but she didn't want to lose her job or the lease on their home next door.

Albert changed the topic, talking about the recent deployment of British warships to Iceland, and Maggie's gaze traveled back up the hill, to the gray house looming near the top. When she didn't see Libby on the hillside, she turned toward the forest. She wasn't worried about the river—Libby had inherited Maggie's fear of water—but sometimes Libby got lost when she wandered off.

She stood again, brushing the wrinkles out of her linen skirt. "I'm going to find Libby."

Rebecca nodded toward the maze, where her three children were presumably playing quite happily together. "Why don't I send Patrick to retrieve her?"

She couldn't tell Rebecca that Libby might run screaming if the Garland's oldest son attempted to corral her back. The woman had no idea what it was like to have a child who not only isolated herself but seemed to like the isolation. All three of Rebecca's children were what society deemed normal. With a capital *N*.

"There's no need to interrupt his play," Maggie said, trying to be polite. "I'll check in the forest."

Walter stood beside her. "I'll go with you."

The two of them walked side by side into the trees, the silence awkward between them.

Three years ago, they had called something of a truce. They focused on their individual work, and when they were home, they were civil to each other. They'd even tried to conceive a child together. Maggie had hoped another baby, their own child, might help heal the rift in their marriage, but she'd yet to become pregnant. Walter didn't say it outright, but she knew he thought her tryst with Elliot had somehow inhibited their ability to have children.

It had certainly infected their relationship.

She'd shattered the idol he had made of her long ago, but from the day they married, she had been faithful to him, and she intended to continue being as faithful to their vows as he was.

Safety and remoteness—the very reasons they'd chosen this place to make their home—also meant that Walter had to give up his writing career. There were no shipwrecks in the quiet Cotswolds or discoveries of mines left over from the war. There was no theft to speak of and when a death occurred, it was either from natural causes or an accident, neither of which interested the editor at the *Standard*. As far as she knew, Walter hadn't written anything of significance since they left Clevedon, and it saddened her.

"You worry too much about Libby," he said. "She'll never grow up if—"

She stiffened. "If what?"

"If you don't help her face her fears."

Maggie plucked a leaf off a tree, scrunching it up in her hand. By the time Maggie was five, she was living in a strange house far from her home, caring for herself and her brother. "I don't want Libby to grow up before she's ready. I want her to enjoy her childhood."

Walter lifted a branch so Maggie could walk under it. "You're going to have to start letting go soon, Maggie, or you might not be able to let go at all."

"She's only five. . . ."

"She needs to be coaxed instead of coddled."

Maggie crossed her arms to help calm her mind, capture her muddled thoughts. "I'm not coddling her."

No parent should ever let go of their child—not completely—but Walter could never understand. His parents hadn't sent him away during the war to live with a family they'd never met. Even though his father was gone, Walter's mother still telephoned every Sunday to speak with him. She didn't cling to him, but she hadn't let go either.

When Walter stopped walking, Maggie glimpsed over to see Libby sitting under one of the giant trees that overlooked the river, her copy of J.M. Barre's *Peter Pan* clutched in her lap. She took a deep breath, relieved that Libby hadn't wandered too far this time.

She'd read *Peter Pan* to Libby at least a hundred times. Libby couldn't read yet, but she knew sections of the book by heart—the parts about Wendy's love and Peter's shadow, the fact that fairies were so small they only had room for one feeling at a time.

But even more than the story, Libby liked to immerse herself in the pictures. The magic. Sometimes it seemed as if the book world became Libby's reality. Maggie didn't understand Libby's need to escape; her real life was good and safe. But Maggie loved her daughter with all her heart, and even though Walter could be stern, Maggie knew he cared about her too. If these pictures made Libby happy, then Maggie wanted to embrace them with her.

"Libby," Walter called as he stepped forward to retrieve her.

She didn't respond.

"Please," Maggie said, resolute. "Let her be."

If Walter tried to force her into the throngs of children, Libby's contentment would unravel. Then she would wail, embarrassing all of them like she had last month when Walter tried to force her to swing at the park.

He studied Libby, sitting above the riverbank. "She needs to exercise."

"She's exercising her brain."

"She must learn to play with the others—"

"But not today," Maggie said, tugging on his sleeve. "I fear—"

He shook his head. "We can't keep living in fear."

"I'll tell her we're leaving soon."

"Maggie—"

"Please," she begged.

"She'll never learn if we don't help her," he said.

She shook her head. "This isn't the way to help."

He rubbed his temples, his forehead creased with frustration. But he relented, sighing before he retreated back through the trees. Maggie turned and watched Libby for another moment.

On one hand, she thought they should learn to appreciate Libby's uniqueness—there was nothing wrong with playing quietly by oneself. On the other hand, she wanted Libby to have the childhood the Nazis had stolen away from her and her brother. She wanted Libby to have friends, a host of them, who would come for tea parties and to play dolls and whatever else girls did these days. Maggie had spent most of her childhood—most of her life—afraid, but Libby and the other children in this village had nothing to fear. They didn't have to worry about bombs crashing into their home or being shipped off to strangers who lived far away or losing their parents to war.

Her books said mothering came naturally to women, but sometimes it didn't feel natural to her at all. If only her mother had lived. She could have taught Maggie the proper way to care for a child.

As Maggie sat down by her daughter, Libby pointed to a picture speckled with pixie dust. "It's magic," she said.

"Indeed," Maggie agreed. "Beautiful magic."

She turned the page to a colorful illustration of Peter Pan with Tinker Bell fluttering at his side. "Mummy?"

Maggie glanced over and met her daughter's earnest gaze.

"Tinker Bell can fly," Libby whispered as if it were a grand secret.

"Yes, she can."

"Someday I'm going to fly."

Maggie whispered back. "One day, I think you just might."

IN THE FIRST MONTH AFTER Libby started primary school, her teacher telephoned three times, demanding that Maggie come down to her classroom. When Mrs. Hoffman called this afternoon, she said Libby was inconsolable. That she was screaming and flailing and acting like a two-year-old. Again.

Maggie cringed at the disdain in the teacher's voice.

She rushed out of the head housekeeper's office in Ladenbrooke, past a gallery of marble busts and family portraits, then through the pantry and kitchen until she reached the servant's door. Outside she hurried through the gardens and the wrought-iron gate hinged between the manor and her cottage.

Her bicycle was in the cottage shed, and she quickly retrieved it before speeding down the long hill into Bibury.

The school was located next to St. Mary's Church, and as Maggie leaned her bicycle against the ivy-covered building, she heard laughter from one of the classrooms. But Libby wasn't laughing. She found her daughter on the sticky tile floor of the dining hall, chunks of macaroni clumped in her hair and beans mashed around her feet. Libby was clenched up in a ball, her blouse soaked. Mrs. Hoffman sat primly on the bench across from her with her hands neatly folded on the lines of her long, brown skirt.

As Maggie knelt on the floor, she saw a bruise on her daughter's arm. Fury twisted in her stomach. Who had done this? And why wasn't the teacher caring for her?

"Libby," Maggie whispered gently beside her.

Instead of responding, Libby rocked back and forth, murmuring something to herself as she clutched one of her legs. Maggie leaned close to her daughter's lips to hear her words.

"Stop," Libby moaned as she rocked. "Stop—"

"They've stopped, sweetheart." Maggie put her hand on Libby's shoulder, trying to reassure her, but Libby flinched. Maggie placed her hand back in her lap. "Mummy is here."

Maggie looked at Mrs. Hoffman and saw contempt instead of compassion on the woman's face. She had so hoped Libby's teacher would understand. "What happened?" Maggie demanded.

"Libby threw her lunch and several of the children reciprocated." Mrs. Hoffman didn't show an ounce of emotion.

Maggie struggled to contain herself. "Libby's hurt."

"She's angry, Mrs. Doyle. Not hurt."

Anger surged through her, the same anger perhaps that Walter felt when he slammed his fist into Elliot's face. She wanted to slap every inch of condescension off the teacher's face, but she clutched her hands together instead. Her gaze fell back to her daughter's face, the lips pressed together in fear, eyes clenched shut as if she could block out the world. "I'm afraid you're wrong, Mrs. Hoffman."

"Some of the other children were irritated as well—"

"Irritated?" Maggie's voice climbed, and she struggled to keep from screaming at the woman in front of her. "My daughter is a little more than irritated."

Mrs. Hoffman stood. "There are better ways for her to get attention."

Maggie gently rubbed her daughter's arm. Libby cringed again, but then she began to relax. "She isn't trying to get attention."

The teacher didn't seem to hear her. "Libby doesn't just need love, Mrs. Doyle, she needs some discipline. Starting at home."

The woman's words burned, as if she'd branded her. *Failure*. For the past five years, Maggie had studied and searched for the right ways to care for her daughter, discipline her even on the rare times she deemed it necessary, but clearly she was still doing something wrong.

Her stomach turned again.

Or maybe there was nothing she could do. Perhaps in that moment when she'd leaned over the railing in Clevedon, she had cursed Libby for life. If only she'd known the future—she never would have contemplated harming her beautiful girl. Libby was her child, and she would fight for her as long and hard as she must.

Mrs. Hoffman towered over them, her hands on her hips. "She hit another student, on her head."

Maggie's anger flared again. "Was that student throwing food at her?"

"Libby started the fight," Mrs. Hoffman said, stepping back. "And I will expect an apology tomorrow."

Maggie rubbed both of Libby's arms and her daughter slowly melted into her, hiding her face in Maggie's shoulder. "And I will expect the child who did this to her to apologize as well."

"I can't promise—"

"Then Libby will not be apologizing for hitting someone when she clearly asked her to stop."

"The other child's parents will be upset."

Maggie scanned the cafeteria. "I don't see the other child curled up in fear."

"No, Libby is the only one who seems to have a flair for drama."

Maggie tightened her grip around her daughter. "The other child's parents aren't my responsibility, Mrs. Hoffman. God has only given me one child, and I am responsible before Him to protect her from harm."

The disdain on the teacher's face dissolved into something more like pity, but the pity angered Maggie even more. They didn't need to pity her. She and Libby would be fine. And one day her daughter would learn to be stronger.

Maggie sat straighter. "I need a towel."

Minutes after Mrs. Hoffman left, one of her pupils returned with a washcloth, and Maggie gently sponged off Libby's face while the other student looked on with curiosity. "You can return to your classroom," she told him.

"Mrs. Hoffman said to wait until you're finished."

She tossed the washcloth to him, then she lifted Libby and carried her frail body outside. Dark clouds clung to the sky above Bibury, preparing to soak them both if they dared walk back up the hill. She took Libby down the street, toward the post office that shared space with the village store, but before they reached it, the window of sky opened. Libby dug her face into Maggie's sleeve as the icy rain drenched them.

Maggie had never felt so alone.

A small car pulled to the curb beside them, and in the driver's seat, she recognized Daphne, one of the Sunday school teachers at the parish church they attended outside of town. A teacher who seemed to like Libby.

Daphne stepped out of her car, her hazel eyes burdened with concern. "Can I take you home?"

Maggie glanced over at the post office and then nodded. She had to get Libby out of the rain.

As Daphne drove up the hill, Maggie held Libby in her lap, and when they reached the cottage, she quickly carried her daughter inside. As she helped Libby change into dry clothes, she saw not only a bruise on Libby's arm but also one on the back of her leg.

Her heart felt as if it might rip in two. Sometimes Libby couldn't seem to remember what happened when she lost control, but the only time her daughter had harmed someone was when she'd felt threatened.

What had the other children been doing to her?

Downstairs, Daphne had started a fire in the sitting room. Maggie placed Libby on the couch before she collapsed onto one of the chairs, blinking back her tears as rain pelted the windows. Libby stared at the embers like the bruises hadn't happened. Like she couldn't feel pain.

Maggie felt plenty of it for both of them.

Daphne slipped *The Tale of Peter Rabbit* off the bookshelf. "Do you mind if I read to her?"

Maggie shook her head slowly, and the young woman sat

down beside her daughter and began to read the words of wise Mrs. Rabbit: "You may go into the fields or down the lane, but don't go into Mr. McGregor's garden."

As Daphne told the story of the good bunnies—Flopsy, Mopsy, and Cottontail—Libby looked at the pictures. Maggie silently begged God to take out His wrath on her and not her daughter. She'd never seen Libby provoke a fight, but if one of the other children had teased her—

She would never send Libby to a mental home, but she wished they could afford to send her to one of the independent schools. Right away. And she wished for a friend she could be honest with about herself and her daughter.

Quietly she slipped into the kitchen to make tea for her and Daphne.

Every morning for the past three years, she'd faithfully made the Croft family beds and polished brass and completed every other task the head housekeeper assigned her. And when the Crofts were in town, she did her best to stay out of sight.

Part of her wanted to pack up the car and run again, but the cottage was a good home for their family, and even if neither she nor Walter particularly liked their work, no one here knew about their past. Walter often worked late at his job though sometimes she wondered if his late nights were more about avoiding the realities at home than the comings and goings of mail in Bibury.

Still, Walter hadn't left her, even after all she'd done, and she was grateful for that. If only he would step up and care for Libby as he had done in those first months of her life. Libby needed someone to protect her from the kids—and adults—who belittled her for her differences, almost as if it were a sport they were guaranteed to win.

But teasing her daughter wasn't the same as cricket or croquet.

When Maggie returned, carrying two cups of hot tea, Libby had fallen asleep in Daphne's lap. "She doesn't take to many people."

Daphne's dark-brown hair lay straight over her shoulders, and the dimples on her cheeks deepened with her smile. "We've been friends at church since she was three."

"Thank you for reading to her," Maggie whispered as she set down the cups.

"I like her." Daphne gently pushed the hair out of Libby's eyes. "She sees things that other people miss."

Maggie wanted to hug her. "That's true."

"And she doesn't seem to care what anyone else thinks of her." Her smile faded. "She reminds me of one of my cousins."

"Where is your cousin?"

"He's ill," Daphne said, her eyes sad. "His parents had to send him away to a special home when I was younger."

"My brother was sent away too, when he was a baby."

"Was he sick?"

"No." Maggie swallowed hard, contemplating whether or not she should share a bit of her story. She decided to take a risk. "We were both orphans and—the people who cared for me didn't want to care for him as well."

Libby squirmed and then rested her head back on Daphne's leg.

"I want to be a nurse one day," Daphne said. "So I can help people who are hurting."

"You would make a fine nurse." Maggie reached over and gently lifted Libby in her arms. "I'm going to tuck her in for the night."

Daphne stood and slipped her arms into the long sleeves of her overcoat. "Perhaps I shall stop by tomorrow."

Maggie nodded, her heart lifting. Daphne was almost ten years younger than she was, but age shouldn't matter one bit between friends.

14

Instead of the classical music Ella deemed stuffy, Heather listened to light rock on the British station as she drove back through the Cotswolds. The rock music seemed more appropriate anyway. When she was growing up here, it was the only music she'd liked.

She cruised around the winding, narrow lanes and then up and down grassy hills dotted with sheep of all sizes, some as big as cows. In a caffeine-accelerated state, she'd driven Ella to the airport long before the sun rose, then waited in the lobby until her daughter's flight departed to Dulles.

On their drive into Heathrow, Ella had urged her one last time to contact Christopher Westcott. She informed her daughter that such inquiries rarely ended well, but Ella claimed she couldn't possibly know if that was true. Still, she would never call Christopher. A long time ago, she'd rehearsed a conversation between them—repeatedly—but she wasn't certain what she'd say to him now.

When she was about fourteen, she'd ridden on this same winding road after a day trip to London. She and Christopher had been friends for as long as she could remember, and on that particular drive, she told her mum that she was starting to like him beyond their friendship and thought Christopher might like her too. At the time, she'd thought her mum would be pleased since she and Christopher's mother were friends. Instead, she surprised Heather with a harsh rebuke, saying she needed to wait until she was much older to go steady with any boy.

She and Christopher didn't officially begin dating for two more years, but they spent most of their summers together. Heather learned she could tell him just about anything, and not only did he listen, he understood her.

That car ride had been the last time she'd talked to her mum about the passion stirring in her heart. She didn't even talk about Christopher again until he invited her to a church social one weekend, the summer after she turned sixteen. When she asked her mum if she could attend, she'd said no, stating Heather was still too young to go without a chaperone. But she hadn't felt young anymore. She'd met Christopher at the church that night, and that one event marked them as a "couple" in the eyes of their friends, if not their families, for months to come.

The sign for Bibury popped her back into her current reality.

She must focus on finishing the task in front of her. The estate agent her solicitor recommended—a woman named Brie Reynolds—was scheduled to come look at the house in two days.

She needed to stop reflecting on the past and put the cottage on the market as soon as possible so someone else could call this place home.

"HE'S NOT MARRIED!"

Heather rubbed her eyes and took a quick glance at the clock beside her bed. It was one in the morning, and though the pounding music from Ella's ring had startled her, she still wasn't fully awake. "Did you land at Dulles?"

"Two hours ago," Ella said. "I decided to do some digging while I had Wi-Fi."

Heather was afraid to ask—

"Professor Westcott was married," Ella told her, "but his wife passed away eight years ago from cancer."

"That's so sad."

Ella kept talking. "I tried to find information about Aunt Libby as well, but no luck. I did find an article about your Oliver Croft."

She elbowed herself up on her pillows. "My Oliver Croft?"

"The reporter said the police suspected foul play."

"Where did you read that?"

"I'll text it to you right now." Ella clicked her tongue against her teeth. "There could still be a murderer on the loose in Bibury."

Heather looked through the glass at the spattering of stars across the sky. "We don't know that anyone killed Oliver."

"That's the problem—we don't know what happened to him or to my aunt Libby."

"My sister was ill."

"That's what your parents said—"

In the background, Heather heard the final boarding announcement for the flight to Phoenix. "I have to go." Ella's voice sounded distorted, as if she was running toward the gate. "I didn't wake you, did I?"

"Go catch your plane."

"Love you, Mom."

"Love you too."

Seconds after Ella disconnected the call, a text message flashed on her phone. She glanced back at her pillow but curiosity won out and she opted to read the story from the *Evening Standard* before she returned to sleep.

The article was short.

SON OF LORD CROFT DROWNS IN BIBURY

Last Tuesday the body of Oliver Croft, age 17, was found in the river near Ladenbrooke Manor, the family's country home in Gloucestershire. Croft attended the prestigious Tonbridge School in Kent and was planning to attend Oxford University in September. Local police are investigating for foul play.

Heather sat up on the pillows and read the story one more time. Three sentences to describe a tragedy that must have ripped through the heart of the Croft family.

She laid down and closed her eyes again, but sleep evaded her so she pulled her long hair back into a sloppy ponytail and climbed downstairs, into the small basement below the cottage. A solitary lightbulb cast shadows into the corners as she scanned the room. The boxes down here weren't neatly organized like the boxes in the stable, and there were stacks of old furniture alongside an assortment of plastic tubs. For hours, in the light of the single bulb, she sorted through old dishes, silk flower arrangements, pieces of pottery, and dozens of children's books.

In a corner, she found the old light table that Granny Doyle had given her when she was a child. Under it was a flat wooden box that had been painted with bright-pink, yellow, and mint-green stripes. Inside the box Heather found colored pencils in different states of sharpening and a sketchbook bound together by metal rings.

The title on the front of the sketchbook was written in bold cursive: *Libby's Book of Butterflies.*

One of the edges was folded, and she smoothed it with her hand, reverently, to honor the sister she'd never known. Then she stepped back under the light and flipped through the first pages. There were beautiful paintings of butterflies, their wings bright from the watercolors.

Did her sister create this book or did someone make it for her?

Mum had loved her gardens, but Heather had never known her to do any kind of artwork. She'd always been busy planting her flowers and working as a hairdresser and caring well for their family.

Intrigued, Heather slowly turned the pages. The butterflies were unique in their brilliance, each one with a magical name.

Golden Shimmer. Moonlit Fairy. Lavender Lace.

Under the butterflies were short descriptions. Like they all had different personalities. Her favorite was the Autumn Dancer, colored a vibrant orange and red with speckles of teal. It reminded her of a leaf, clinging to its branch before the autumn winds blew it away.

Autumn Dancer flutters among the flowers, chasing the last rays of sunlight until her haven is swallowed up by the night. Her sisters are asleep now, hidden under the fronds, but she doesn't care. She dances alone in the twilight, embracing the warmth of the golden hour, her wings sweeping past silky petals of the late summer blooms. In the safe cocoon of her garden, she dares believe that no harm will ever enter the gates. This is her world of beauty and peace, of sweet nectar and life, completely unspoiled by the footsteps of danger or the silent mockery of time.

Heather read the description twice. The cadence of the words was almost as beautiful as the paintings. It was like an entire community of these butterflies lived in the gardens of the artist's mind.

She'd never seen her father draw anything other than a map, and while she'd been told her grandfather had been an artist in London, he died in the Blitz, years before Libby was born.

With all the flourishes and flowers, these pictures seemed to be created by a young woman anyway. At least one who was young at heart.

Heather turned the page again to a pink butterfly named Rosa Belle, and she smiled as she read the description. Rosa Belle was a very proper butterfly, invited often to take tea with the queen in the gardens behind Buckingham Palace.

Heather liked to color when she was a child, sometimes for hours at her light table, but as she grew older, her mum discouraged her interest in pursing a career as an artist. Heather enjoyed breathing new life into damaged pieces of artwork, though looking back, it was strange that her mum didn't encourage her desire to be creative when she'd loved to create her own sort of beauty in the gardens behind their house.

She flipped through the book of butterflies until she reached the last page. Then she turned again to the front.

Her eyes refused to stay open any longer, so she climbed back up the steps to her room and turned out the light, pulling the blanket to her chin.

Later in the morning she'd do a little digging, like Ella had done, to find out who had created the butterflies.

And perhaps, as she dug, she could find out what happened to her sister as well.

15

OCTOBER 1963, LADENBROOKE MANOR

I'm quite sorry," Lady Croft told Maggie, though she didn't sound the least bit sorry. "Libby can no longer stay here while you work."

Maggie reached for the polished banister, clutching it tight. A hundred questions collided in her mind, but before she asked a single one of them, she knelt down to speak softly to her nine-year-old daughter on the bottom step. "Why don't you go read in the library?"

Libby shook her head, continuing to draw in her sketchbook. "I don't want to read."

"You can look at the picture books if you'd like."

Libby glanced up as if to decide whether or not Maggie was telling the truth before she handed over her sketches. Maggie brushed the wrinkles out of her dress as she stood, her gaze trailing Libby as she scurried down the great hall. Her daughter still wasn't very good at reading, but she loved the artwork and photographs she discovered in books.

Slowly Maggie turned back toward the woman who had employed her for seven years.

The Crofts' nanny was long gone now, but after she left, Lady Croft had permitted Libby to shadow Maggie in the house after school or play in the gardens while Henry, the head gardener, worked outside.

Maggie lowered her voice so the other staff wouldn't hear. "Has she done something wrong?"

"It's not that . . ." The sternness in Lady Croft's light-gray eyes flickered. She was several years older than Maggie and usually quite direct in her instructions and her answers.

Maggie persisted, frustrated at Lady Croft's refusal to answer. "Have I done something wrong?"

Lady Croft shook her head, seeming to regain her composure. "Libby is much too old to follow you around."

"She doesn't just follow me. She sits and draws—"

"She acts like a toddler," Lady Croft said.

Her simple activities made people like Lady Croft think she was simpleminded as well, but Libby was very bright and creative. "She doesn't distract me from my job."

Lady Croft drummed her manicured nails on the banister. "Perhaps not, but she is an inerrant distraction for my children."

Maggie leaned back, focusing on the gardens through the immense window that mirrored the steps.

Now she understood what Lady Croft was refusing to say. Sarah, Lady Croft's teenage daughter, attended a girls' school in London, but even when she was home, Sarah Croft no longer cared whether or not Libby was in the house. The Croft's son was much different. From the time Libby could walk, Oliver would trail her around the nursery, trying to make her smile. Even though he was eleven now, Oliver's interest hadn't waned.

His parents had sent him away to a boy's school last year, but this term he was attending an exclusive school about a half hour from Bibury. When he returned home in the afternoons, he often searched for Libby and tried to pull her out of her make-believe world.

The nanny had been pleased about Oliver's fascination with Libby when they were young—it kept him entertained—but as the children grew older, Oliver's persistence irritated Libby even more than when she'd been in the nursery.

"Can she play in the gardens after school?" Maggie asked.

Lady Croft shook her head again.

"But she won't hurt any—"

Lady Croft cut off her words. "I'm sorry, Maggie. You must respect my decision."

Nodding, Maggie stepped away from her, and she bid goodnight to her ladyship before tears began to flood her cheeks. Then she walked slowly through the corridor to retrieve Libby from the library.

She needed this job, but even more than her work, she wanted her daughter to thrive.

Even though she hadn't succeeded in her studies, Libby had adjusted to the rhythm of school. Still, Lady Croft's gardens were her sanctuary. A place where she could dance with the butterflies and savor every color of the season. A place where no one teased her.

What would she do when Maggie told her she couldn't return?

Oliver and Sarah thrived in both their studies and friendships, and Lady Croft thought all children should be as perfect as hers. Maggie was well acquainted with imperfection—in herself and her family. Instead of looking down at Libby or fearing what they didn't understand, Maggie wished others could see the beauty in her daughter. The bright worlds she created when she was alone. The wonder at all of God's creation.

Lady Croft may not respect Libby's differences, but if she would take the time to get to know her, perhaps even she—like her son—would be fascinated by Libby's enchantment with all things beautiful.

THE NEXT DAY, INSTEAD OF eating lunch, Maggie rode a bus over to the Woolworths in Cirencester to purchase two trowels and two bags of tulip bulbs. Then she left her post a few minutes before Libby arrived from school and met her daughter by Ladenbrooke's back gate. Instead of taking her up into the manor, Maggie guided her past Lady Croft's gardens and into the garden that would become their own.

Libby had spent most of her childhood at Ladenbrooke, but she didn't belong there. Instead, Maggie wanted her to appreciate her home, the place where she'd always be welcome.

Even though Maggie didn't have much time or money to create an elaborate garden—nor could she and Walter hire a gardener like the Crofts did—she could plant some flowers alongside her plot of vegetables. In time the flowers would grow and then the butterflies would come. And perhaps Libby would be happy roaming in her own world behind their cottage.

Maggie handed Libby one of the trowels, and the two of them worked side by side for an hour, digging into the soft dirt and planting the bulbs. As she turned the soil, Maggie glanced over at her daughter and pointed down to the small hole Libby had dug. "You're doing an excellent job."

Libby flashed her a smile. "The butterflies need flowers."

"Yes, they do, and you're going to give them the most exquisite display in Bibury."

Libby covered her bulb with dirt and patted it. "They will want to play here."

"Every day," Maggie said. "And you can play with them for as long as you'd like."

"Forever," Libby whispered.

"Forever, it is."

Libby rarely expressed emotion, but Maggie knew she felt things, deeply. That's what most people didn't understand. Libby's heart ran as deep as her imagination even though she guarded it with defenses that would make Her Majesty's Armed Forces proud. Maggie feared an arrow might blaze through Libby's defenses one day and pierce her heart, the entire fortress caving in upon itself.

She wished there was more she could do to protect her daughter.

Lady Croft wasn't the only mother to critique her parenting. A few weeks ago, after church, one woman took it upon herself—like Mrs. Hoffman had four years ago—to lecture her about Libby's need for more discipline. Then another mother pulled her aside at school recently and said that Libby clearly needed a mother who didn't withhold affection from her. If Maggie expressed her love more freely, Libby would love other children.

Did she need to discipline Libby more? Love her more?

Doubt made her brain twist and twirl like the seawater during a storm. Guilt made her second-guess all of her decisions along with her present state of mind. Had she been withholding affection from the girl she loved?

Her heart ached for her child, but whatever happened, she would not send her away to one of the homes for children who struggled with their mental capabilities. She regretted so much in her life, but she didn't regret giving Libby life. She knew well that it wasn't God's perfect will for her to become pregnant before she married, but Jesus loved children. He loved Libby too, no matter who her father was. And He understood Libby even more than Maggie did.

She only wished He would tell her how to mother her daughter well.

She dug deep into the dirt and planted her bulb, her anger driving her to work even harder. Libby mimicked Maggie's digging and planting, and then she whispered to each tulip as she planted it, coaxing it to grow. Maggie was keenly aware that Libby would never be like the Croft children, but she didn't really want her to be like anyone else. She wanted Libby to be exactly who God created her to be.

An hour later, Walter came home and found them still digging in the old flower beds, trying to make them new. Libby ran to him, wrapping her dirt-plastered hands around his sleeve to tug him toward the gardens.

He stuck his hands in his pockets as he examined their work. "What are you doing?"

"We're making flowers!"

He glanced back and forth with curiosity between Maggie and her. "You *grow* flowers, sweetheart—"

"Not our daughter," Maggie explained. "Libby makes them."

It probably seemed like the most minor of points, a simple technicality in word choice, but Maggie knew it meant everything to Libby. In her was the innate desire to create.

Libby pointed at a small mound. "This one will be blue," she said then pointed to another mound. "And that one will be red."

She skipped around the flower bed, naming all the colors for him.

Walter kissed her on the head. "They will be spectacular."

In his gaze, Maggie saw the growing love he had for her. Perhaps Libby disappointed him at times, but she didn't think Walter had ever stopped caring about her.

16

JUNE 1968, LADENBROOKE MANOR

A wooden seat circled the turret that overlooked Ladenbrooke's gardens. Oliver sat on the bench, binoculars in hand, his eyes focused soundly on the girl who roamed among the yellow and purple iris below. He didn't like being anyplace else in the house—the portraits of his ancestors were creepy, their eyes seeming to follow him wherever he went, and everything was *valuable,* as his mother liked to say.

V-a-l-u-a-b-le.

Sometimes she spelled it out just like that, as if he were six instead of almost sixteen.

He took every opportunity to avoid being in the house, and when he was home on holiday, he spent most of his time in the village, playing cricket or rugby with the other boys in town. Anything to keep from wandering the halls of a house that seemed to be falling apart over their heads.

In recent years, he'd noticed some of the *v-a-l-u-a-b-l-e-s* disappearing as well—porcelain vases, tapestries, marble busts. More than twenty years after the war, his parents were still struggling to keep the manor intact. Money didn't flow like it once had, and his parents had even begun selling off some of their property. His father sold the old bothy to the Doyle family sev-

"Your flowers will be the most beautiful in all of England," Walter said, stepping into her imaginary world.

Libby gave him a curious look, and he blinked hard as if he were fighting back tears. Maggie couldn't stop her own tears from falling, but wiped them off quickly with the back of her glove.

"The flowers are thirsty," Libby said before she bounded toward the house to fill her watering can.

Both Maggie and Walter watched her rush away. "She loves you so much," Maggie said.

He looked back at the messy mounds of dirt. "She's going to be okay, isn't she?"

"She needs to make things. Just like you used to do."

He met her gaze. "Writing is different."

Maggie watched Libby hop onto the back patio. "I don't think so."

"She'll be disappointed when the colors are different than she imagined."

"Or maybe she'll embrace the colors that the flowers chose on their own."

Walter was silent for a moment before he spoke again. "You're a good mother, Maggie."

Her insecurities about her parenting skills began to subside as she smiled up at him. "And you're a good father."

"But I'm not her fa—"

She stood up and reached for his hand, silencing his doubts as he had silenced hers. "Yes, you are."

He gave the slightest nod and her heart warmed when she saw the hint of a smile.

Libby had become much more than an obligation to him, and she had no doubt he loved her.

Not a single one.

eral years back, and Oliver was thankful for that. Libby no longer came to the house after school, but at least she could still sneak into the gardens.

Sometimes she explored in the afternoons and sometimes she came in the evenings, right before the darkness conquered the light. Once the sun went down, he couldn't see her anymore, and on those evenings he was highly annoyed at the sun for giving up the fight.

His mother's flowers won all sorts of prizes for their beauty, but he thought Libby, with her brilliant copper-streaked hair and striking blue eyes, was more beautiful than anything found in a garden. She was an enchanting princess, reigning over a comely court.

He'd known Libby was a princess since they were children. She'd captivated him long before he started school, and for years, he'd been trying to win her attention. Some people thought she was crazy, but she wasn't. She was ethereal. Magical. Like a fairy or butterfly.

If only he could be like her. Happy and free.

She seemed to understand what so many people did not. That happiness was not found in trying to pigeonhole one's self into another's ideal. Happiness was found in embracing all you were created to be.

She twirled again in the twilight.

Libby seemed to draw energy from the flowers. She didn't hurt the gardens or the butterflies, but his mother still didn't want her on their property. Earlier this summer, his mother directed Henry to padlock the gate between the cottage and manor, but in the afternoons, when Mother was overseeing one of her many committees, Oliver removed the gardener's lock. And after Libby left for the night, he'd lock up the gate again.

His mother took credit for the prized flowers of Ladenbrooke, but she never worked in the gardens herself. She hired Henry and a staff of three other gardeners to fulfill her vision, so she hadn't discovered his magic with the lock. She rarely visited her gardens, but she'd ordered Henry to notify her immediately if Libby returned.

Fortunately Libby had managed to evade Henry's watch—or perhaps the head gardener looked the other way instead of reporting Libby whenever she visited the gardens.

Oliver didn't understand—why couldn't his mother just let Libby dance?

But neither of his parents were fond of the girl who'd captured his attention. If they knew he watched her up here, they would probably banish him from the tower forever. It was foolishness really, how they tried to control his every move, as if they could control his thoughts and his heart along with his actions.

He longed to be free like Libby, but his parents treated him more like a piece of pottery—shaping and molding him into the distinguished Lord of Ladenbrooke.

No one had ever asked him if he wanted to be lord.

Two days ago his father's man descended on the gardens, presumably to escort Libby back to the gate, but Oliver had rushed down the stairs as fast as he could and told the man to leave Libby alone. The man was conflicted, but he finally relented to the junior Croft, though he later told Lord Croft about their intruder.

Over dinner his mother had ranted about Libby's presence on their property along with the state of Libby's mind. Mother said she would appeal to the local authorities if Mr. and Mrs. Doyle didn't stop their daughter from trespassing.

Oliver told his mother that Libby was as harmless as the butterflies, but his mother thought Libby was a nuisance—a distraction—and she didn't have time for either.

Oliver, however, had plenty of time.

The door into the tower creaked open, and Oliver shifted his focus away from the window. He braced himself for an inquiry from his parents, but his sister stepped in the room instead.

Sarah flipped on the light overhead, and he shielded his eyes, the bulb blinding him for a moment.

"You're late to dinner," she said, her white-gloved hands balled up on the waist of her pleated dress. The ends of her blonde hair were flipped up, and she wore a teal green hat that matched her dress and a double strand of pearls.

He shrugged. "I was busy."

Sarah glanced down at the binoculars in his lap. Then she switched off the light and stepped toward the window. Her nose an inch from the glass, she scanned the shadows below them until her gaze stopped on the one shadow moving through their mother's flower beds. "It's Libby, isn't it?"

"Does it matter?" He stuffed his binoculars into the bench under the window seat.

"Apparently it matters to you as much as it matters to our mother."

He stiffened. "Please don't tell Mother she's here."

"She'll find out either way," Sarah said, twisting the pearls on her neck.

He shook his head. "Libby comes almost every night at this time."

Sarah sighed. "You like her, don't you?"

He looked back out the window, but he couldn't see her anymore. "Very much."

"Father would have an awful fit if he heard you say that."

"Then don't tell him," Oliver begged. "Don't tell anyone."

"Come along to dinner," she said as she stepped back toward the door. "I'll keep your secret."

He held the door open for her. "Thank you, Sarah."

Mother scolded them both for being late, but he didn't care what his mother, or, for that matter, what his father, thought—about dinner or the girl next door.

Libby was good and pure. Full of life and laughter. She might never love him like she loved the butterflies, but one day he hoped she might love him just a little.

One day he would win her attention and perhaps capture a small bit of her heart as well.

17

Adrienne crossed her legs in the leather seat next to Christopher, and she looked almost threatening in her black skirt, tights, and long black boots. Adrienne worked in admissions at Oxford, and even though she was thirty-six, it seemed half the population of male students along with their tutors were vying for her attention. For some reason, perhaps because he hadn't vied, they had become friends, bonding over their mutual love of rowing and reading, though his choices in literature were much different than hers.

He'd sold his car a long time ago, preferring to walk or bicycle around Oxford, so this morning he drove her convertible through dozens of tiny villages that dotted the Cotswolds. Adrienne was a smart woman who enjoyed a good story—and she seemed to enjoy his company most of the time, until he began talking about theology or his passion for writing. She was able to feign interest for a while but inevitably changed the subject.

His younger brother said his relationship with Adrienne was a "rebound," but it had been eight years since he'd lost his wife. He wasn't thinking about marriage right now, and Adrienne didn't seem the least bit interested in discussing marriage either. Though if he was gut-honest with himself, he did want to marry again one day. It might be too late to start a family, but he longed to settle into a relationship with a woman who didn't have to pretend to enjoy their conversation.

Adrienne was talking about a new restaurant opening outside Oxford, run by a renowned chef from one of the foodie shows. Christopher tried to pay attention to her words, but as their car crawled through the countryside, his focus was diluted. His anxiety, off the charts.

He'd tried to convince Adrienne to come another weekend, but she wouldn't budge on their plans. He'd already canceled the trip twice in the last month, and when he suggested rescheduling again, she asked if he was embarrassed to introduce her to his family. He wasn't embarrassed, though after his experience with Lauren, he was hesitant. And nervous.

It didn't help his nerves to know Heather was home.

Adrienne was adept at managing people whether it was her employees or the men who sought her mobile number. He had no doubt she would manage his family well also, and everything would be fine. Tomorrow, instead of staying in Bibury, he'd take her to one of the tourist spots in another town. Shakespeare's birthplace. Warwick Castle. Winston Churchill's childhood home.

Anyplace far from Willow Cottage.

Having grown up as friends, he and Heather had spent much more time together than he and Adrienne ever could with their busy careers. Time was the beauty and perhaps curse of young love. You could devote seemingly endless hours getting to know each other.

It was easy to idealize the past, but dwelling on it was unbeneficial for him as the best memories of his youth all had Heather in them. In Oxford, he'd managed to escape most of the memories, even when he visited Walter, but he couldn't seem to get away from the memories in Bibury.

After all these years, he still didn't understand what had happened between him and Heather. One night he had professed his love for her, saying he wanted to marry her. She'd accepted his proposal but then left for London the next day without even saying good-bye. In the months that followed, she refused every attempt he made to contact her.

He'd given her his heart along with the promise of the future, and she had rejected and humiliated him.

Instead of avoiding Heather this time, perhaps he should seek her out. Leave his personal baggage on her doorstep and move on. Once he saw her, reality would come crashing down, and then he could finally let go.

They passed through a village, and Adrienne glanced around at the stone cottages and gardens as if she was just realizing they'd left Oxford. "It's beautiful out here."

He smiled at her. "You should have come sooner."

"I tried." Her lips scrunched together into a pout.

"You didn't have to wait for me."

"It would have been a bit awkward to visit my boyfriend's home without my boyfriend."

He cringed at the word *boyfriend*, but knew he needed to stop being so uptight. "You have a rotten boyfriend."

Adrienne pulled down the sun visor to reapply her lipstick in the mirror.

"Are you nervous?" he asked.

"Not a bit."

"They're all going to love you."

She flashed him a smile. "Of course they are."

HEATHER PACKED *Libby's Book of Butterflies* into her handbag and stowed it in the basket on her old bicycle as she prepared to ride down the hill. To find out about Libby, she must visit the one woman she'd been avoiding ever since she'd come home.

Mrs. Westcott was the town midwife, and though she'd been much younger than Heather's mother, they had children the same age. Growing up, it had always seemed to Heather as if Mrs. Westcott and her mum were peers. She was one of the few people who came to visit often during Heather's childhood, and as far as she knew, the only friend of Mum's that was still alive.

After she crested the hill by Ladenbrooke, Heather spread out her legs and began to soar down toward Bibury. She and Christopher used to race like this when they were teenagers, not a single care anchoring them to the ground. They may have both grown up, but in her mind, Christopher would always be handsome and reckless and completely free from the cares of this world.

His confidence had shaken her when she was younger. Sometimes she'd felt like she was clinging to the tail of a kite, bobbling along behind him. Her home was quiet—reserved—while the Westcott house was crazy loud and fun. Christopher once said he liked coming to her cottage to get away from the noise, but she hadn't understood the value of peace at the time.

Her feet back on the pedals, she braked in front of the Westcott home. Their renovated farmhouse was much larger than her parents' cottage and, despite its age, in mint condition. The flower beds in front were free of weeds, and the family had replaced their thatched roof with slate.

She slipped the butterfly book from her bag and walked up the steps, just as she'd done countless times in her teens. It was so strange to be back here, standing on the stoop like she was waiting for Christopher to answer the door again.

She knocked tentatively on the front door, and seconds later, the door swung back.

"Oh my goodness," Mrs. Westcott exclaimed. "I'm so glad you've come."

Heather smiled at the kindness in her welcome. Mrs. Westcott's white hair was cut short, a pixie style, and her face was pale with the exception of a dark crimson shade on her lips.

Seconds after she answered the door, Mrs. Westcott's welcoming smile fell into a nervous one, the lines of her lipstick tightening like a wide rubber band. "I was hoping you would visit, but . . ." The woman didn't finish her sentence. Instead her gaze traveled over Heather's shoulder as if she was looking for a car.

"I rode my bicycle," Heather explained. "Should I come back another time?"

Mrs. Westcott looked down at the sketchbook in Heather's hand. At the pink-and-golden butterfly on the cover. "Where did you find that?"

"In my parents' basement," she said, holding it up. "I was wondering if you could answer some questions about my sister."

Mrs. Westcott opened the door wider. "I only have a few minutes."

"I can come back tomorrow."

But Mrs. Westcott waved her inside, and Heather stepped over the threshold into the home that had once been as familiar as her own. The last time she was here, she and Christopher were supposed to be filling out forms for college at the kitchen table, but at the time, it had been almost impossible for her to focus on paperwork.

Mrs. Westcott pointed toward the plaid couch for Heather while she sat on an upholstered chair, drumming her fingers on the arms. "I'm sorry I don't have time to offer you tea today."

"I won't stay long," Heather promised, glad she didn't have to make small talk this afternoon.

"Will you come back for tea another time?" the older woman asked.

"Of course," Heather replied. Christopher was living in Oxford now and their teenage years were far behind them. It was absurd for her to continue avoiding this place.

She slid the book across the polished coffee table in front of Mrs. Westcott. "Did my sister paint these butterflies?"

Mrs. Westcott touched the edges of the cover as if it were sacred. "Libby was a beautiful artist."

"My parents never talked about her."

"It was probably too hard—"

"I wish they'd let me get to know her through their stories."

Mrs. Westcott lifted her hands, softly drumming her fingers together. "Did you know your mum had a younger brother?"

Heather shook her head.

"She lost him not long after the war." Mrs. Westcott inched further back on her chair.

"It's hard to lose someone you love when you're so young."

"But my parents weren't young when they lost Libby."

"No, but your mother tried hard to shield herself and you from this loss. She tried to create—" Mrs. Westcott hesitated.

Heather understood what it was like to shield someone you loved, but she didn't know why her parents had to shield her from the memories.

"She never wanted to hurt you," Mrs. Westcott said.

Heather leaned forward. "I found some pictures of my parents holding Libby's hand when she was a girl. They looked so happy."

"They adored both of you."

"Could you tell me how she died?"

Mrs. Westcott glanced up at the clock over the fireplace mantel. "That isn't my story to tell."

"Whose story is it?"

Mrs. Westcott shook her head. "It doesn't matter anymore."

Heather looked down at the book, flipping the page to the Autumn Dancer shimmering with bright orange, red, and golden browns. "It does to me."

Mrs. Westcott reached for the book and pulled it onto her lap. "As you grow older, you realize some things that happened in the past should probably remain there."

Heather managed a smile. No matter how many years went by, she suspected that Mrs. Westcott would continue to think of her as a child. "I'm old enough to realize that."

"Of course you are." Mrs. Westcott gingerly touched the picture of the butterfly. "I'm surprised your mother kept this."

"Why would she get rid of it?"

Mrs. Westcott didn't answer her question this time. Instead, she leafed through the pictures until she found a bright-blue butterfly rimmed with red.

"Libby wasn't well." Mrs. Westcott sighed as she closed the book. "She broke your mum's heart."

"I'm not here to judge her," Heather said. "Or my mother."

But even as the words left her mouth, she realized they weren't completely true.

"Now that your father is gone . . ." Mrs. Westcott's voice trailed off as she slid the book back onto the table. "Perhaps I should tell you."

A strange sense of foreboding crept up her spine.

"It happened so long ago—"

"Before I was born?" Heather asked.

The woman slowly nodded her head.

Heather scooted to the edge of her seat. "Did you know my sister?"

"As much as anyone could know her, I suppose." Mrs. Westcott glanced at the clock again.

Heather lifted the book off the table. "Perhaps we should talk on Monday?"

Before Mrs. Westcott replied, a car pulled into the driveway, the gravel rumbling under its tires. "Oh dear," she mumbled as she hopped up from her chair, her eyes fixed on the front window.

Heather stood quickly. "I'm sorry—" she apologized. "I've stayed too long."

She stepped toward the picture window, but Mrs. Westcott took her arm, bustling her away from the glass. "You should probably use the back door."

18

JULY 1968, LADENBROOKE MANOR

Oliver's family had returned to London, like they did every year before his mother opened up their gardens. This year he had petitioned his father for permission to stay in the manor over the weekend. At first, his father had refused his request, so Oliver had to up the stakes. He said he needed to stay behind to practice cricket with his team.

Finally, his father relented.

His parents didn't socialize with anyone who hadn't obtained upper-class status, but the game of cricket leveled society's rigid structure. It was the one place where he was allowed to spend time with friends from the middle and even working classes. His father, of course, always assumed his son would win the games against those in a lower class, but Oliver wasn't nearly as athletic as his father liked to think. There was no cricket practice this weekend, though his father was much too busy to bother with details like that.

When the gardens opened, Oliver donned a tweed cap and sunglasses and then wandered incognito among the visitors. He had watched Libby from the tower, but it had been so long since he'd been close to her. He'd worried for days that the Doyles wouldn't come. . . .

But they had, and while Mr. and Mrs. Doyle visited with another family, he followed Libby to a quiet bench in his mother's white garden. He didn't disturb her, standing instead back by an arbor where he could study her as she studied the butterflies.

Libby pulled her knees to her chest and slowly rocked back and forth as she watched two butterflies dance among the white-and-silver tips of petunias, lilies, and phlox. She was completely lost in her world until three girls stepped close to the bench, local girls who were fourteen or fifteen. Close to her age.

Edith was the name of the tallest girl. She and her gang giggled whenever they came near Oliver in the village, but this morning their laughter wasn't nervous or innocent. It was ugly.

Libby ignored the girls' teasing, folding her head between her arms, but they were relentless, calling her awful names.

Imbecile. Idiot. Simpleton.

And his heart reared to defend her.

He'd only meant to watch Libby, not to frighten her as he'd done so many times when they were younger, but he couldn't allow anyone to torment her.

He rushed toward the pack before they insulted her again. "Good afternoon, ladies," he said though his pleasantry didn't sound pleasant at all.

The laughter dissoved into giggles.

"Hello, Oliver," Edith said. Her blonde hair was held back with a blue hairband, and she smiled at him as if she were daring him to flirt back.

He wasn't the least bit interested in flirting, stepping instead toward the bench. "If your mum heard you use those names, she'd box your ears."

Edith laughed again as she flung her hand toward Libby. "My mum thinks she's stupid too."

"Then, perhaps, someone should box her ears as well."

She clasped her hands together, her laughter fading. "We're only having a bit of fun."

"It's not so much fun for Libby."

Turning away from Edith, he sat down on the bench. "Hiya."

Libby lifted her head slowly from her hiding place, like a turtle sneaking a peak from its shell.

Then he looked back at the regiment of prim and proper girls before him. "Libby is one of my best friends."

"We didn't know—" Edith said, the confidence in her voice waning.

"I can assure you that she's not an idiot or a simpleton, but I'm not certain about our present company."

"We didn't mean anything by it," another girl said. "She just—well, she never *says* anything."

"That's because you aren't listening," he said as he draped his arm across the back of the bench. Libby sat a bit straighter. "Besides, some people consider contemplation a virtue—and ignorance a vice."

The girl huffed at his insult, and the trio began to back away. When he turned back toward Libby, he heard one of the girls whispering about the impudence of the younger Lord Croft. Perhaps he was an idiot too. . . .

"I'm sorry they weren't playing nice."

Libby rocked again. "I don't want to be their friend."

"I don't want to be their friend either," he said. "But I sure wish you'd be mine."

She didn't reply, but she didn't scoot away either like she'd done when they were children. Or ask him to leave. As people milled around, they sat there together, watching the butterflies.

"Those girls are as annoying as the mosquitos down by the river." He'd meant it to be funny, but she didn't laugh. "But you—"

He studied her again like he'd done when they were kids. "You are different."

When she turned, the look in her blue eyes was one of curiosity and the slightest hint of appreciation.

"I know your secret," he whispered.

She shook her head. "I don't have secrets."

"You aren't really a butterfly."

"I know that."

"You're really a princess. A butterfly princess."

Her eyes grew wide, and then she laughed. Not a giggle like the other girls or the falsity of forced laughter. Her laugh came from the depths of her heart. She wasn't nervous. Libby was free, not caring one whit what anyone else thought about her.

Oliver wished she would care just a little about what he thought, but if she cared too much, her focus might turn inward like the other girls, painfully aware of what she said and did when she was around him. She might no longer dance among his mother's flowers.

As he laughed with her that morning, something passed between them. Something he couldn't explain.

No longer would he be satisfied with watching Libby dance from afar. He wanted to dance right beside her.

WALTER CALLED LIBBY'S NAME WHEN he stepped through the front door. Usually she was waiting for him in the sitting room when he came home from work, but sometimes she got caught up in looking at the pictures of a book she'd borrowed from the lending library or sketching a flower she'd seen in the gardens.

He knocked on her bedroom door, and when no one answered, he opened it. Libby wasn't inside, but her window was open. The breeze fluttered the gauzy pink curtains and jangled the glittery beads strung down from the canopy, making them dance like marionettes over her bed. Maggie had picked out colors reminiscent of a magical garden, and together she and Libby had created a bright space that thrived even on the gloomiest days.

The colors were beautiful, but the rest of the room was not. Markers, pencils, pieces of paper, and books were strewn across the bedcovers, spilling over onto the floor. He'd repeatedly asked Libby to make her bed before school and clean up her room when she returned home, but she always seemed to forget. At least she said she forgot. There was a fine line between defiance and distraction, and he wasn't always certain which it was for her.

He wanted to smooth out the wrinkles on her bed, but he resisted the urge. She must learn to care for herself or she would never be able to live on her own.

One of Libby's sketchbooks lay open on the messy bedcovers, and he sat down on the mattress to look at the flowers she'd drawn at Ladenbrooke. Libby was fourteen now, and in the last few years, he'd come to realize that she was as smart as the next person. Sometimes she feigned ignorance to get out of what was required of her, or stayed silent so she could slip away. Unfortunately her silence made people doubt her intelligence.

Sometimes Walter wished she would yell, even at him. Scream or shout or even cry. But if she was ever angry, she never expressed it. She did express hurt sometimes, and love, but only to a select few and only in her peculiar way. Her smiles were rare, but he treasured every one sent his way.

Thirteen years had passed since he'd slugged Baron Bonheur in that alley. It had taken almost as many years to build up all that had been destroyed in those few seconds.

How many times had he regretted listening to Mrs. Bishop that morning? If he had been away from the village, off reporting about someone else's problems, he never would have found Maggie and Elliot together. Never would have known that Libby wasn't his daughter by birth. Never would have given up his career as a writer and newspaperman.

But sometimes he also wondered if he'd prevented something worse from happening between that man and Maggie. He didn't know what—nor would he allow his mind to conjure up any potential scenarios—but now, after more than a decade in hindsight, he thought he might have saved his family in that alleyway. Or at least, that's how he chose to look at it.

He and Maggie had suffered plenty in those early years, but they had slowly grown to love each other. Perhaps they were even stronger because of all they'd gone through together. Libby may not look like him, but no one here seemed to care. With the exception of the reddish tint to her hair, she was the spitting image of her mother. And when people asked about Libby's lovely hair, Maggie just said she got it from her father's side of the family.

He flipped through the pictures in Libby's sketchbook. He wished he understood the way her mind worked. At age twelve, the smartest students in England transitioned into grammar school while the rest of the kids attended a secondary modern school to learn a trade. Libby would never attend grammar school nor had she shown much interest in pursuing a trade. But he was growing to appreciate her eye for beauty in their everyday life, details that most people overlooked. Some of the flowers in her book were still crude pencil drawings, but he had no doubt that Libby would bring them to life. She saw a rainbow of colors where other people saw only black and white.

He set Libby's sketchbook back on her crumpled bed. She was obsessed with color, along with beauty, and she had the uncanny ability to deflect the cares of the world and appreciate all of creation—whether she or God had created it.

Walter walked to the back of the cottage and found Maggie outside, kneeling among the blossoms of spring flowers as she plucked out the weeds. Standing by the patio door, he admired his wife's tenacity. The years together had taken them on a windy road, far from each other at times and then remarkably close as they hugged the side of a mountain that neither of them could climb alone.

One of the hardest times had come two years ago when Lady Croft found Libby wandering in the gardens of Ladenbrooke. She treated his daughter like a common criminal and then proceeded to dismiss Maggie as if she'd been a conspirator with Libby's crime. After almost eleven years of faithful service, his wife became unemployed.

Maggie had fretted for a few days after being relieved of her position, but then she poured herself into her own gardens, working religiously on planting and fertilizing and ridding the soil of weeds that threatened to harm her flowers and vegetables. The flower gardens were both to entice Libby to stay at home and to keep Maggie's hands busy.

They'd cut back on their expenses, grown more vegetables among the flower gardens, and then Maggie had gone back to school to become a hairdresser. For the first time since they'd married, she was excited about the possibilities before her.

If they were still renting, Walter had no doubt the Crofts would have evicted them from the cottage, but Lord Croft sold them the old bothy before Lady Croft's dismissal. Instead of paying rent to the Croft family now, he and Maggie were dependent on the local savings and loan. He preferred it that way. His income from the post office was steady and sufficient enough to pay the monthly mortgage.

Maggie renamed their home Willow Cottage after the elegant tree that draped over the river below the house. A farmer bought the field and forest on the hillside behind the cottage, the land between their garden and the River Coln, but the Doyles could use the path through the field whenever they liked to picnic by the water. Both Maggie and Libby were afraid of wading in the river, but they liked to sit under the willow and watch the current rush by.

He scanned the gardens, but he didn't see Libby.

A few years back, when Maggie first began to garden, Libby had been disappointed that her flowers hadn't grown into the colors she'd selected for them. She'd returned to sketching flowers on paper instead of planting them.

Maggie had singlehandedly turned their two acres of backyard into a regular Garden of Eden. She'd created a formal garden and a whimsical one, and then she'd asked Walter to plant hedges in a rectangle shape to create a secret garden. He hadn't said anything to Maggie, but he wasn't sure how they could refer to the garden as secret when the entrance was as plain as day to anyone visiting behind their house. Still, he'd accommodated her and played along with her illusion that it was hidden.

He walked toward his wife and kissed her on the cheek. "Where is Libby?" he asked.

"Drawing in her room."

"Not anymore," Walter replied with a shake of his head. "But she left her pencils scattered across her bed."

Fear flickered in her eyes. "Did you check the gate?"

"Not yet."

Maggie sighed.

The wrought-iron gate separated the cottage from the manor. The Croft family from the Doyles. Even though Lady Croft had released Maggie, Libby still didn't respect the differences in their classes or their property. She thought she belonged on the Ladenbrooke side, but the local authorities did not.

The Crofts were supposed to padlock the gate, but some days the lock seemed to disappear and Libby would wander over as if she were the Lady of Ladenbrooke. She didn't understand why she couldn't be in the gardens. She'd practically grown up in the old manor house, freely roaming the grounds throughout her childhood. She didn't seem to care about returning to visit the house, not like she cared about Lady Croft's flowers. He and Maggie tried to contain her on their side of the wall, but they continued to fail at their attempts.

As she stood, Maggie tossed her handful of weeds into a pile. "I'll find her."

Walter shook his head. "I can do it this time."

Maggie searched his face, as if trying to determine if he was sincere.

"I want to get her," he said. "She needs to understand what the Crofts will do if she keeps trespassing."

Maggie took off her gloves. "I don't want to frighten her—"

"A little fear is better than having the Crofts dictate her future." While he wanted to help her conquer her fears on one hand, when it came to the gardens at Ladenbrooke, he needed her to be afraid.

"Please be gentle with her," Maggie said as he stepped away.

He didn't respond. Gentleness wouldn't help Libby understand the realities of life.

The gate in the wall was open, the padlock dangling from the handle on the opposite side. Walter glanced up at the grand house on the hillside. He didn't see anyone on the lawn, so he descended down the path through the gardens. If he saw anyone, he hoped it would be the head gardener. He knew Henry from his mail route, and Libby knew him as well from her earlier years playing in the garden.

Libby wasn't among the flowers in the formal garden or under the arbor of grapevines, so he moved down the terraces on the hill. She wouldn't be too close to the river, but she might be hiding among the trees.

"Libby?" he called out.

Light danced on the leaves, shifting shadows over his path as the sun started to set. He called her name again as he stepped out of the trees, toward the old maze.

This time he heard her respond. "Shh . . ."

He followed the sound of her whisper until he found her sitting by the lily pond.

"We have to go," he said.

She pointed at a moss-green butterfly with black spots, hovering above a bed of red and orange poppies. "She's trying to find a home for the night."

He eyed the butterfly. "How do you know?"

"Because she's usually asleep by now." Libby's gaze remained on the creature. "Butterflies can't fly at night, you know."

He didn't know—didn't know anything about butterflies except what Libby told him.

"Their wings only work when they're warm," she explained. "They would die without sunlight."

He held out his hand, trying to urge her to stand. "We can't let the Crofts find you here."

"Their wings move like this." Instead of taking his hand, she shaped a figure eight in the air. "They fly back and forth so they don't miss anything."

"Your mum is going to start missing both of us if—"

"The poisonous ones don't fly nearly as fast as the others." Her hand slowed. "More like this."

He wanted to grab her shoulders and shake them, jolting her back to reality.

"Some of the adult butterflies only live about a month," she said wistfully. "Only a month to play in the gardens."

"You need to stay in the gardens Mum planted for you."

She finally acknowledged his words with a shake of her head. "It's not the same."

"Why not?"

"My friends don't come into our garden."

"The butterflies?" he asked.

When she nodded, he sighed. Perhaps it was hopeless to make her understand right now. Perhaps he simply had to play along. "Have you invited your friends into our garden?"

She crossed her arms over her chest. "They wouldn't come."

"Let's try again," he begged.

Before she replied, he heard a rustle on the other side of the hedge behind them. Then he saw a figure of someone moving between the tangled branches.

"Who's there?" he called.

The person stopped moving.

"Who is it?" Walter called again, but no one answered as he stepped toward the tall hedge.

He heard rustling again, the sound of someone running. He wanted to pursue whoever was on the other side, but they would be long gone before he rounded the hedge.

When he glanced back at Libby, she didn't seem worried about someone watching them.

He put his arm around her. "We have to get you home."

She didn't move, her eyes still on the butterfly. "I wish I could help her."

"You can, Libby," he said, searching quickly for a reason behind his declaration. "You can encourage her to fly away."

She seemed to consider his words before curling her fingers over the edge of a boulder and beginning to stand. The butterfly flittered toward the maze, and for a moment, he thought Libby might chase after it, but she remained at his side.

"She will find a safe place," he assured her.

She looked up into his face, not quite meeting his eyes, and then slowly nodded, seemingly content in his certainty. He thought it strange that a girl so unaccustomed to anxiety would be concerned about this butterfly and not about the person on the other side of the yews.

They couldn't go back up through the gardens and the gate now. Whoever had been watching them may already have alerted Lord or Lady Croft to their presence. They needed to find another way around the wall.

He eyed the forest that hid the river. While he wanted her to be afraid of the Crofts, he no longer wanted her to fear the water.

Perhaps this was the perfect opportunity to help her confront this fear of the river once and for all. Confront and conquer it. It was plenty warm enough for them to wade through the water. They only had to traverse about fifteen feet until they reached the shore on the other side of the wall.

"We have to hurry, Libby."

She looked back at the flowers.

"If we don't go now, you might never see your friends again."

She rubbed her arms. "Like in Mr. McGregor's garden?"

"Exactly," he said. "Like Mr. McGregor and his garden."

The sun had almost set, casting long shadows over them as she followed him down to the river. He reached for her hand, but she shook away his grasp as she always did when anyone except Maggie tried to touch her.

She studied the river and then looked down at her toes. Her voice trembled when she spoke again. "I don't like the water."

"I know," he said. "I will carry you."

She started to back away from the bank, and he decided it was time to be completely honest with her, to show her that she could be strong in the face of what she feared. "If the Crofts find you here tonight, they'll have you sent away."

"I don't like the water," she repeated.

"You won't be able to live at the cottage with your mother and me anymore."

She shivered.

"You won't even be able to visit Mum's garden," he continued as he took off his shoes.

Her gaze fell to the current, swirling around in the center.

"But you'll be safe if you let me carry you to the other side."

When she looked back up at him, he could see the wavering in her eyes as she decided whether or not to go with him.

"You have to trust me, Libby, or some bad things might happen to all of us."

She didn't argue anymore.

He rolled up his trousers, and then with his shoes in one hand, he leaned over and swept his daughter off the ground. She was delicate. Fragile. More like the flowers she loved than the trees.

As he stepped into the water, she circled her arms around his neck and he held her close to his chest. She may not let him take her hand, but she freely gave affection on her own terms. Like when she was afraid.

Stones poked into his feet as they slipped around an overgrown bush. The cold current rushed around his ankles and then his shins, but he didn't let either deter him.

He couldn't remember a time, even when she was a toddler,

that Libby had allowed him to hold her. Not that he had tried very hard. He'd allowed his own bitterness, his disappointment with life, to distract him from being a good father, and he feared it was too late to mend it. Yet Libby trusted him enough to let him carry her over her greatest fear. In her heart, she must know he wanted what was best for her.

The strands of leaves on the willow tree dangled over the water like the beads around Libby's bed. He ducked under the canopy of leaves, and in the fading light, he could see the field in front of him. In seconds, they could move out of the river and onto the path that would lead them home.

He took another step, but this time he didn't feel the smooth surface of a river rock under the water. This time a broken stick speared the sole of his foot.

His body reacted against his will, his foot recoiling back up above the surface as he leaned sideways, Libby's screams piercing his ear. He tried to anchor himself again, but it was impossible on the slippery stones. Dropping his shoes, he reached behind to protect them both from a hard fall.

Water splashed over Libby as they landed in the river, water soaking through his trousers, across Libby's lap.

She shoved away from him, her eyes wide in terror.

"I'm so sorry." He quickly regained his footing and reached for her.

Shaking her head, Libby backed away even farther. Then she slipped on one of the rocks and screamed as she fell into the current.

He tried to help her out of the water, but she shook her head again, her tears mixing with the river. On her hands and knees, she crawled through the water until she reached the other side.

He retrieved his socks and the shoe that hadn't been stolen away by the current. Then he climbed up the grassy bank beside her.

Libby's arms were clutched around her knees, her entire body shaking as she rocked. When he sat beside her, she scooted away from him.

"It was an accident," he tried to explain, devastated that he'd lost control when she needed him to be strong.

He put his hand on her shoulder, to comfort her as much as himself, but she moved away again.

Dejected, he sat down on the rock beside her and watched the current flow by.

Perhaps Maggie was right. They needed to protect Libby from harm instead of forcing her to confront her fears.

19

AUGUST 1968, LADENBROOKE MANOR

The scent of lilac and lavender drifted inside through the open windows, beckoning Libby to come play. She tiptoed through the dark hallway, pausing only to listen at her parents' door. Through the crack, she heard Walter's steady breathing.

She hadn't been back to the gardens in a week, ever since he'd dropped her in the water.

She shivered at the memory.

Mummy said Walter loved her, but it didn't matter what she said. He was always wanting her to do things she didn't want to do. Things that scared her. He wanted her to play with children who teased her. Read books instead of draw. Go to school when she didn't learn a ruddy thing except that she was different from everyone else.

Walter said he loved her, but he didn't much like who she was.

And sometimes she didn't much like who she was either.

Soft moonlight enveloped her path, guiding her toward the gate like creamy white petals leading a bride to the altar. Walter didn't understand—she needed to be in these gardens. The beauty of it breathed life into her. Filled her very soul.

She pushed down the latch, testing it slowly to see if it was locked on the opposite side. Her heart leapt when it opened.

The lady left her gardens every autumn now when the flowers began to die, and Mummy didn't seem to care if she visited the gardens when the lady was gone. But in the summer, when the flowers were blooming, when the air smelled sweet and the butterflies danced in the breeze, Mummy and Walter didn't want her to explore.

Yet this was her sustenance. Her magic. She needed to be here as much as the butterflies needed their nectar to fly.

Quietly she closed the gate and hurried across the brick path until she reached the circular rose garden. In the center of the roses was the most lush carpet of grass. She tossed her shoes into the air, the soft grass tickling her toes. Then she stretched out her arms and twirled in the moonlight.

Some people thought the rays of the moon were cool, like the rays of the sun were warm, but they were wrong. The light from the moon was as warm as the sun, a lovely, golden warmth that electrified her from the inside.

"Libby," someone whispered from the other side of the rosebushes.

She stopped her dance, her hands falling to her side. It was him again. Interrupting her. As if he couldn't stand the thought of her being alone.

Some nights she liked seeing him, but nights like this when the moon was full, when the light and flowers were luring her outside, she just wanted to dance.

Sighing, she moved toward the trees. "Oliver?"

He stepped out from behind the trunk of an elm, into the moonlight. His hands were in his pockets, and he grinned at her in that sheepish way that made the girls in Bibury act all weird.

Last week she'd been trying to sketch in the park, and he'd walked right over to her with an ice cream cone in each hand. He didn't even ask. Just handed her one and then sat right down on her blanket like she needed company.

Edith and her friends had walked by, laughing like they always did. They tried to get Oliver to come walk with them, but he refused. Edith glared at her when they left, as if she'd tethered Oliver to the blanket.

For some reason, Edith and her friends didn't like her at all.

"Can I dance with you?" he asked.

She hiked up her nose a notch, crossed her arms over her chest. "I only dance by myself."

When he laughed, her chin fell again. She loved to study the colors on a flower, the patterns on a butterfly wing, but she'd never really studied a face before.

Was Oliver teasing her like the girls in the village? She stared at his eyes, but couldn't tell. "It's not funny."

"It seems to me that you are always dancing with something, Libby. The butterflies or the breeze or the starlight."

Something shifted inside her with his words. He'd never mocked her like some of the other children did. In fact it seemed as if he might understand a small part of her.

She never danced alone, but it was a secret. And it scared her that Oliver knew her so well.

She turned away. "I have to go home."

"I want to be your friend," he said.

"I already have friends."

"But I want to be your friend forever."

She considered his words.

"Come with me," he said, pointing back to the trees.

"Where would we go?"

He reached for her hand. "To the river."

Her skin bristled as she stared down at their hands knotted together like the vines over the lady's arbor. No boy had ever touched her, but as he held her fingers gently in his, a strange feeling coursed through her. Not disgust or worry. Something closer to happiness, like the feeling of the grass under her toes.

Oliver used to annoy her when they were kids, always wanting her to play with him, but he didn't bother her as much anymore.

"Come with me," he whispered again.

She shivered. "Not to the river."

"We'll go someplace else then." He clicked on his torch and light spread across their feet, erasing the warmth from the moon. "Have you been up in the tower?"

She turned toward the path of light and then looked back at him, confused. There were three towers in the manor, but the lady wouldn't let her inside any of them.

"I'm not allowed in your house."

"Not that tower." He grinned. "The old folly in the maze."

She followed him across the paths of the lady's gardens. And then into something like a tunnel between the yew bushes. She didn't like the branches and leaves scratching her face, didn't like the canopy above them that blocked the moon and stars.

She tugged on his hand. "I want to go back."

"The tower's right there," Oliver said, pointing up to the tip of a structure between the bushes.

She hesitated again. "I don't know—"

"We won't stay long," he promised, placing his other hand over hers, cradling her fingers.

She'd spent most of her life trying to ignore Oliver, wishing he would leave her alone, but in that moment, her heart seemed to break free. She wanted nothing more than to be with Oliver in his folly.

As she clung to his hand, he guided her through the bushes, through the corners and crevices and winding turns of the maze. When they reached the tower, he stepped inside first and the light from his torch flooded the ground floor. Cobwebs hung from the low ceiling, and she shivered again. She liked creatures that flew among the flowers, not ones that liked to hide.

He urged her toward the circular stairs, but she refused to move.

"Are you afraid?" he asked.

She didn't want to be afraid of anything—not the river or other people or spiders—but still the fears pressed against her.

He squeezed her hand again. "You don't have to be afraid with me."

She nodded and warily began to walk toward the stairs with him. He tested the first step and then the second one. When he deemed each step safe, she climbed up after him.

"My great, great-grandfather built this tower," Oliver said. "The village thought it was only a folly, but it wasn't."

Intrigued, she glanced up the steps. "What was it?"

"His secret place." Oliver reached for her hand. "He used to bring his mistress up here."

The way Oliver said it was like the other kids who shared secrets near her, laughing together over a common bond. As she grew older, she realized they were often laughing at her. Oliver wasn't teasing her though. She was missing something, but couldn't figure out what it was.

"Why didn't he take her to the house?" she asked.

"Because his wife didn't want her there." He said the words in a low voice, so serious, as if she would understand his secret.

Something seemed to click in her mind, a few pieces falling into place.

"Like the lady doesn't want me in your house."

His eyes looked sad, and she wished she could bring the light back into them. "Something like that."

"Why does it make you sad?" she asked quietly.

"Instead of marrying the woman he loved, my grandfather had to hide her in a maze."

Her ignorance frustrated her. Why was Oliver upset over something that happened so long ago?

"He wanted to be alone with her," he said as they neared the last step. "Even in a big house, it's hard to hide when so many people are watching you."

"Perhaps they shouldn't have tried to hide."

He glanced back at her. "Perhaps."

They emerged onto the top floor, a circular room that was just as musty as the entrance below. She released his hand and hurried to look out one of the windows along the stone walls. He turned off the torch, and beyond the maze, she could see the moonlight playing on the flowers.

His hand touched her shoulder, and she jumped. He removed his hand, moments passing between them in silence, and then he placed his arm around her. This time she only shivered at his touch.

"Libby." He turned her slowly toward him. "Please dance with me."

She couldn't see his eyes in the shadows, but she could hear the intensity in his voice.

"I don't know how to dance with a person."

"I will teach you."

She wasn't certain she wanted to learn, but he took her right hand into one of his and curled the fingers of his other hand around her waist. In the darkness, he stepped right. She didn't know what to do at first, but he guided her toward him before taking another step.

"My family is leaving for London in the morning," he whispered as if he were telling her another secret.

Usually the thought of the Croft family's migration pleased her, knowing she could roam free in their garden without anyone to stop her, but tonight she didn't want Oliver to go.

She slowly followed him around the perimeter of the room. "They have my life planned out," he said.

"Why do you let them plan it?"

"I don't have a choice." He stopped dancing, but he didn't let go of her waist or her hand. "But you can choose, Libby. You are just like the butterflies."

Her legs stopped moving, but her heart danced at his words.

"No one can contain you."

She smiled up at him, her long hair falling over both of her shoulders.

"If someone trapped you, I'm afraid you might—" His voice trailed off.

She stepped back. "What are you afraid of, Oliver?"

"I wish I could be more like you." He gently folded her hair behind her ears. "I'll be back next summer."

She nodded in the silence, and again she thought he wanted something more from her, but didn't know what it was.

He leaned down, whispering in her ear. "Will you wait?"

"For what?"

He hesitated before speaking again, as if he were afraid to answer her question. "For me."

She'd waited for the flowers to bloom each year, for the cocoons to birth new butterflies, and for her other butterfly friends to find their way home. But she'd never waited for a person.

People were much less predictable. Except Oliver perhaps. He came back every summer with the flowers and butterflies.

"I'll try," she said.

This time, when he pulled her close to him, she didn't flinch.

"LIBBY?" MAGGIE CALLED SOFTLY AS she stepped onto the back patio. She scanned the gardens behind her house even though she knew Libby wasn't there. No matter how hard she worked to convince her daughter to stay on this side of the wall, she couldn't keep Libby out of the gardens next door.

It was long past midnight, and she considered waking Walter to tell him Libby was gone. But he'd felt so guilty after dropping her in the water, and in his fear for her, he'd be furious to know she'd left again.

Maggie called Libby's name one more time, hoping she wasn't far, but there was no answer.

Slipping through the open gate, Maggie hurried through the familiar gardens. Moonlight settled over the flowers, and the estate was quiet and surreal. Just like her daughter.

She glanced up at the darkened windows of the house, hoping she wouldn't waken the occupants or their dogs. The dogs weren't allowed in the gardens, but if they began barking, Henry would come out to check on them.

She eyed the trees in front of her. Libby wouldn't go anywhere near the river, especially after what happened last week, but she liked to hear the sound of the water. Perhaps she was sitting along the bank.

A bright light flashed through the lower terrace of the garden, above the maze, and Maggie stopped. Then the light held steady from the top of the folly, like a beacon.

Had Libby climbed the old tower?

If Lord or Lady Croft saw the light, they would probably phone the police.

"Libby?" she called louder this time.

She'd never been inside the maze, but she had no choice now. The yew hedges blocked most of the light as she moved through the narrow passage, the spindly branches poking her skin. When the path ended, she turned back to try another. And then another.

As she drew closer to the folly, laughter filtered out from the tower, soaring like one of Libby's butterflies on the breeze. Stunned, Maggie stopped walking. Then Libby laughed again, but this time her laughter was followed by the laugh of a man.

Maggie's heart began to race as memories flashed back in her mind. Elliot and her at the cave. Her own tumbling emotions as she longed for his return. And how she'd wanted to sail away with him.

But Libby didn't want to escape, did she?

Her daughter wasn't old enough to have a suitor, and even if she was, she wouldn't know how to act with a man. He would take advantage of her and leave her—

Her stomach rolled as she rushed through the tower's doorway, following the path of light up the steps. She found Libby upstairs, dancing in the arms of Oliver Croft.

Libby grinned when she saw her. "Hello, Mummy."

But Oliver didn't smile at her. Instead his laughter dissipated into the walls of the folly. "Mrs. Doyle?"

Her head—and her heart—felt as if they were about to explode. She still saw Libby as a child, but even though her daughter may wrestle with the emotions of an adolescent, her body was maturing into one of a young woman. A beautiful woman.

Libby was too young, much too young for—for *this*.

She may not understand what was happening, but Oliver Croft was almost two years older and knew exactly what he was doing.

"Move away from her," Maggie commanded, her voice steely.

When he stepped away, Libby reached for his arm, but he shook off her hand. "Mummy, you remember Oliver."

Maggie nodded slowly. "Oliver is the respected son of Lord and Lady Croft."

"I'm sorry—" he muttered, guilt etched in the nervous lines around his eyes and lips.

Confused, Libby looked back and forth between them before she spoke to the man next to her. "Mummy doesn't mind me coming into the gardens."

"I do mind," Maggie replied, trying to calm her voice. "Oliver, you should know better . . ."

"We were only playing together," Libby said. "Like when we were kids."

Maggie didn't respond. Oliver knew just like Maggie did that Libby never wanted to play with him when they were children.

Maggie reached for her daughter's hand, but Libby pulled it away. "I'm staying here," she insisted.

Anger collided with fear inside her. When she looked at Oliver again, it felt like her heart was on fire. "Go home," she said, her voice so hard she barely recognized it.

He took a step back toward the stairs.

"And stay away from my daughter."

When he paused by the railing, his eyes on Libby, Maggie stepped between them. "I hear you're going to marry Judith Perdue."

Oliver glanced down at his feet. "My parents want me to marry her when I finish at the university."

"I'm sure your parents want what's best for you."

When he looked up at her again, the fire in his eyes matched hers. "They want what's best for them."

She took Libby's hand and guided her around Oliver.

"Good-bye, Libby," he said, his voice low.

And Libby smiled at him.

Her heart raced as she led Libby back out of the maze. How could she make her daughter understand what could happen if she continued to entertain a man like Oliver Croft? And how was she supposed to keep Libby from returning to Ladenbrooke if Oliver lured her over?

The Crofts would be gone for months now. Probably until next summer.

Oliver was sixteen, and for the first time, she agreed with Lady Croft. They must—at any cost—keep Libby and Oliver apart. But even with a lock, how would they keep Oliver away? He could come to their house when she and Walter were gone.

"Walter would like Oliver," Libby said as they walked back through the flowers.

"No, he wouldn't," Maggie said. "You mustn't tell your father that you saw the Croft boy."

"Why not?"

She paused. "He might hurt Oliver."

Libby slowed her walk. "Why would he hurt him?"

Maggie thought for a moment. The only time she'd ever seen her husband get violent was when he pummeled Elliot in the alleyway. "He wants to protect the women he loves."

"I think Oliver might love me too."

The spider of fear crept up the back of her neck again.

They had to keep this night a secret—from Walter and the Crofts.

Somehow she would stop Libby from returning to the folly.

20

Curiosity anchored Heather's feet to the carpet as Christopher emerged from the convertible, wearing an olive-colored shirt and dress trousers. His warm smile was exactly as she remembered except this time he wasn't smiling at her.

He quickly rounded the car and opened the passenger door. The woman who stepped out was a foot shorter than him and so petite that Heather thought at first she was barely out of her teens. Her dark hair felt straight over her shoulders, and she looked as if she could command an army.

Christopher's wife may have passed away, but he was most definitely not single.

Heather backed away from the glass and then spun around, mortified at the thought of Christopher knowing she'd been gawking at him and his—whatever she was.

When Mrs. Westcott turned toward her, she saw worry reflected in the woman's eyes. "Her name is Adrienne," she explained. "Would you like me to introduce you?"

"No, I—" Heather shook her head. "I think I will use the back door."

She rushed through the kitchen and into the sunroom. Voices

echoed behind her, and she hurried outside, down the path between the house and detached garage to her bicycle. All she needed to do was pedal quickly away while Mrs. Westcott distracted everyone inside the farmhouse.

She pushed her rickety bike around the shiny black convertible then climbed onto the seat. It was a short driveway. It would take her only seconds to—

The front door slammed behind her, and she heard whistling. Her heart collapsed within her, and even though she knew she should pedal away, her feet fell to the ground.

"Hello," Christopher called out.

She didn't turn around. Couldn't turn. She lifted her right foot again to push off, but it was too late. Christopher Westcott was beside her.

"Can I help you?" he asked.

Slowly she took a deep breath before looking over at him. "Hello, Christopher."

His eyes grew wide, as if he'd seen a ghost. "Heather?"

She nodded.

He groaned, and she felt his rejection fresh again. How was it, twenty-five years later, she still felt the wounds as acutely as she did when they were teenagers. "What are you doing here?" he asked though it sounded more like an accusation.

She inched up her chin, straightening her back. She had done nothing wrong. "I was just visiting—"

He glanced toward the front door. "It's not a good time for us to visit."

"I didn't come to see you, Christopher. I came to see your mother."

At least he had the decency to look embarrassed.

She teetered on her bicycle. "I thought you were in Oxford."

"I'm only here for the weekend." He paused. "I'm sorry about your father."

Her shoulders softened a bit.

"Christopher?" Adrienne called behind him, and he glanced back and forth between Heather and the door.

As Adrienne stomped toward them, Heather wished she could run again as she'd done years ago, but she hadn't come to the Westcott home to threaten anyone. Nor had she returned desperate to rekindle any sort of relationship with her ex-boyfriend.

"Oh dear," Mrs. Westcott said from the front porch.

Icy shards seemed to shoot from Adrienne's gaze. "Who's this?"

Sighing, Heather stepped off her bike again, and when she looked back up at Christopher, she saw the anxiety in his eyes. And the anger. As if she'd flown across the Atlantic to ruin his life, almost three decades after he'd broken her heart.

She tapped her foot. If only the gravel drive would open up and swallow her whole.

He cleared his throat. "Adrienne, this is Heather Doyle. She's—"

"My last name is Toulson now," she interjected. "And I'm a friend, from long ago."

"It has been a long time," Christopher said, a sharp edge piercing his words.

The younger woman glanced back and forth between them. "I'm Adrienne. Christopher's friend now."

Heather stretched out her hand in an attempt to be civil. "It's nice to meet you."

Adrienne didn't echo her sentiment, but she shook her hand, her grip remarkably strong for such a small woman. "Did you say Doyle?"

Heather nodded. "That was my maiden name."

Adrienne looked up at Christopher. "As in, *Walter Doyle*?"

Heather glanced between them. She was missing something but didn't know what. "Walter was my father."

Adrienne's eyes were still focused on Christopher's face. "You never mentioned that Walter had a daughter."

Heather glanced toward Mrs. Westcott on the stoop then hopped back on her bicycle

"Thank you for your help," Heather said before finally pedaling toward the street. She didn't know if they were watching her ride away, but she held her head high, pretending like pride in oneself was overrated.

Christopher looked every bit as good as he had when they were teenagers, and he probably had dozens of women, college students even, tripping over themselves to be with him. She was a relic in comparison.

But then again, no matter how good Christopher looked, he was older than her.

Ella said his wife had passed away eight years ago. Was he going to marry this woman now? Perhaps they were already married.

It shouldn't matter—didn't matter—to her.

After parking the bicycle beside Willow Cottage, she plucked her handbag with the butterfly book out of the basket and fled into the sitting room. Inside she pulled the window shades down and sank onto the couch.

She hadn't been stalking Christopher—she hadn't even known he was home—but her heart still pumped voraciously. For years, she'd wondered what she would do if she saw him again, and now she knew.

She'd regress.

Slipping her cell phone out of her handbag, she checked her voice mail. Three new clients had called asking for her assistance and two current clients wanted updates on their projects.

She should leave her past in the past and immerse herself back into what she knew well—work that was challenging but predictable. Relationships with clear boundaries to ward off the unknown. Blemished artwork that could be restored.

The beech tree outside the window blocked the afternoon sunlight so she turned on the lamp and began flipping through Libby's butterfly pictures again, trying to distract herself from her encounter with Christopher and Adrienne. Mrs. Westcott was hiding more from her than the impending arrival of her son and his date. Something about Libby made her feel uncomfortable and Heather wasn't certain how to siphon off the truth. And it wasn't like she could go back and ask Mrs. Westcott about it again, at least not until she was completely, absolutely certain that Christopher was gone.

She closed the book and stood. There was no point in sitting here, commiserating about what might have been. Libby was gone, and Christopher had moved on a long time ago in his relationships.

She changed into jeans and a T-shirt then borrowed her mum's gardening shoes, gloves, and trowel along with the worn kneeling pad she'd used as a girl.

Pink foxglove and violet clusters of verbenas struggled for survival among the weeds behind the cottage. It felt good to yank out the plants that were choking the remaining flowers and pile them up beside her. It was all part of her struggle for control, she supposed. Order along with a steady pace to calm the mind.

Mum used to do the same thing when she got frustrated, kneeling beside her and telling her stories about her childhood in South London as she pulled out fistfuls of weeds. Heather had been intrigued by the war, fascinated that her mum could remember hiding in a shelter and German planes flying overhead. The darkness in London and the fear she'd felt before she was evacuated to Clevedon.

In hindsight, she was glad her mum shared that small part of her life. She only wished she'd told her more—about the brother she had lost and what happened to her first daughter.

When Heather was a child, she remembered being sad that her mum's parents—her grandparents—died long ago. Her father's mother—Granny Doyle—lived until Heather was thirteen, but she only came to visit once a year, during the spring. They never went down to Kent to visit her.

She yanked out another handful of weeds as she looked down at the overgrown hedges that surrounded her mum's secret garden and the bench where Christopher had first kissed her. It was also the place where he'd asked her to marry him.

As they grew older, their friendship morphed into a powerful attraction they deemed love. Their parents both said they were too young to make promises for the future, but at the time, they hadn't felt young.

In hindsight, their parents were exactly right.

The sun had begun to set, but she didn't want to go back inside. Instead she tugged out another weed and added it to her pile.

No matter what happened, she wouldn't let Christopher Westcott break her heart again.

CHRISTOPHER SILENTLY CHIDED HIMSELF AS he walked up the hill in the darkness, away from the streetlamps in the village. If only Heather hadn't caught him by surprise this afternoon—he

could have controlled all the mixed emotions that erupted inside him. He was no longer nineteen and naïve, but for some reason, in her presence, he still felt awkward.

Of course Heather had stopped by to see his mother. He shouldn't have been so presumptuous to assume that she would seek him out after all these years.

And then he'd been the slightest bit disappointed that she hadn't come to visit him.

She'd looked beautiful with her golden-brown hair tied back, wearing a simple white blouse and jeans. And she'd looked so very different from Adrienne.

He groaned again, loudly this time. He was here to put the past behind him, not conjure up old feelings, but it would help if Heather had lost some of her beauty over the years.

After Heather left this afternoon, he'd told Adrienne the truth—that he and Heather had dated, almost thirty years ago, long before he married Julianna. There was nothing between Heather and him now, just like there was nothing between Adrienne and her old boyfriends.

Adrienne said he was fooling himself.

This was exactly why he hadn't wanted to come home this weekend. Unnecessary confusion when there was nothing to be confused about. He'd tried to explain to Adrienne that his feelings for Heather died with his teenage years, but she said that anger is still a feeling. She also said he may not feel love in his heart toward his old girlfriend, but plenty of strong feelings remained.

He should have been honest with Adrienne about his reasons for wanting to postpone their visit. They could have waited to return until Heather was back in the States.

The evening with his family hadn't been a disaster, but it was just as strained as the meeting with Heather had been. His sister started talking about Julianna twice and awkwardly dropped the conversation. Then his brother mentioned he'd seen Heather Doyle in the village yesterday. Mum shut him down, but not before his brother asked what had happened between them. When dinner was over, Adrienne feigned a headache and then locked the door to the guestroom.

Mum went to bed early as well, but he hadn't been the least bit tired.

Away from the village, a thousand stars showered the canvas of black above him, and in the light he could see the imposing gray stone of Ladenbrooke's towers among the trees. Its eerie presence was woven into the fabric of their town, like the River Coln and Rack Isle. One rarely spent much time reflecting on the familiar things of life—like the presence of a home that had been abandoned for as long as he remembered—but things that had once been so familiar to him felt oddly foreign tonight.

As he crested the hill, the towers disappeared behind the ivy-draped gray wall and iron gate.

In the months before Walter died, his friend talked often about his former neighbors. At one point, Walter asked Christopher to send Lord Croft a letter, but then changed his mind. He thought it odd at the time, but Walter wrote incessantly in the weeks before he passed away. Christopher figured Walter had paid his dues in this life and paid them well—he could write whomever and whatever he wanted in his final days.

Even though Ladenbrooke intrigued him, Christopher had only been inside the walls one time. About ten years after the Crofts vacated the property, he and four of his buddies followed the wall down the hill, past the side entrance, until they found a place with enough footholds in the ivy and stone for them to shimmy over. The light from their torch beams reflected off the manor windows, and they tried to open the massive doors so they could explore inside, but the doors were as secure as the property's front and side gates.

When they couldn't get inside the house, he and his friends decided to explore the old gardens, fanning out as they crept toward the riverbank to search for Oliver Croft's grave. But they never made it to the river.

One of the boys started screaming that he'd seen a ghost, and even though Christopher didn't believe the boy saw any kind of apparition, it didn't matter. His friend believed he'd seen one—an enchantress in a blue gown—so their excursion was over. The kid ran back toward the wall, and they all followed.

They'd done such silly things when they were younger. Believed in the craziest things. Like haunted gardens and ghosts. And love that lasted for a lifetime.

Christopher stood beside the gates of Ladenbrooke again, at a crossroads of sorts. He could turn back to check on Adrienne. Or he could continue walking over this hill to visit the cottage on the other side.

Perhaps what he really needed, what he and Heather both needed, was reconciliation. Not that Heather still thought about the past—she'd moved on after she first left Bibury, and over the years, he thought he had as well—but clearly all was not resolved.

He tried to look past the wall, to see if the lights were still on at Willow Cottage, but he couldn't see the Doyle's home.

It wasn't his place to judge Heather, but he couldn't seem to help himself. If she had visited her father more often, perhaps she would have known that he and Walter had become good friends. If she hadn't run to America and left them all behind, she would have known a lot of things.

He shook his head to clear his mind. He hated this ugly bitterness that kept creeping up inside him. He talked all the time about the power and freedom of forgiveness, but it was hard to live it.

If the lights were on in the cottage, perhaps he'd knock and try to finally sort out what happened so long ago with the woman he'd once loved for what he thought would be a lifetime.

Then he would forgive and forget what was behind them.

21

SEPTEMBER 1968, WILLOW COTTAGE

Libby turned the lever, but instead of opening the gate, the wrought iron caught on something. Libby shook it again, trying to make it move, but she was trapped. On the wrong side.

Her fingers searched the rusted iron until they found something new hanging on her side of the gate. A cold piece of metal. A claw clutching the gate closed. She shook the gate again as if she could break the barrier, but it wouldn't budge.

She fell against the slats, devastated. Had Walter locked her out this time?

Her parents told her that she must stay away from the gardens in the summer, like Peter Rabbit had to stay away from Mr. McGregor's gardens so he wouldn't end up in a pie. Not that the lady would eat her, but they said the lady might send her away.

But the lady wasn't even home now. Mummy was busy working at the beauty shop this afternoon and Walter was delivering mail.

Why wouldn't they let her play while they were gone?

Through the slats, she could see a flutter of butterflies dancing above the flowers. Without her. Soon it would be winter, and they'd fly away. She wouldn't be able to dance with them again until spring.

"Come here," she whispered, trying to lure her friends toward Mummy's garden. "Please—"

But they ignored her.

She shook the gate one last time, tears streaming down her face. Then she looked at the stone wall on both sides of her. If she couldn't go through the break in the wall, perhaps she could go over the stones. The river terrified her, but she wasn't afraid to climb.

Determined, she inched left along the wall then anchored her sturdy shoe against a rock as she pulled herself up, climbing steadily until she could see the butterflies dancing right beneath her.

But before she propped her leg over the top of the wall, her hand began to slip and suddenly there was nothing else for her to grasp. Teetering, she slipped backward and fell, scraping her knee on the rocks before she landed back on the grass.

Limping, she stepped back from the wall and glared at it as if she could make it crumble.

How she hated that wall. Any walls.

She hurried back to her bedroom and curled up on her bed, her legs clutched close to her chest, her bloodied knees staining her blouse as she rocked herself back and forth.

What was she supposed to do if she couldn't dance?

Eyes closed, she imagined the butterflies soaring over the petals, riding the tail of the breeze. She imagined a fairy leading their dance, her wings shimmering in the sun.

Then one of the butterflies seemed to come alive in her mind, like a character on the silver screen. Twirling in the sunlight that spilled through the window.

She was pale blue, laced with gold, and Libby could see her, inside and out, every detail on her slender body, every color on her wardrobe of wings.

Libby released her legs and sprung down onto the rug on her floor. Under her bed was a box with her old sketchbook and colored pencils. She hadn't wanted to draw in a long time. She'd only wanted to be among the flowers and butterflies.

But if she couldn't be with her friends, perhaps she could entertain them in her room.

The sketchbook in hand, she hopped back on the bed and began drawing the blue butterfly who'd twirled in the lamplight, but her butterfly looked so dull on the paper. Nothing like the butterfly she'd seen moments before.

She—Libby Doyle—was a creator, and her creation begged her for more.

Rushing to the bathroom, she filled a paper cup with water. In her parents' bedroom were tubes of special paint. And a brush. Mummy once told her she'd kept the paints to remember her father—Libby's granddad—but what better way to remember him than to use his paints to birth another life?

Life. She wanted to breathe light and color and life into her friends.

She tucked the box of paints under her arm and retreated back to her bedroom, locking the door behind her. Then she rolled back the rug to lay her paper on the hardwood. With a firm squirt, blue paint leapt into the bowl. She dipped a brush into it and began to give life.

For hours she played with the colors, adding streaks of gold paint onto the sheer blue wings before her, then reaching for a new paper to craft the lines of another friend. Nothing else mattered more than the picture before her. Nothing could stop her from making new friends . . . until someone knocked on her door.

"Go away," she shouted, angry at the interruption.

Walter called her name, and she gripped the paintbrush

tighter between her fingers. He'd dropped her into the river, kept her away from her friends. Now he would try to stop her from painting, and she wouldn't—*couldn't*—stop.

She dabbed her brush back into her paint.

Minutes later, Mummy called her name from the other side of the door. Then Walter said they were going to unlock it if she didn't open it on her own.

Sighing, Libby put down her brush and as she walked toward the door, the aching in her heart returned.

"What are you doing?" Mummy asked when she opened the door.

"Painting."

"Where did you get paint?"

Libby nodded toward her parent's room across the alcove. "From your special box."

Mummy twisted her hands together, her voice sounding sad. "You should have asked."

"You would have said no."

Walter's eyes were focused on the bedroom floor, flush with papers and paint. He couldn't be angry about the mess. He hadn't given her any time to clean up.

Mummy pressed her lips together for a moment before speaking again. "You missed dinner."

Had she? She didn't even know what time it was. "I'm not hungry."

"I'll bring you a tray."

She didn't care about food or sleep or anything else tonight. She didn't even care about going back to the gardens. All she wanted was to paint.

She returned to the floor, and a tray appeared beside her with a sandwich, glass of milk, and some cubes of cantaloupe. She didn't know who brought it in, but she picked up a piece of the cantaloupe and examined it. The color matched some of the roses in the lady's garden, exactly what she needed for the flowers she'd drawn behind her butterfly.

Yellow, white, and a dab of red—she combined them on her plate until a soft peach colored her palette.

Walter thought she should grow up, like the lady wanted Oliver to do, but grown-ups didn't spend their nights dancing in gardens. Or painting. "I will stay a girl forever," she whispered, changing the lyrics from *Peter Pan*. "And be banished if I don't."

She began to paint her butterfly.

"I'll never grow up," she chanted as she worked.

It wasn't until the first rays of dawn spilled across her paper that she began to feel sleepy. Her floor was covered with pictures and papers, but where others might see a mess, she saw a new world. There were flowers and trees and butterflies she'd brought to life with her hands. And her heart.

A lot of people thought she wasn't good at anything, but it wasn't true. She was good at making things.

She dropped her brush into the water and, fully clothed, stretched out onto her wrinkled bed, smiling as she closed her eyes.

Oliver may be gone, the garden door locked, but no one could take away her butterflies.

Someone pounded on her door again, and she rolled over, exhausted. She didn't want to eat or even paint now. Just sleep.

Seconds later, Mummy nudged her shoulder. "It's time for you to get up."

She shook her head, her eyes still closed. "It's Saturday."

Her mummy leaned closer. "Daphne's here to visit you."

Lifting her head, Libby saw someone else in the room. It was her former Sunday school teacher, wearing a pretty green polka dot dress.

Daphne sat down on the edge of her bed, scanning the floor of the room. "It looks like you've been busy."

"Why are you here?" Libby asked.

"I asked her to—" Mummy started, but Daphne interrupted her.

"To play with you, of course. While your parents go to work."

Libby shook her head again. "I don't want to play."

But Daphne wasn't deterred. "We can read together instead."

Libby almost said she didn't like books, but that wasn't entirely true. Words on a page didn't make much sense to her, but she loved to look at pictures. And listen to the stories.

Daphne smiled. "We're going to be the best of friends."

She inched up on her pillows. With Oliver gone, and her butterflies locked in the lady's garden, perhaps it would be good to have another friend. Perhaps Daphne could even find a way for them to get into the gardens.

Libby fought to keep her eyes open a bit longer to study her new friend, but she lost the battle.

As she drifted away, she heard Daphne say, "I'll wait until she wakes up."

"Don't let her sleep past ten," Mummy replied.

MAGGIE WAS ATTEMPTING TO GIVE Mrs. Reynolds' rather limp hair a permanent wave in the Bibury Beauty Shop when a white Cadillac pulled up to the curb.

"Now who could that be?" Mrs. Reynolds asked as Maggie wrapped a strip of her hair around the rod and basted it with lotion.

"Probably someone on holiday." Though in the late-autumn months, when gray clouds plastered the sky and puddled the sidewalks, visitors rarely came to explore the gardens or castles in the Cotswolds.

The driver stepped out of the Cadillac and rushed around to the curb. When he opened the door, Lady Croft stepped onto the sidewalk, dressed in a tailored suit, taupe pillbox hat, and pearls hanging around her neck and dangling from her ears.

Maggie put down the bottle of solution in her hands, a mixture of curiosity and dread stirring inside her.

A shopping bag from Harrods hung from one of Lady Croft's arms as she eyed the sign over the beauty shop. Then she opened the door and marched into the salon.

Maggie nodded toward her. "Good morning."

Lady Croft was no longer her employer, but still every muscle in her body seemed to tense in her presence.

"I need to speak with you," Lady Croft said.

There was no back room in the tiny shop, only a closet. "Should we step outside?"

Instead of responding, Lady Croft dumped her bag, filled with letters, onto Maggie's hairdresser stand. Mrs. Reynolds turned her attention downward, pretending to be engrossed by the copy of *Vogue* in her lap.

Lady Croft crossed her arms. "Tell your daughter to stop sending him letters."

Stunned, she stared down at the envelopes before picking one up. It was addressed to Oliver, in childlike handwriting, but there was no return address. "Libby didn't write these."

Her daughter wasn't capable of writing a letter to anyone.

Lady Croft swiped the envelope from Maggie's hand, but instead of ripping it open with her gloves, she reached for a pair of scissors and slashed the top. A colorful picture of a boy and girl, holding hands in a garden, fell on top of the pile.

It seemed Libby's fixation on flowers and butterflies had evolved to include the boy who wandered the gardens with her.

Lady Croft's eyes flashed with anger. "Is your husband still the postmaster?"

Maggie looked back down at the stack. "He is."

"What's wrong with him—"

Maggie stiffened. "There's nothing wrong with Walter."

"Then tell him to stop delivering her mail."

Mrs. Reynold's eyes remained fixed on the magazine as Maggie curled her fingers over the back of the chair, facing her former employer. For the first time she realized that she was actually taller than Lady Croft by an inch or two. "Clearly you need to tell Oliver to leave my daughter alone."

"He doesn't want to see her—"

Maggie snorted. "Then why does he keep inviting her over?"

"Oliver does nothing of the sort."

Maggie picked up the bottle again and turned to Mrs. Reynolds. Then she pointed the tip of her lotion toward an empty chair, speaking to the lady who stood trembling beside her. "If you'd like me to set your hair, you'll have to wait for an hour. If not, I suggest you find your way back home."

Lady Croft didn't move, holding the shopping bag like a shield in front of her. "Lord Croft and I have plans for Oliver, and I won't let some—" She stopped herself. "I will do anything to protect my son."

Maggie met her gaze in the mirror. "And I will do anything to protect my daughter."

22

JULY 1969, LADENBROOKE MANOR

Libby wore her prettiest dress as she glided through the backyard, a shimmering, blue one like Grace Kelly had worn in *To Catch a Thief*, before she became a princess. The moon was a perfect crescent, shooting rays of silvery light across the garden.

After almost a year of waiting, Oliver had finally returned.

She hadn't seen him yet, but somehow he'd climbed the tree outside her window and left the loveliest bouquet of purple-and-bronze dahlias on the windowsill, tied together with twine, and a simple note that said to meet him by the gate tonight. At midnight.

Or at least, that's what she thought the note said. After writing the time, he'd drawn a clock with both hands pointing to the top.

It was half past now, and she hoped she hadn't missed him.

"Oliver," Libby whispered through the wrought-iron slats.

When he didn't answer, she waited for him in the shadows. Her fingers trembled against the metal, her heart racing. The family had been gone all winter and spring, but she hadn't forgotten him for one single day. Not even a minute.

Had he received her pictures?

She'd sent dozens and dozens of them, but he hadn't sent any letters in return.

It didn't matter now. Oliver said he would come tonight, and he never lied to her.

What would he think of her and her new dress and her sandals instead of saddle shoes?

Her gaze roamed over the dark garden on the other side. For months she'd visited this gate, longing to be among the lady's flowers as they bloomed in the sun and curled up in the rain. But even more than the gardens at Ladenbrooke, she'd wanted to be with Oliver.

He was her friend. Forever.

Her hands twitched at her sides, and she pinched the gauzy material on her skirt. Oliver had always known her as a girl, but she'd changed since last summer. She was a young woman now—a woman who had other friends.

She no longer attended school, but Daphne came almost every day after her work at the hospital for a visit. Daphne had married six months ago so she didn't stay as long as she used to, but Libby liked it when her friend read to her.

During the day, while Mummy worked, she spent hours in her room, drawing and painting butterflies and fairies and new flowers that were even more beautiful than those of the lady's. These flowers were planted in the soil of her heart, rooted down inside her. Their blossoms opened slowly in her sketchbooks and on the paper her mummy brought her, revealing the secrets of their beauty to no one but her.

Now that she was fifteen, visiting the flowers didn't interest her as it once had. Instead she preferred drawing them alongside her butterfly friends.

Daphne was a friend as well, but Libby didn't long for her company like she did with Oliver. That was the reason she'd failed school again. How could she concentrate on silly numbers and such when Oliver kept wandering into her mind?

She much preferred the study of Oliver Croft.

She was done with school anyway. For good. She didn't have a job nor could she attend the secondary modern school for another term. Once she failed her classes for the second year, no one pushed for her return.

She didn't care. Butterflies didn't need to attend school and neither did she.

Something rustled on the other side of the gate. "Oliver?" she whispered again.

"Hello, Libby." His fingers settled over hers, and she smiled at his touch. "I missed you."

She grasped his hand through the iron slats. "I want to see you, Oliver."

He quickly released her fingers to unlock the gate.

OLIVER SHOOK THE IRON SLABS that separated him from Libby. The padlock was lying on the ground, the only thing that kept him from seeing the girl who'd danced through his dreams all year, but still the gate didn't budge.

"Walter put a lock on this side," she said sadly. "He doesn't want me in your garden."

His parents didn't want her here either, but he needed to see her, more than anything.

"You belong here, Libby." And he belonged with her. "Can you climb over the wall?"

"I already tried," she whispered. "But I fell."

He could smell the lilac scent of her lotion through the gate, could see the copper strands of her hair glowing in the moonlight and her silky dress ruffling in the breeze. Libby Doyle was no longer the pretty girl he admired. She'd grown into an absolutely stunning woman.

He touched her fingers through the gate again, and electricity shot through him.

She was fifteen now, no longer a child. And he was almost seventeen. A man who knew exactly what he wanted—and what he did not want. He'd never wanted to follow in his father's steps as lord of this manor or anything else.

The past school year he'd spent mingling with Judith Perdue and other debutantes in London, and most of the young women—Judith included—treated him with great respect, even awe. Like he already ruled over Ladenbrooke Manor.

Libby didn't treat him like royalty. She treated him like a friend.

But he wanted so much more than a friendship from her.

How he wished he could marry her, all proper-like, instead of marrying Lord Perdue's youngest daughter.

Blast his future! He had to find a way to see Libby tonight, in the folly. "We'll have to go through the river," he said.

She pulled her fingers away from his. "I can't."

"I'll meet you down on the bank."

She didn't answer.

"Libby?" he whispered, afraid she'd left.

She was silent, and he ached, ached for her and everything he wished they could be together. Ached to be with her for the rest of his life.

"Please, Libby," he begged.

"I'm afraid of the water."

He reached for her hands again, kissing the top of her fingers. "I'll take care of you."

LIBBY WRAPPED HER ARMS AROUND Oliver's neck when he lifted her. She'd dreamed for months about seeing him again, but she'd had nightmares about water her entire life. Falling into the river alone, struggling for air. She feared she'd be trapped under it forever.

Oliver kissed her head as he stepped into the water, and she clung to him. He'd said he would take care of her. He wouldn't drop her like Walter had done.

Still she was terrified. Squeezing her eyes shut, she tried to pretend they were dancing in the folly instead of wading through the river, but the nightmare flashed through her mind again. She was at the edge of the water, screaming, begging whomever held her not to let go. She never knew who held her back, but she wished she could thank him.

And then she realized she was shaking in Oliver's arms as well. "Don't worry, darling," he assured her. "We're almost there."

When she opened her eyes, she saw him smiling down at her, confident and handsome and strong. And she realized that he wasn't walking anymore.

Gently he placed her bare feet on the grassy bank.

"You didn't drop me," she said, breathless.

"Of course not."

He handed her the sandals he'd strung over his shoulder, and she strapped them on. Then he reached for her hand. A strange shyness swept over her as she took it. He was used to her quietness. Perhaps he wouldn't notice this change in her as well.

But he seemed to notice that something had changed because he pulled her close and kissed her. The pulse from his kiss threaded itself through her skin like the sticky strands of a web, all the way to her toes, capturing her wholly, body and soul.

They followed the path of moonlight through the forest, to the maze, and he guided her up the stairs of the folly.

When he turned on the lantern, she gasped. The dust and cobwebs that littered the floor last August had been swept away, replaced by dozens of colorful silk pillows and satin blankets. There was a basket, overflowing with fruit, and a cooler she opened to find different flavors of soda pop on ice. And a bottle of champagne.

He lit two candles, then turned off the lamp.

"Do you like it?" he asked.

She rubbed away the goose bumps on her arms. "I feel like a princess."

"You are a princess." He reached for her hand and twirled her around before pulling her close. "And I, dear lady, am your prince."

23

Heather?"

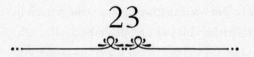

The trowel trembled in her hand even as her heart leapt. She turned slowly to watch Christopher walking toward her in the darkness, instinctively pushing her hair behind her ears. If only she could hide among her mum's remaining flowers.

"I—" He hesitated, pointing at the lantern beside her. "I saw your light and wondered if we could talk."

She stabbed her trowel into the dirt. "Aren't you supposed to be with your guest?"

"She needed some time to herself." He folded his arms over his chest. "Why are you working out here so late?"

"I needed some time outside."

He stepped back. "I'll leave you alone."

"No—" she started and then stopped. This was a discussion that was long overdue. "What do you want to talk about?"

He glanced up at the archway to her mum's secret garden, and she wondered for a moment if he remembered their last night together as well as she did. "Do you want to join me for a walk?"

She should be exhausted after spending most of last night rummaging through the basement, but even though it was after ten, she didn't feel the least bit tired. At least not with Christopher so close.

Instead of answering his question, she tossed her gloves onto the kneeling pad and stood up beside him.

"Should we walk down to the river?" he asked, lifting his lantern.

She shook her head. "There's a field of rapeseed growing between here and the forest."

He cocked his head slightly, a tentative smile on his lips. "I bet we can find a path."

She followed him past the arched entryway, to the edge of her parents' property. They didn't find an official path, but barriers like that never seemed to stop Christopher. In lieu of a trail, they waded together through a sea of gold, the lantern light skimming across the tips of bright-yellow blossoms until they reached the grove of trees. The rush of the river current grew louder as they moved through the forest.

After they stepped up onto the riverbank, she sat on a flat boulder next to the weeping willow tree and Christopher lowered himself on a rock near her.

"I have so many memories of you and your mum working in that garden," he said, his eyes focused on the river. "You wanted to be just like her when you grew up."

She studied the gilded sheen of light that skimmed across the water, her mind wandering back to the pleasant memories with her mum. She had wanted to be just like Maggie Doyle when she grew up, with a family and a husband who loved her for a lifetime. She loved being a mother, but unlike her mum, she'd failed miserably in her marriage.

"Instead, I became me."

"And who exactly are you?" he asked.

Christopher had wandered, unbidden, into her dreams over

the years, but she'd always wakened and run away from her memories by immersing herself in the busyness of her work. Now she wanted to run again like she had so many years ago, back across the ocean if necessary, instead of sitting here with this man who pretended to care when he hadn't really cared at all.

"Your dad told me you restore artwork."

She tilted her head. "I didn't know you and my father were friends."

Christopher threw a rock into the water, black ink spreading across the light. "We've been friends since I was in graduate school. I always wanted to be like him when I grew up."

"A postman?"

He shook his head. "A writer."

She pondered his words for a moment. She knew her father had written when he was younger, but she'd never seen him writing when she was home. It saddened her that Christopher knew a part of her dad that she'd never known. "What did he write?"

"He poured himself onto paper in his last years, like you used to pour yourself into your paintings."

She rubbed her hands together. "It's been a long time since I painted."

"I thought you'd be an artist when you grew up."

"There are plenty of people creating art," she explained. "Not so many taking care of what we already have."

"I liked your art."

She cleared her throat, not wanting to talk about herself anymore. "I hear you're an official fellow at Oxford."

"It sounds lofty, doesn't it?"

The limbs over the river swayed in the breeze. "You were never one for loftiness."

"I can fake it pretty well."

She stretched her arms around her legs, pulling them close to her chest. "You were able to fake a lot of things pretty well."

He reached for another rock and threw it in the water. "Are you trying to make me mad?"

"No." She paused. "I've just had a lot of things I've wanted to say to you over the years."

"And I've had a lot of things to say as well." His gaze met hers and she looked away. "Perhaps we should say them now."

"Perhaps." But even as she spoke, her thoughts scrambled in her mind. She'd rehearsed her lines over the years, in case she ever saw Christopher Westcott again, but she had wanted to pummel an arrogant, conniving man with her words, not the one being kind to her right now. And the one who'd been kind to her father.

"Heather—" His gaze lingered on the river. "What happened to us?"

She didn't reply for a moment, surprised at the directness of his question. "You know exactly what happened."

"I showed up to take you to a dance but you'd already left for London—" He leaned toward her. "For months, I took a bus to the city on my days off school to talk to you, but you were never there. And you never returned my calls."

She'd ignored his calls but—"I didn't know you came to London that many times."

"Your roommate wasn't particularly excited to see me."

"She knew I was angry at you."

He cocked his head. "Angry?"

"Okay, I pretty much hated you."

"And now—" he started. "Do you still hate me?"

"Some days."

"Tonight?"

"Not so much," she said, the anger at him turning inward

for her weakness. Christopher was the one who'd cheated on her. He was the one who pretended to love her, the one who'd asked to marry her, while he was out with Britney Garnett on the side.

"I didn't even know you'd married until I saw the announcement in the paper."

"It was for the best—" she said.

"Not the best for me. Or your parents."

"But it was best for—" She stopped.

"For who?"

She shivered. This place, along with this man, unnerved her. Of all the lines she'd rehearsed during the past decades, the conversations she'd repeated in her mind, this was not one of them.

Christopher's cell phone rang. He pulled it out of his pocket and glanced at the screen before muting the call. Then he looked back over at her.

"You said you'd marry me," he said, his voice so low she could barely hear it above the sound of the current.

"Only because I thought you'd be faithful."

"I was faithful to you until the day I found out you'd married someone else."

She released her legs and crossed her arms over her chest, angry with him now for his lies.

"You knew I loved you, and yet you ran away. If I knew where you went, if I'd known you were going to marry—" His voice cracked. "I would have broken down the door if I had to, Heather, but you hid yourself while I racked my brain to figure out what I did wrong.

"And I still wonder," he said, searching her face in the lantern light. "What went wrong?"

Her hands trembled. Finally, after all these years, she had the opportunity to confront his deception. Get the vindication she'd sought. Finally she could tell him the truth. "That night in the garden, you told me you wanted to marry me. You got down on your knee and gave me the ring you bought at Woolworths."

"I remember it well."

And so did she. It had been warm that night. Starlight had rained down on them, and her mum's garden smelled sticky sweet. Heather was preparing to start her first year of college in London, Christopher his second year at Oxford. Both of them spent the summer working at a shop for tourists in town, and during the long evenings, they biked in the hills and walked along the river. Sometimes, when both her parents were working, they hid out behind Willow Cottage.

After their glorious summer, Christopher had met her in the garden and slipped down onto one knee. He didn't have the money yet to buy a diamond, but she accepted the brass band with a pink opal and told him she didn't like diamonds much anyway. And she'd given him everything that night, thinking they would marry—

Her parents hadn't been as excited about the proposal as she had been, but at the time, she didn't care.

The next night Christopher was supposed to take her to one more dance before they left for school, but instead of dancing with her, he'd been out with a girl a year younger than Heather. Her gift to him had meant nothing, and it shattered her heart. And her ability to trust another man.

"I wanted to marry you," he said.

"Then why were you fooling around with Britney Garnett?"

He lurched back like she'd thrown a stone at him. "What?"

"You never came that last night to take me to the dance. Mum said she saw you and Britney kissing near Arlington Row instead."

She took a deep breath. "The next day, I drove over to Oxford to talk to you, but you seemed to be quite occupied with another woman there."

"That's why you wouldn't return my calls," he said slowly.

"I gave myself to you, Christopher, and you crushed me."

He opened his mouth slowly, as if he were still forming the words, when the phone in his pocket began to ring again. He took out the phone and then looked back and forth between it and Heather.

"Is it Adrienne?"

He nodded.

"You better take it."

"I'm sorry, Heather," he said as he stood, though she wasn't sure if he was sorry for taking the call or for what happened long ago.

When he answered his phone, he apologized to Adrienne too—for not answering the first two times she phoned.

Heather felt numb as she crawled into her bed that night. Alone.

She had been so angry back then—at herself and at Christopher. At least she had finally been honest with him.

Or almost honest.

Perhaps it was time to tell him about Ella as well.

PART THREE

For many years, I thought Maggie's sin had stained our family, ruined any hope for our—*my*—future. While I was busy criticizing the splinter in my wife's eye, I should have been chopping up the log in my own.

Even though it's small, a splinter can cause tremendous pain, and if someone doesn't pull it out, an infection can spread through an entire body. Or an entire family.

Instead of criticizing, I should have helped Maggie heal.

Perhaps God's heart isn't to punish sinners. Perhaps it's to wash away the guilt from our sins, the pain of our hardship, and bring us back to Him.

The aftermath of sin might remain, like the destruction after an earthquake, but He cleanses it from our souls so we can rebuild, healing our wrongs from the inside out.

Libby wasn't a punishment. She was a blessing.

Maggie, Elliot, and I—we all had choices. But Libby had no choice. When she was afraid, I should have been there beside her, encouraging—not forcing—her to overcome her fears.

Maggie asked for my forgiveness, and I refused to give it for far too long. My stubbornness came between all that was right. And I hurt too many people.

I've tried to make my amends.

Some in life. Some will have to wait until after death.

I pray Heather will understand.

24

DECEMBER 1969, LADENBROOKE

Oliver's folly was terribly cold. Clouds hid the warmth of the moonlight along with all the lovely stars that offered Libby comfort when she couldn't sleep.

She pulled another blanket over her chest to shield herself from the winter air, but her trembling wouldn't stop. Something was wrong with her, but she didn't know what it was. Or what to do.

Rubbing her hands up and down her arms, she tried to warm herself under the blankets, stop the shaking, but she couldn't rid herself of the cold.

She'd left home weeks ago, afraid Mummy would take her to a doctor, and she hated the men who asked her all sorts of strange questions and probed her skin with their tools.

Oliver was the only man she wanted to touch her, but he'd been gone for months now.

If he was here, he'd know what to do.

Walter had been searching for her in the evenings, calling her name over and over in the gardens, but whenever he came close to the folly, she hid, afraid he would force her to conquer her fear of the doctors. She'd thought about going to visit Daphne, but her old friend had a husband and a baby to care for now. Besides, on the last day Daphne had come for a visit, Mummy had given her money.

Daphne wasn't really her friend. Libby was her job.

She'd been neglecting her real friends for too long—the ones who would fly alongside her if only she had wings. But winter was here now and the butterflies were gone along with most of the color in the lady's garden. All that remained were the lonely browns and greens. And the fiery red of the heather.

Sometimes late at night, she snuck away from the tower and stole through the unlocked servant's door in the back of the manor to borrow items from the lady's pantry. She never stayed long, afraid Henry or someone else would find her wandering the house. Last time she'd found some tonics in the lady's medicine cabinet, but even with the tonics, her ailment remained.

She didn't like feeling sick. Didn't like the queasiness when she moved or the growth in her belly. And the darkness—it felt as if it might swallow her.

She pressed against her stomach, trying to make the lump go away, but it was as hard as one of the stones by the river.

Wind rattled the glass, confusion and sickness overwhelming her as she rocked on the thin mattress. Was this what it felt like to die?

Death wasn't something she'd thought about much. The rector spoke about it at church, but her mind usually wandered during the talking. She'd much preferred thinking about color and movement and all manner of things to a cold body in the ground.

If she was dying—would God take her in or would He mock her, reject her, like so many of His people?

She closed her eyes and pretended that Oliver was here, loving her. He had said he would make a way for them to be together. Forever.

And Oliver never broke his promises.

She rocked back and forth again.

Part of her wanted to die, but she didn't want to die alone.

WET FLAKES FELL BEHIND THE cottage, more slush than snow. Maggie stood on the back patio, her heart grieving as she watched the gray slurry from the skies mask her garden. Libby was out there someplace, alone and cold, and all Maggie could do to rescue her daughter this time was pray.

Libby had been gone a month now. She'd packed up a small suitcase one Tuesday night, along with a new sketchbook, and disappeared while Maggie and Walter were sleeping.

When Walter found her room empty, he'd gone straight to the local police. The captain said he would look for her, but Walter wasn't convinced. Everyone in town knew about Libby and her strange ways. Many thought she'd run away for good.

Perhaps they were right. It wasn't odd for Libby to leave during the night, but in the past, she'd always come home by morning. Maggie couldn't bear to think her daughter wanted to stay away from her.

Several days after Walter's visit to the station, Maggie petitioned the police as well, but they were so condescending she wanted to scream. She canceled her appointments for a week and spent her hours searching around Bibury. Then she expanded her search to the surrounding villages, a picture of Libby in hand, but no one recognized her daughter.

Something was wrong. Maggie knew it deep within, and it terrified her. She'd always been able to fix the wrongs for Libby before—the teachers who thought she was slow, the children who'd mistreated her, even the night she found her daughter with Oliver Croft.

She rubbed her hands together to warm them.

The scaffolding she'd built under her daughter's feet was collapsing, and if she didn't know where Libby went, she couldn't do anything to fix it this time.

Maggie moved back across the path to the wrought-iron gate, as she had done every night since Libby left the house, but it remained locked. Had it been a horrible mistake to keep Libby out of Ladenbrooke while Oliver and his family were gone?

Maggie once hoped the gardens behind their house would renew Libby's body and mind, but perhaps her time at Ladenbrooke was more than just enjoying the flowers and her butterflies. Perhaps it was her daughter's only means of feeling free. Independent. While trying to protect her, she and Walter had taken away the one place where she thrived.

Where would Libby go if she couldn't enter the gardens?

She'd never cross the River Coln, but still Walter had waded across to Ladenbrooke the morning after Libby disappeared and then returned over and over in the evenings, searching for her.

Fear gnawed on Maggie's insides, gorging itself like a tapeworm on her regrets. Ever since she'd seen Oliver holding Libby's hand in that folly, more than a year ago now, the memories of her and Elliot haunted her again. She'd been swept off her feet by an older, dashing sailor, but she'd never thought Libby could be swept away like that.

For months Libby seemed to pine for Oliver as Maggie had once done for Elliot, but this past summer, even when Oliver was home, Libby never fought with them about the lock on the gate. She'd thrown herself into her painting, and Maggie was glad she had something to distract her.

Oliver might enjoy Libby's company, but he didn't love her

any more than Elliot had loved Maggie. If he were like Elliot, he'd want to claim Libby for himself, without offering her a future.

Oliver had seemed to awaken something in Libby's heart. Part of her might have rejoiced at the maturation in her daughter's emotions, but Libby was far from ready to be in a relationship with a man—especially one like Oliver who wanted the only thing he couldn't have.

No one ever talked to Maggie when she was younger about the ways of men and women or how babies were made, but she had told Libby that neither storks nor gypsies delivered them. Libby hadn't been horrified by the truth as some children might have been nor did she seem curious to learn more. Instead, she only seemed bewildered by Maggie's explanation.

If her mother had survived the war, Maggie liked to think she would have talked to her about the relationship between men and women. Instead, Elliot had been the one to explain how a man loved a woman. And how a woman was supposed to love a man. Yet their first time together wasn't as magical as Elliot claimed it would be. Instead it had scared her. She'd known in her heart what she was doing was wrong, but still she met Elliot at the cave, desperate for what she'd thought was love.

Walter had never forgiven her for carrying Elliot's child or for deceiving him. But how could he really when she had never been able to forgive herself? She wasn't even certain that God had forgiven her.

She pulled her house robe tighter around her chest.

What happened wasn't Libby's fault. It was hers alone. If Walter found out about Libby and Oliver, he would think Libby was just like her mother. And Maggie feared he would stop searching for her.

She scanned the drifts of muddy snow again. Where was her daughter tonight?

She prayed Libby was safe. That no one would harm her. That she had food and a warm, dry place to sleep.

She walked back into the house and started the electric kettle, but she didn't make herself a cup of tea. She'd hardly eaten anything since Libby left them. How could she savor the warmth of food or tea when her daughter might be hungry tonight?

"Why are you up?" Walter asked from the shadows, slouched in one of the sitting room chairs. He rarely smoked the cigarettes he kept hidden in his church shoes, but an acrid cloud billowed around him now.

"I was hoping the snow would bring her home."

"I don't think she's coming home," he said, resigned.

"She's warm, isn't she?"

"I don't know."

Her gaze wandered back toward the dark window. "I pray to God that she is."

"I hope God listens to you."

She flinched. Sometimes she didn't know if he was trying to be optimistic or if he was condemning her for her past, sentencing her again and again.

Guilty.

She switched on the lights of the Christmas tree, trying to brighten the sitting room, and sat down in the upholstered chair beside him. "We may have started our marriage wrong, Walter, but have we done everything wrong?"

"We did our best." His chair creaked as he spoke. "Now Libby has to choose how she wants to live her life."

"But she can't choose. She doesn't know what is right and wrong."

He took a drag on his cigarette. "We all know the difference between right and wrong."

CALGARY
PUBLIC
LIBRARY

Country Hills Library
Self Checkout
March,11,2020 12:04

39065145598924 2020-04-01
Shadows of Ladenbrooke Manor : [a novel
]

Total **1 item(s)**

You have 0 item(s) ready for pickup

Your Calgary Public Library membership give you access
to Libby, a FREE online ebook and audiobook app.
Ask Library staff how you can get Libby today!

To check your card and renew items
go to www.calgarylibrary.ca
or call 403-262-2928

It always came back to the same worn argument. Walter thought Libby was more capable than what Maggie gave her credit for. Maggie thought Walter's expectations for her were impossibly high.

A knock on the back door interrupted their quarrel, the sound prickling the hair on her arms.

She shouldn't allow herself to hope, but she couldn't stop the surge that rushed through her. The door was unlocked, as it always was. Libby usually just walked in.

She glanced over at Walter in the hue of Christmas lights, and he slowly crushed his cigarette in the ashtray before rising from his chair as if he didn't want to allow himself to hope either.

The knock came again, harder this time, and Maggie trailed her husband through the kitchen, holding her breath as he opened the door.

On the other side, in the darkness, stood a young woman, her stringy hair wet, her threadbare coat covered with snow.

Maggie's heart collapsed within her. "Libby?" she whispered.

The woman nodded.

It was Libby and yet she looked nothing like her daughter. Her simple beauty was washed away. And her stomach. *Dear God.*

Maggie caught herself on the edge of the counter.

Libby was pregnant.

25

DECEMBER 1969, WILLOW COTTAGE

Anger raged through Walter as he stared down at Maggie's daughter. He'd spent the past fifteen years toiling to provide for her like she was his own, pushing her to succeed even when Maggie thought she would fail. But Libby wasn't his. Never was and never would be. She'd followed right in her mother's—and her father's—footsteps.

After all he'd done for her. After all he'd desired for her future. He had wanted a different life for Libby, and yet she betrayed them.

Libby's shoulders were hunched, her gaze on the ground. "Something is wrong with me."

He folded his arms tight over his sweater. "I daresay it is."

Maggie pressed her fingers into his arm. "Walter . . ."

He waved her hand away. "Whose child is it?"

Her eyes grew wide, her voice cracking when she spoke again. "What child?"

Maggie tugged on his sleeve. "She doesn't understand."

"I think that she does." He didn't take his eyes off Libby, searching for the truth like he'd done the day she was born, except back then he'd been searching for the truth from her mother. He wouldn't be played the fool again. "Who's the father?"

Maggie reached around him, taking Libby's hand. "Come inside or you'll freeze."

"What child?" Libby repeated, staring at him.

"She doesn't know," Maggie said, trying to push him out of the way, but he wanted—needed—someone to tell him the truth this time.

"Where have you been?" he demanded.

She looked back up at him, those big, beautiful eyes not as innocent as they'd once been. "With the butterflies."

"There are no butterflies in December."

She held up her sketchbook, wet from the snow. Inside were her pictures.

"Did someone hurt you?" Walter asked.

"No—"

His voice trembled. He hated asking these kinds of questions, but if Maggie wouldn't do it, then he must. "Did someone force you to do something you didn't want to do?"

"He'd never force me."

"Who, Libby?" He pressed. "Who wouldn't force you?"

She began to cry again.

"You have to go back to him," Walter said.

Maggie gasped. "You don't mean it."

He ignored her. "Go back to the baby's father."

Libby's cries grew louder, and Maggie pushed around him. "He doesn't mean it."

But he did mean it. A baby should be with its mother and father. No good had come from this pasting together of a family. No matter how strong the glue—nothing could hold them together.

Libby shivered, and Maggie began to cry with her. "This is my fault," Maggie said.

"Libby is old enough to choose."

"I should have—" Maggie started as she shook her head, defeated. "I've ruined everything."

Libby tried to step around him, but he wouldn't budge. "Go back to him, Libby."

She sobbed, and then turned and ran away.

Stunned, Maggie stared over at him for a moment before following Libby into the night.

Walter fell back against the doorpost, sobbing as well, deep from his gut. He was only forty-one, but he felt like an old man, tired and aching in every joint. No matter how he'd tried to keep everything together, his family had fallen apart.

MAGGIE CHASED LIBBY BACK THROUGH their garden and into the field beyond. She called out her name, but Libby didn't listen, just as she hadn't listened when she told her to stay away from Oliver.

Walter would never forgive her and now Libby—

Her husband hadn't kicked out Libby. After all these years, it was really Maggie that he was ridding himself of. He had stayed with her out of duty. Obligation.

Walter could leave them if he must, but she would not—could not—allow Libby and the child to go back to whatever squalor she'd been living in.

She found her daughter in a heap in the field, sorrow heaving from her chest.

"I'm going to have a baby," Libby said, the shock permeating her words.

"The doctor will have to decide."

Libby shook her head. "No doctors."

Snow fell on Libby's face, and Maggie brushed it away. She remembered well hanging over the railing in Clevedon, not caring about the cold or her fear of the water or even her life. Thank God, Walter had found her and offered her a new life.

Tears slid down her cheeks. Walter hadn't just saved Maggie's life back on the promenade. He'd saved her daughter's life as well and now she prayed he would help her save Libby one more time.

She rubbed Libby's arms. "We have to get you warm."

"Walter won't let me back in."

"Yes, he will."

"You tried to tell me. About babies. But I didn't know—"

"I know you didn't."

A sob escaped Libby's throat even as her hands curled over her stomach. "I don't want a baby."

"We'll figure everything out later, darling."

Libby collapsed onto her, and Maggie wrapped her in her arms. Never before had Libby come to her with any sort of sadness. Any suffering.

Perhaps her daughter had never felt pain like this before.

No matter what anyone said about her emotions, Libby felt things more profoundly than other people. Her ability to deflect sorrow or pain, to see the goodness and beauty in almost everything, was a cocoon of sorts to ward off a mortal wound. Oliver may have been the first one to chip away at the shell of Libby's cocoon, but Walter, in his anger, cracked it open.

Libby shook as she cried in Maggie's arms. As they both cried. She'd longed for her daughter to need her, to reach for her when she was in pain. To communicate like other mothers and daughters. But now, as Libby sobbed, she wished she could weave the cocoon back around Libby's heart again.

She didn't know how long they sat huddled together in the

snow, the pain boring through her soul. Then Walter was there, his hand on her shoulder.

"Come inside," he said.

Carefully he helped Maggie stand, but Libby wouldn't let him touch her.

Maggie reached for Libby's hand, and she slowly led her back to the warmth of their home.

26

Brie Reynolds knocked on Heather's front door, two minutes before nine. Heather never thought to inquire about the estate agent's maiden name, but the moment she opened the door, Heather realized that she'd invited the woman formerly known as Britney Garnett into her home.

Christopher's other woman.

Brie looked quite proper, dressed impeccably in a navy skirt with a matching jacket, navy pumps, and what looked like glitter flaked on the rim of her glasses. She kissed both of Heather's cheeks, explaining that she'd worked in Paris for five years before returning to England and preferred the French way of greeting.

"It's so nice to see you," Brie said, stepping back. "I was just talking to my sister-in-law the other day about you—do you remember Edith Reynolds? Her name's Edith Lane now."

Heather shook her head, wondering how this woman could be so friendly to her when she'd been sneaking around with Christopher long ago.

"I suppose you wouldn't remember most people from around here, since your parents sent you away for school." She smiled as she set her leather bag on the coffee table. "I was wondering whatever happened to you. I heard you'd gone to London after you and

Christopher broke up but then poof—" She snapped her fingers. "You were gone. Years later, I heard you went to the United States."

"I met an American in London," Heather said. "We eloped—"

"How romantic!"

She didn't tell her that their marriage lasted only six years.

Brie glanced around the room and then walked toward the back window. "I've been wondering what you were planning to do with this cozy space."

Heather leaned against the stones that framed the fireplace. She didn't want to work with Britney turned Brie, but she needed a real estate agent and Brie Reynolds was supposed to be the best in the area.

"I want to sell it," she explained.

"Then let's get it sold." Brie pulled out her cell phone and began tapping on her keypad with her manicured nails.

A wave of sadness swept through Heather, her heart clinging to the past in spite of her desire to let it go. But she had traveled here to clean out the rooms and put her parents' house on the market, not dwell on Christopher or the memories in this cottage. It was time to say good-bye.

She showed Brie the small kitchen and dining area to the left of the sitting room; then Brie followed her up the steps. Brie clicked her tongue as she examined both of the bedrooms and the one bathroom that separated them, opening up closet doors and the bathroom cabinet as she tapped notes into her phone.

When they finished upstairs, Brie peeked into the basement and retreated quickly back up the stairs, into the kitchen. "You still have a bit of work to do before we can put it on the market."

"I'll clean out the rest of the boxes."

Brie slid onto a bar stool by the kitchen counter. "The clutter must go, of course, but there's more to it."

Heather flipped on the electric kettle beside the refrigerator before turning back toward her. "What else do I need to do?"

"You'll need to repaint the bedrooms along with the kitchen. The windows need cleaning of course, and if you want to hire a gardener to help you with the lawn, I can recommend a couple of good ones."

As Brie rattled off a list of tasks, Heather's mind whirled, trying to remember it all. She would finish sorting through the stuff first. Then she would hire someone to do the maintenance.

Brie glanced up from her phone. "How long has it been since the thatch was replaced?"

"I have no idea."

"Your parents bought the house from the Croft family, didn't they?"

Heather nodded. "The Crofts sold it to them about fifty years ago. While my mother was working for them."

"The Crofts need someone to help them dig out of their rubble now." Brie typed something else into her phone. "The entire house is going to be ruined if they don't renovate it soon. I've been trying to convince Lord Croft to sell Ladenbrooke to the National Trust before it's beyond repair, but he won't even entertain the idea."

Heather took a canister of teabags out of the cupboard. "Have you been on their property?"

"No, but my sister-in-law used to be sweet on the Croft's son, before she met her husband, of course. She tells the grandest stories about visiting the place. Have you been there?"

Heather smiled. "I used to sneak over when I was a girl to play."

"They say the place is haunted now. It has been, I suppose, since that nasty business with Oliver."

Nasty business. The words caught Heather off guard. It seemed strange to talk about the loss of a son, the devastation of an entire family, in such a casual way.

"What do you think happened to Oliver?" she asked.

Brie's eyebrows rose. "In the end, the police said he drowned by accident, but I don't believe it. . . ."

The teapot clicked, steam billowing up from the spout.

"I think he committed suicide," Brie confided, as if she were sharing a secret.

Heather shivered. "How tragic."

Brie didn't let the sentiment linger for long, smiling when she spoke again. "Some buyers like the idea of a ghost or two hanging around, especially if they plan to convert the place into an inn."

"I'm afraid you won't find any ghosts in our cottage."

The woman glanced around the room again, as if searching for something. "There doesn't have to be an actual ghost, just the hint of one that links it to the past."

"We have plenty of links to the past here."

Brie's gaze rested on the cover of the butterfly book and she picked it up, flipping through the pictures. "These are beautiful," she said. "Did your sister draw them?"

Surprised, Heather leaned across the counter. "How do you know about my sister?"

"Edith went to primary school with Libby. When I told her I was coming here today, she talked like she and Libby had been best friends." Brie set the book down. "But then again, my sister-in-law thinks everyone is her best friend. She works at the Tesco now, over in Cirencester, and has a whole posse to keep her company."

Heather lifted the kettle of hot water. "Would you like some tea?"

"That would be splendid."

Heather filled a mug and passed it across the counter before pouring a cup for herself. Both women steeped bags of Darjeeling in their water.

"Edith wanted me to ask you about Libby."

Heather lifted her teabag out of the water and put it on a saucer. "What about her?"

"She wanted to know if your parents ever found her."

Heather set down the mug, confused. "Libby died before I was born."

Brie's neatly plucked eyebrows arched. "Edith said the police were searching for her around the time Oliver died. She thought it was a romantic tragedy, of sorts. Like Romeo and Juliet."

Heather inched her mug away from her, her mind whirling. "Your sister-in-law thinks Libby and Oliver committed suicide together?"

"Or died of broken hearts." Brie took a sip of the tea. "Edith likes to create drama, but she swears they were lovers. In secret, of course."

Was it possible that her sister wasn't sick at all? Perhaps Libby had fallen in love with the boy next door and—

After Oliver drowned, what had Libby done?

If there was any truth to Brie's story, it made sense why her parents would have kept the cause of Libby's death secret. They were probably heartbroken at their loss as well. And ashamed.

"Where is the Croft family now?" Heather asked.

"They're living outside London. In Woldingham," Brie said before returning to the business at hand. "We'll want to get your cottage on the market right away. Once the sunshine disappears, no one sells much around here until April."

The longer Brie talked, Heather realized she wouldn't be returning to Oregon next week. She needed to finish this job before she returned to the restoration work waiting at her studio, but now, even more than the work at the cottage, she didn't want to leave England until she found out what happened to her sister.

"I can finish the work here in the next three weeks," she said.

"Excellent." Brie took another sip of her tea, and it felt so strange to be sitting here, drinking tea with the woman who had—well, she wasn't sure exactly what the relationship was between Christopher and Brie. She replayed the conversation with Christopher last night in her mind. He'd seemed surprised by her accusation.

Brie stood. "Do you have any more questions?" she asked as Heather escorted her to the door.

She felt odd asking her about Christopher but knew that she must, no matter how uncomfortable it might be. "It's a little off topic—"

Brie stopped on the stoop. "You can ask any question you'd like."

"Back when we were teenagers, did you and Christopher ever—" She took a deep breath. "Did you ever date?"

"Of course not," Brie said with a little wave. "My sights were set on Alan Reynolds from the time I was sixteen, though it took a few more years before he noticed me."

She studied the woman's face as if she could cypher the truth behind her glitzy glasses. "There was nothing between you and Christopher?"

"He only had eyes for you, Heather. Surely you knew that." Brie slid her phone into her purse. "You should ask Christopher's mother about Libby. She knows everything about everyone in this town."

Heather forced a smile. "Perhaps I shall."

After Brie left, she sat down on the front stoop of the cottage. Had her mum lied to her about seeing Christopher and Brie—or Britney—together? Or was Brie embarrassed by the truth? And at this point in her life, did she really need to find out what happened?

Twenty-five years ago, she'd cried in her mum's arms, her heart crushed that Christopher had betrayed her. Never once had she doubted the story—probably because she'd begun questioning whether Christopher Westcott really loved her or if he'd proposed marriage so she'd give herself to him.

She'd been up most of that night grieving, wondering what had gone wrong. They were supposed to say good-bye the night of the dance, but he'd left without seeing her and then when she found him and a female student huddled together in the lobby of the dormitory. . . . in hindsight, it could have been innocent, a study date perhaps, but at the time, her emotions were in overdrive, reeling from the betrayal.

She'd returned home without talking to him and ripped off his brass ring. Then she left for school in London and refused to take his calls.

Leaning back against the house, her gaze wandered over to the stone wall where on the other side, the Crofts lost their son around the same time her parents lost their daughter. Mum had told her Libby was sick but—

If her mum lied to her about Christopher, had she lied about Libby as well?

CHRISTOPHER STEPPED THROUGH THE IRON gates, into the pristine quadrangle of Magdalan. Wisteria draped across the honey-brown buildings around the lawn, and flowers clustered near benches occupied by both scholars and tutors. This college, like all the older colleges in Oxford, was fortified with stone walls, centuries old, to separate the students from the townspeople, curbing the animosity between Town and Gown.

And with good reason. Back in 1355, there was a confrontation between the students and a local innkeeper over the quality of the tavern's wine. A riot ensued, and sixty-three scholars were killed along with thirty townsmen. For almost five hundred years, on St. Scholastica's Day, the town and its mayor had to pay annual penance for the slaughter until a mayor in the early 1800s refused to participate. The tradition ended, but the old wound was easily reopened.

His visit to Bibury ended late Friday night when the old wound inside him had been ripped open as well. He'd been honest with Adrienne about his visit with Heather and tried to reassure her they were just two friends, reconnecting after the death of her father, but he hadn't convinced Adrienne, or himself for that matter, that it was completely innocent. Adrienne had said there was no misunderstanding—she was just the only one willing to admit it.

It had been a long drive back to Oxford.

He walked into the chapel at Magdalan this morning and sat down on one of the hard pews. Wooden statues of the saints stared down at him; music from the organ above wafted through the narrow room. Closing his eyes, he prayed silently for wisdom and peace and direction. God knew the truth about what happened long ago between him and Heather. Perhaps He could reveal it now to both of them.

Christopher had known Britney Garnett from school, but she had been younger than him, and he certainly never met her near Arlington Row. He didn't even remember socializing with her as a student.

But he did remember the night he'd come to take Heather to the dance, a bouquet of wildflowers in hand. Mrs. Doyle had opened the door before he knocked and told him that Heather had already left for London. It was no surprise then that Mrs. Doyle told Heather a story about him and Britney. Heather's mum had consistently tried to thwart their attempts to be together. Of course, it didn't help that in his immaturity, he'd proposed marriage before they were ready. At the time, he hadn't been thinking about consequences, and he would give just about anything to undo his actions that summer.

He'd been honest with Julianna about his relationship with Heather, and he had loved his wife with all his heart. But still he'd wondered what happened so long ago. . . .

It was his mum who'd given him back the brass ring—a silly token of his affection for Heather, as cheap as how he'd treated her their last night together. In his mind, he knew God's forgiveness had washed over him, but it still felt like he paid penance every time he returned to Bibury.

Had his mother somehow conspired with Mrs. Doyle to keep him and Heather apart?

After the organist stopped playing, he stood up and stepped under the dark paneled doorway, into the sunlight. As he strolled the path alongside the quad, he called his mum.

"Is Adrienne angry?" she asked.

"Terribly."

"Oh dear—"

"It was a misunderstanding."

"Of course," she replied quite unconvincingly.

"I need to clear up something else with you." He turned a corner into another quad with a meadow of bluebells. "Back when I was in college, you said Mrs. Doyle brought back the ring I gave

Heather. You said Heather decided she didn't want to marry me after all."

There was a long pause before his mum replied. "You were both so young."

"Not too young to hear the truth."

"We thought you'd do something you would regret," she said.

He leaned back against a brick wall. "Did you and Mrs. Doyle plot against us?"

She didn't answer his question. "We were afraid, for both you and Heather."

Two young scholars walked by him hand-in-hand. "What were you afraid of?"

His mum sighed. "It's a long story."

"I have plenty of time."

27

DECEMBER 1969, WILLOW COTTAGE

Maggie paced in front of the fireplace, the lights from the Christmas tree glowing behind her. For a lifetime, she'd longed for the Christmas she'd dreamed about as a child—of love and gifts and slowly sipping eggnog while her family savored one another's company.

She'd wanted her husband and daughter together for Christmas, but not in this way. Now she wished the light of Christmas would shine into the hearts of the two people she loved more than anyone else. That hope would flood their hearts.

Sometimes the barrier between Libby and Walter had seemed as impenetrable as the stone wall that separated Ladenbrooke from Willow Cottage. But walls weren't impossible. She wasn't certain whether she should quietly traverse this one or knock it down, but one way or another, the barrier must go.

Libby refused to see Walter, and he wouldn't cross the threshold into her room. It broke Maggie's heart to see the people she loved at such odds, but she and Walter couldn't quit now because Libby was having a child. They must put aside their animosity to save Libby's child.

Their grandchild.

She was only thirty-five years old and about to become a

grandmother. No one in their village suspected that Walter wasn't Libby's biological father so whether he liked it or not, he was about to become a grandfather.

He stepped into the sitting room. "How long do we have?"

Maggie didn't know when the baby would arrive. Libby refused to talk about Oliver, but the Croft family left for London in August so Libby would be at least four or five months along. "Maybe April?"

"You need to get some sleep," he said.

"I'm not tired."

"I wish you would be honest with me, Maggie."

She rested one arm on the back of a chair. Her secrets, she feared, were one of the reasons the wall remained up between all of them. "I suppose I am tired." She pressed her fingers together. "I'm just trying to figure out what we're going to do with a baby."

Walter crossed his arms. "If she won't tell us about the father, then there is only one thing we can do."

She had no clue as to what that one thing might be—her head was clouded with the possibilities. And responsibilities. "What is it?" she asked.

"We'll find a good family to care for him."

Her sharp intake of air almost choked her. "You'd give Libby's child away?"

"She can't care for a baby," he said, sounding shocked that she'd consider another option.

"This is our grandchild!"

He shook his head. "It's not my grandchild."

The same old argument except this time it was about Libby's baby.

Maggie folded her arms over her chest. She hadn't expected to be a grandmother at such a young age, but the idea began to take hold. Perhaps a baby was exactly what their family needed to bring them closer together.

"I don't know if she'll give up the baby," Maggie said.

"She may not have a choice."

Maggie sat down in the chair. She would never press Libby to give her baby up for adoption. Quite the opposite. "Of course she has a choice."

"People will ostracize her," Walter said. "Just like back in Clevedon—"

"People already ostracize her."

"We will send her to stay at a home," Walter said. "Just until the baby is born."

"And then we separate them?"

"I don't know, Maggie. I don't know what the right answer is."

She rubbed her arms, her voice small. "I'm afraid there is no right answer."

He sighed. "Then we must make a choice. Right or wrong."

"At least we don't have to choose now."

"Mummy?" Libby called out from her room upstairs.

Maggie slipped quickly up the steps, into Libby's bedroom. "What is it?"

She moaned quietly. "My stomach hurts."

"What do you mean it hurts?"

Libby moaned again, and Maggie's chest felt as if it might implode.

She reached for her daughter's hand. "How often is it hurting?"

"All the time."

Maggie sat on the bedcovers beside her. "Does it come and go?"

Libby didn't say anything.

"Up and down." Maggie gently lifted her hand. "Like the wings of a butterfly."

"Butterflies don't hurt."

Maggie leaned over and kissed her forehead, tasting the salt from her sweat. "I know, honey."

"But babies do."

"Yes, sweetheart." Maggie's heart turned. "Sometimes they hurt a lot."

Libby groaned, and more than anything, Maggie wished she could take away her daughter's pain one more time.

Walter stepped into the room. After glancing at Libby, he turned toward Maggie. "I thought you said the baby would come in April."

Maggie looked up at him. "I was approximating. I don't know when the baby was conceived."

His face blanched. "I don't want to talk about the conception."

"Maybe the baby is early," she said, releasing Libby's hand.

"Just like—" He stopped himself. Sometimes he seemed to forget that the baby he thought to be early was actually full-term. "I'll get Doctor Upton," he said.

Maggie shook her head. "That man can't keep a secret."

"I thought you didn't care what people thought."

Libby groaned again, and her mind raced. There was only one person who might do this for them. One person who could take care of Libby and their secret as well.

"We don't want anyone to know quite yet." She kissed Libby again. "I'll be right back, sweetie."

Libby reached out and grabbed her. "Where are you going?"

"To get Daphne."

Libby let go of her arm.

LIBBY DIDN'T SCREAM LIKE MOST women Daphne had helped through childbirth. At least, not until the very end. Clutching her mum's hand, Libby pushed when Daphne commanded her to, waited when Daphne told her to stop. Then she let out one long, horrible wail that shook the glass on the window.

And a little girl was born.

The baby was tiny but perfectly and wonderfully made. As Daphne sponged olive oil on the girl's wrinkled skin, Maggie prepared a hot water bottle.

Last year she'd stepped down from the midwife training when she found out she was expecting, but she knew enough about midwifery from her nursing classes, not to mention the birth of her son four months ago.

There were no complications with Libby's delivery, but Daphne felt as if she were reeling from a bit of shock, as one child brought another into the world. Even as she tried to stay focused on her work, Daphne felt sad for the girl she'd befriended long ago. The girl who'd never wanted to grow up.

How strange that she and Libby had both become mothers the very same year.

Daphne weighed the baby on the scale that Walter brought into the room along with the cot Libby used fifteen years ago. He placed the baby cot beside Libby and then retreated back into the hallway.

"She's too small," Maggie said, standing over Daphne's shoulder.

"She's five pounds."

"That's how big Libby was when she was born."

"Was she premature?" Daphne asked.

Maggie shook her head.

Daphne wrapped Libby's daughter in a blanket and spooned droplets of sugar water into her mouth. The winter sun had awakened outside the window, casting a dull sheen across the snow, and the pains of exhaustion were wearing on her. She'd been up most of the previous night night comforting her son.

She looked up at Maggie as she fed the baby girl. "You'll need to get a birth certificate."

"Not yet," Maggie said. "We need some time before we tell anyone about her."

Libby's eyes were closed as she rested on the pillows, and Daphne wished Maggie could sleep as well. Her friend's eyes were swollen, her skin blotched, and the worry creasing her face frightened Daphne.

She hated keeping secrets, but she'd do just about anything for Maggie and Libby. And now for Libby's daughter as well. "We can discuss it later."

Daphne placed the baby in the cot alongside a hot water bottle to warm her little body. Then she slid her fetoscope back into her bag.

Maggie escorted her down the steps, into the sitting room. "Thank you for doing this."

Daphne nodded. "I'm glad she's healthy."

"A miracle," Maggie said, holding out Daphne's wool coat.

"Who will notify the father?" she asked as she buttoned her coat.

"Libby won't tell us his name."

Daphne moved toward the door. It was her job to care for people's well-being, not to judge or search out facts they wanted to hide, but she couldn't stop herself from wondering about the man who'd been with Libby. "It's not my business to pry—"

Maggie stopped her. "She said she loves him, whoever he is."

"He'll want to know he has a daughter."

Maggie shook her head. "I'm not so certain."

Daphne slipped on her Wellingtons. While her husband would try to console their son while she was gone, her own breasts were crying for relief. "I'll check back on her later today."

Maggie nodded. "Thank you."

Daphne stepped out into the slushy snow. Her house was a short walk away from the Doyle's home, and she prayed no one would see her in this early-morning hour.

She would do her best to protect Libby and her family, but it would be impossible to hide a baby from the entire village for long.

Shivering, she hurried through the cold.

Some things, she supposed, she'd never find out, but in her heart, she suspected that Maggie knew exactly who fathered Libby's child.

28

MAY 1970, WILLOW COTTAGE

Maggie rocked the baby as Libby sketched on the floor beside them, singing quietly in the space of their sitting room. Heather had given them a scare in those early days, but at five months, her lungs were strong now, and she wasn't afraid to use them.

Maggie never thought she would be so happy to hear a baby cry.

Sometimes she worried the milkman or a neighbor might hear the cries, but so far no one except Daphne knew about her birth. Maggie realized they couldn't keep their secret forever, but for now she savored it. Peace had finally come to their house with this little one.

Libby seemed to be adjusting to her role as a young mother. She named the girl Heather after the magenta-and-white blossoms in Ladenbrooke's gardens. Butterflies loved the heather, she'd said, and the plants thrived even in the winter.

Maggie loved the baby by the same name. With all her heart.

Heather squirmed and cried again. "I think she's hungry," Maggie said.

Libby looked up, seeming to hear her daughter's cries for the first time. Then she glanced back and forth between her colored pencils and the baby. "Should I feed it?"

"Yes, you should."

Maggie stood, and Libby switched places with her in the rocking chair. Maggie helped her situate Heather against her bosom, and her cries stopped as she ate, contented at her mother's breast. Libby seemed distracted however, her gaze wandering to the window. To her knowledge, Libby hadn't been out to the cottage gardens since Heather's birth.

"Do you want to go outside when you're finished?" she asked.

Libby looked back at her, her toes shoving off the rug with a steady, soothing pulse. "Are the flowers blooming?"

Maggie nodded as she collected Libby's drawings into a neat pile beside her.

Libby's eyes returned to the baby in her arms. "I don't know—"

"You can love her and the flowers at the same time."

Libby nodded, but Maggie saw the doubt in her eyes. She wished her daughter could reconcile the conflicting emotions inside her, the dual tugging on her heart.

She'd been so proud of Libby during these months. Maggie had never thought a baby could bring so much healing into their home, but Heather had done that. Her birth brought a sort of normalcy into Libby's life. Consistency that her daughter needed. Libby may not be as old or as doting as other mothers, but she'd been faithful with her responsibilities.

Perhaps Libby had simply needed to grow up.

She wished, of course, that there had been another way for Libby to grow into womanhood, but for the first time, Maggie felt a glimmer of hope for her daughter's future.

She had taken a leave of absence from the beauty shop, and Libby had stayed hidden in the cottage for the remainder of the winter and then the spring. The rector and a few friends had telephoned, but no one except Daphne and the milkman knocked on the door. And she never let the milkman step inside.

Most of their friends had stopped phoning. Maggie told those who did ring that Libby had returned home after Christmas, and she was attending to her daughter's health. Walter said the same thing when people inquired after her at the post office.

Daphne still came once a week to check on both Heather and Libby. She had no more concerns about Heather beyond her lack of a birth certificate—something which Maggie intended to remedy soon—but she had some concerns about Libby's despondency. Maggie thought her daughter might have a bit of the "baby blues." In time, her sadness would fade.

Maggie slipped into the kitchen to stir the vegetable soup she'd made for dinner to go along with the egg and watercress sandwiches Libby liked to eat.

When she walked back into the sitting room, Heather was finished eating, but Libby wasn't drawing or singing to her baby. She was staring back out the window.

"Go see the flowers," Maggie said.

"It's the butterflies I miss."

The familiar ache pressed against Maggie's heart, her desire for Libby to have real friends, the kind who wanted to talk about dances or clothes or even art. Now that she had a baby, there was little hope that Libby would ever have friends her age, but at least she had her family. And her butterflies.

"Go then," Maggie urged. Sitting inside, pining for butterflies, wouldn't do her any good.

Libby put Heather into her little cot, but the moment she walked outside, Maggie picked Heather up, singing softly to the infant. Her arrival into the world may have been unconventional,

but she would have the most conventional life, the happiest childhood, possible.

Walter walked through the door, fifteen minutes earlier than normal.

He glanced at Heather in Maggie's arms as he hung his cap on the rack. "Where's Libby?"

Maggie nodded toward the back window. "Out in the garden."

In his eyes, she saw the same doubt she'd seen in Libby, but he didn't say anything to criticize. Instead he lifted Heather into his arms and sat down in the rocker, holding her tight.

Maggie leaned back against the doorframe and watched them, wondering if he'd ever let go of her again.

THE CREAMY VANILLA SCENT OF clematis breathed life into Libby's lungs. She trailed the vines along the wall, down the hill behind her parents' home and through the path in the forest. At the river's edge, she sat on a rock and dipped her big toe into the current, watching the water swirl around it. The river didn't seem nearly as frightening as it once had. For she had a new fear now, one even more daunting than the water.

How was she supposed to care for a baby?

She had nothing to offer it except milk, and sometimes that wouldn't even console it. The baby's crying frightened her, and she often felt as if her head might explode if she didn't get outside, away from the noise.

Then Mummy would come alongside her and say that it was tired or needed a new nappy or that Libby's hands were squeezing too tight.

Her aching breasts reminded her when it needed to eat, but Mummy said the milk wouldn't last forever. Sometimes when she was younger, in the frantic pace of drawing and dreaming, she forgot to eat or even drink. How was she going to remember to feed another person?

She took a deep breath.

The smell of the flowers was supposed to quench her fears, but all she smelled this time was mud and moss.

Summer was almost here, bringing back the tulips, butterflies, and the promise of Oliver Croft on its warm breeze.

Butterflies needed flowers to survive, just like she needed Oliver Croft. And Oliver needed her more than the baby did.

Baby needed someone like Mummy to care for her.

29

The manager at the grocery market in Cirencester said Edith Lane was working today but not until after lunch. Heather checked her watch and asked for directions to the local library.

Although there was no newspaper in Bibury, the librarian at the main desk said the *Wilts and Gloucestershire Standard* covered the entire region in 1970. They kept all the editions on microfilm, but the librarian had never operated the reader on the back wall. Heather hadn't operated one since she'd attended college in Portland. Between the two of them, they managed to get the reel on the spindle and the film threaded through the glass, rotating forward instead of back.

Her parents had said Libby died before Heather was born, so she scanned through the obituaries in the late 1960s. When she didn't find any mention of Libby, she started foraging for information about Oliver Croft's death.

The first headline about Oliver was published on June 4, 1970. It was quite similar to the one Ella had sent, saying the police found Oliver's body in the River Coln, and they suspected foul play.

She studied the grainy photo beside the article. Oliver Croft was a handsome young man, and in his eyes, she saw a bit of the recklessness she'd once admired in Christopher. Had her sister loved this man as she'd once loved Christopher?

The next article on Oliver was published a month later. The police, it seemed, had no suspects in the case.

She scanned the obituaries and articles for the rest of the year. There was only one more mention of the Croft family. One of the November papers reported that their daughter, Sarah Croft, was engaged to marry a man from London.

If Oliver Croft, the son of a lord, had been murdered, it seemed there would have been a massive search for the person who had killed him.

Perhaps Brie was right. Perhaps there'd been no foul play.

Did the Croft family ever return to Ladenbrooke after Oliver's death? The Crofts and her parents were neighbors, and her mum once worked for Lord and Lady Croft. Did they mourn the deaths of their children together? Or did the wall that separated them remain intact, even in their sorrow?

She turned off the machine and sat back in her chair, sadness looming over her. She had returned to England to close the doors to her past, but new doors kept opening, more questions with fleeting answers.

She glanced at her watch. Brie's sister-in-law should have started work twenty minutes ago. Perhaps she could offer some clarity, at least, to her questions about Libby.

HEATHER FOUND EDITH BEHIND THE meat counter, a hairnet holding back her graying hair. She looked as if she'd been quite pretty at one time, but heavy wrinkles now lined her forehead and eyelids.

When Heather introduced herself, Edith greeted her with a solid handshake. Then she hung up her apron on a hook and led Heather out behind the supermarket, to sit at a picnic table along the edge of the parking lot. Cigarette butts littered the patches of gravel and grass underneath.

Edith plucked a pack out of her shirt pocket and offered Heather one. After she declined, Edith lit her cigarette, took a long drag, and turned her head to blow the smoke. "So you're Libby's kid sister."

The words sounded strange to Heather's ears, but she nodded. "Brie said you used to be friends with her."

She took another drag on her cigarette. "I wouldn't say *friends* exactly."

Heather's cell phone rang, but she muted it without looking at the screen. "What were you?"

She shrugged. "I don't think your sister had any friends when we were kids. She wasn't particularly fond of people except Oliver Croft, of course. All the girls were fond of Oliver."

"Did she and Oliver date?"

"Not officially, I suppose. His parents would have had a royal conniption if they thought he was sweet on her."

"What was wrong with Libby?"

Edith examined her face. "Libby was different than the other girls our age, but that wasn't the main problem. Oliver's parents needed him to marry someone with a truckload of cash."

"And my parent's didn't have enough—"

"No one in Bibury had enough money for the Crofts. They had that huge house to maintain, but they didn't have the income to keep it up."

Heather pulled out the book of butterflies from her handbag. "Do you recognize this?"

Edith scanned the cover. "No, but Libby was always drawing something in one of her books when we were in primary school."

Heather slid the book back into her bag. "Do you know how Oliver died?"

Edith shook her head. "Everyone was hush-hush about it. The police came to our school right after they found his body, asking all sorts of questions. We wanted to know what happened, of course, but they wouldn't tell us a thing."

"Did Libby die before or after Oliver?"

Edith took another drag on her cigarette. "Your sister left school before Oliver's death, and I never saw her again. Then I heard she died, but no one told me exactly when or how. It sounded awfully suspicious to me."

"My parents told me she was sick."

Edith nodded slowly. "She probably was ill. Your sister was very beautiful, but seemed so simple and . . ."

"And what?" she prompted.

"Different," Edith finally said. "Back before most people appreciated differences. Oliver really liked her though, and my friends and I—we were jealous. Unfortunately, I didn't treat Libby very well."

Heather cringed. "You teased her?"

Edith nodded slowly, smoke clouding her face.

Heather didn't ask any more questions, afraid perhaps of what she might hear. Children could be cruel, and if her sister was different from the other girls, and pretty, perhaps they had done more than teased her. Perhaps they had wounded her deeply.

Perhaps her sister, the beautiful young woman who'd been

fond of butterflies along with the boy next door, had thought life was no longer worth living.

DAPHNE WESTCOTT FIDGETED WITH THE case of her mobile phone as she waited outside Willow Cottage, praying that someone—*anyone*—would contact her with an emergency. She looked down at the screen. Thankfully there were four solid bars of service up on the hill.

The slightest hint of a contraction, from any of the five women in her care, would have to take precedent over her talk with Heather today. But even though she'd been waiting for almost an hour outside the cottage, no one had called.

More than thirty years ago, she'd finished her schooling to become a midwife, and it was her hard-won reputation of honesty and reliability that kept her working in the years after most nurses and midwives retired.

She loved her job—the wonder of ushering a new life into the world and helping instill confidence in a new mother to care well for her child. She'd had failures over the years, children who'd arrived in the world with medical conditions she couldn't mend and mothers who hadn't wanted to mother. She couldn't remember every baby she'd helped deliver, but she'd never been able to forget the first baby she'd helped bring into the world. Forty-five years ago.

She sighed.

Her biggest success had also been her greatest failure.

A car rumbled up the gravel in the driveway. She checked her phone again, but it seemed there would be no way out of this conversation. She had to tell Heather the truth this time.

She stood as Heather stepped out of her car. "I thought I'd pay you a visit."

Heather looked at her skeptically. "Don't you have company at home?"

"They left on Friday," Daphne said, but couldn't tell if the woman walking toward her was pleased or disappointed by that news.

Heather motioned toward the door. "Come in."

Daphne stepped into house, and pleasant memories flooded back to her, her years reading to Libby when she was a child, the many times Heather and Christopher played together as toddlers while she and Maggie sipped tea on the patio. "I haven't been in here since your mother died."

"You were a good friend to her."

"I tried to be," Daphne said. "But perhaps not always in the best way."

Heather directed her to the chairs by the fireplace. "Did you come to tell me about Libby?"

Daphne glanced down at the phone in her hands before nodding slowly. "And I've come to ask your forgiveness."

She'd been a decade younger than Maggie, but they had been raising children the same age. For better or worse, they shared the bond of secrecy, started in a moment of desperation and propagated by little lies that started white but blackened over the years.

Heather sat in her father's chair. "I met with a woman named Edith in Cirencester today. She said she knew Libby when she was in school."

"I don't think anyone really knew Libby. . . ."

Heather leaned forward. "What was my sister like?"

Daphne checked her phone one last time and then muted it. "Libby was beautiful and wild and completely enchanted by flowers and butterflies. She was like a fairy, fluttering around all the time, and she was so lost in her own world that sometimes you thought there might have been a bit of magic in her."

"So she did make the butterfly book—"

"I'm sure she drew the pictures, but Libby struggled to communicate when she was a child. With her words and writing." She folded her hands together. "If she was born today, I'm sure the doctors would have a diagnosis and therapy to help her, but back then, no one knew what was wrong."

Heather leaned toward her. "I searched the local newspaper for her obituary, but I couldn't find anything about her death."

Daphne fidgeted with her phone, wishing again she was anyplace but here. Maggie should have shared Libby's story with Heather, but Daphne bore just as much responsibility in the deception.

"Do you know what happened to her?" Heather asked.

"Walter and Maggie loved you, Heather. They both wanted you to have a happy childhood, and they would have done anything they could to protect you." She paused. "Even if it meant withholding the truth."

"Please tell me what happened."

"Libby didn't die, Heather. She ran away."

Heather shivered, folding her arms across her chest. "They should have told me. . . ."

"The rumors about Libby's death started after you were born, and your mother did nothing to stop it. She loved Libby fiercely and when she left—it was almost as if Maggie had to say good-bye in her heart for good."

"Do you know where Libby went?"

Daphne shook her head.

"So my sister might still be alive?"

Instead of responding, Daphne twisted the phone in her hand, looking at the screen again to see if anyone had called. She'd harbored Maggie's secrets for so long, guarding them with all her heart, but it was time, finally time, to let this one go. "Libby wasn't your sister, Heather."

Heather leaned forward. "What was she?"

She took a deep breath. "Libby was your mum."

30

MAY 1970, BIBURY

Maggie pedaled her bicycle up the steep hill, her basket filled with tomatoes and avocado pears from the greengrocer, a rump roast from the butcher, and a tin of cheese crispies from the general store. It was a splendid spring day, the apple trees blossoming and flowers blooming on both sides of the lane.

It was also the first time she'd visited the village since Heather had been born, and it was good to be back in town. People eyed her oddly, as they had back in Clevedon, but no one seemed to whisper when she entered the shops. They had nothing to whisper about.

And she didn't particularly care if they did whisper. Joy had washed over their little family, and while Libby rarely talked, the gardens behind their cottage seemed to breathe hope back to her soul. Heather was a strong baby, demanding the attention of whoever was in the room, and she and Walter were both more than pleased to accommodate her when Libby was outside. Heather's strength—even her discontentment at times—was a blessing to them. With her tenacity, they hoped she would thrive.

Libby continued to mature with her new responsibilities though sometimes Maggie would have to call her in from the garden to feed Heather. Or she slept through the baby's cries and Maggie would have to wake her.

Sometimes Libby's gaze drifted over toward the towers of Ladenbrooke, and for that moment, Maggie lost her entirely.

But Libby was trying her best to be a good mother. She loved her daughter in her own way. Neither she nor Libby ever talked about Oliver, and Maggie didn't think Walter suspected the father of Libby's child. She prayed he would never find out.

At the top of the hill, Maggie braked suddenly, the tin of crispies spilling to the ground along with her bag of produce. Her hands trembled as she tried to hold up her bicycle, and she felt as if she might faint.

The gates of Ladenbrooke were open, and they were never open unless . . .

She breathed deeply, trying to calm the racing in her heart.

Had the Croft family come home?

Oliver may have had Libby last summer, but he couldn't have her anymore. If he even wanted her . . .

She collected the food from the ground and tossed it back in her basket before walking her bicycle past the gate. She couldn't seem to stop herself from staring inside the gap, at the beginning of the treed lane that wound toward the manor.

Hopefully Oliver would stay in London for the next three months to play rugby or row or whatever held his attention these days, but if he came home, Maggie would not let him ruin their family's newfound peace or her daughter's stability. He and his greed, his arrogance, would not destroy everything they'd built.

She pedaled home as quickly as she could and leaned her bicycle against the stable door, trying to calm her heart before she walked inside the house. Once Libby's mind focused on something, whether it was her butterflies or her art or Oliver, it was impossible to deter her. Even if Oliver didn't return to

Ladenbrooke, what would Libby do if she thought he was here?

Surely Oliver would avoid Libby if he knew about Heather. But what if Libby kept their child a secret from him, like Maggie had done years ago when she saw Elliot?

Perhaps she and Walter should try to sell Willow Cottage. Leave Bibury like they'd left Clevedon. They could find a new home where both their daughter and granddaughter would be safe.

"Libby?" she called out as she rushed into the house.

When no one answered, the familiar dread weighed against her heart. She flung open the back door.

"Libby?" This time she was shouting, not caring who heard, but still no one answered.

She rushed back into the house and realized that Heather was in the sitting room, asleep in her cot.

Heather was asleep, and Libby was gone.

LIBBY HURRIED DOWN THROUGH THE field and trees behind the cottage, her feet bidden forward. Her nightmares about the river had subsided, swept away in Oliver's arms, but in his absence, inside the walls of the cottage, she'd felt as if her life was being sucked out of her. Sometimes it almost seemed as if she couldn't breathe anymore.

But this afternoon, under the blue shimmer of summer sky, she felt alive again. Mud cooled her bare toes as rays of sunlight pricked her skin, energizing her. She craved Oliver's touch. His smile. His kiss.

Mummy said that Oliver didn't really love her, but he did. He'd climbed the beech tree this morning to leave another bouquet on her windowsill, but this time he hadn't asked to meet her by the gate. Instead he'd drawn a picture of himself and her by their tower.

The pale-blue dress she'd worn last year no longer fit, but she had a new skirt and blouse, the soft apricot color of the lady's roses. And she wore a pretty silk scarf that Mummy had bought for her, a dozen colors blending perfectly together like the colors that spilled from a setting sun.

She hoped Oliver would still think her pretty.

At the edge of the river, she dipped her toes into the water, surprised by the cold sting when the air felt so warm. Stepping back, she eyed the swift current.

When she ran away last year, the water had been trickling around the rocks instead of racing over them. But she'd waded over to Ladenbrooke then and she would do it again now.

Oliver's face flashed through her mind, and she breathed in the memory as she stepped back into the water. The river streamed around her ankles, the stones slippery under her bare feet. Silvery branches from the willow swept across the surface of the river, and she embraced them in her arms, clinging to the branches and leaves as she inched herself around the wall.

Fear clamped her chest, weighing down her entire body. She hated this—the feeling of being anchored to the ground. She wasn't made to walk or swim. She was made to fly.

And she was made to be with Oliver.

Lifting her skirt, she moved around the tree and then the wall, to the grassy bank on the other side. She twirled once on land, her feet light again. Then she glided up through the forest and into the Italian garden.

Someone moved on the other side of the hedge, and she smiled as she hurried toward the figure, but instead of Oliver, she saw Henry's black hair, peppered with white.

Freezing, she pressed her back into the trimmed topiary of a swan, the pruned branches poking her neck and arms. Oliver had warned her last summer to be careful when she snuck over to Ladenbrooke, saying if anyone saw her in the gardens, she might never be allowed to see him again.

She squeezed her eyes shut and held her breath. If only she could fly away like a real swan.

"Miss Doyle?"

For a moment, she didn't move, hoping the head gardener would pass by, but he didn't.

"You can come out, Libby."

She opened one eye and saw Henry looking back down at her, his left eye twitching. "You have to go home."

She straightened herself then stepped away from the swan's prickly wings. "I'm here by invitation."

The gardener twisted his cap. "Who invited you?"

"Oliver." Reaching into her pocket, she pulled out his picture.

Henry scanned the paper. "I wouldn't call this an invitation."

"You can ask Oliver," she replied, carefully refolding it.

He wiped his face with his handkerchief. "Lady Croft won't be pleased."

"I don't care about the lady," she said, trying to be strong.

His gaze trailed the steps up to the house. "You should care."

"Please, Henry—" she started. "Don't tell her about me."

"She'll find out."

"Not if you—" She struggled for the right words to convince him. "Not if you keep our secret."

He took a step back toward the path from which he'd come. "You mustn't stay long."

When Walter did something that pleased Mummy, she kissed his cheek, so Libby did exactly what she thought her mummy would do. Stepping up on her toes, she strained her neck to kiss the whiskers on Henry's cheek.

He cleared his throat. "You better hurry on now in case the lady decides to take a stroll."

He didn't need to tell her twice. In the distance, beyond the maze, was the tower, and she hurried toward it. Was Oliver there now, waiting for her? It was strange to be meeting him in the daylight instead of the midnight hours.

She passed by the lily pond and the statue of a goddess before stepping into the maze. The path toward the tower might be confusing to some, but it was as familiar to her as the road that led from the village up to her home. The last time she was here, it had been so cold she thought she might freeze to death, if the growth inside her didn't take her first.

How could she have been so stupid to have not known about the baby?

But she knew now. She wouldn't make the same mistake.

Oliver would understand.

Gnats swarmed near the top of the hedges, the hour of dusk their feasting time. Her hands over her arms, she ducked her head and pressed through the insects that drank blood instead of nectar, winding through the maze until she reached the folly.

"Oliver?" she called softly. Then she called his name again, louder this time.

She waited for his familiar whistle, for his handsome face to appear in an open window, but when she didn't see him, she climbed the steps. He was probably waiting for her upstairs with his fancy pillows and champagne.

She smiled at the thought, but when she reached the top, her smile quickly disappeared.

There was no one in the room.

She'd thought Oliver would prepare the room like he had

before, burn his citrus and sage incense to clear away the stench, but the room smelled like rotten food and the floor was cluttered with all the things she'd left behind. Tins she'd taken from the lady's pantry. Pages ripped out from her sketchbook. The torch that needed batteries. Blankets that Oliver had brought down from the house last summer.

She opened one of the shutters, and in the fading sunlight, she sat on the remains of a moth-eaten blanket.

Oliver would be here soon and that was all that mattered.

31

MAY 1970, WILLOW COTTAGE

The postal truck from London arrived late, and Walter worked until half past six, sorting through the mail for the morning delivery. He'd once thought he would spend his life writing, but since they'd left Clevedon, he'd spent his career delivering other people's stories. Sometimes as he worked, the desire to write his own stories rekindled inside him, all sorts of ideas playing in his mind, but he promptly quashed the muse. Instead of spending the evenings with a pen and paper, he now had a little girl who needed him when he came home.

He wore no blinders about the challenges their family faced in the future nor did he know how they were going to reveal Heather's birth to their community, but ever since he'd held Libby's newborn in his arms, he was incredibly glad they hadn't given her to another family to love.

In fact, he hadn't been this happy since his first year of marriage, when he thought Maggie had hung the moon and his daughter sprinkled the stars. Still, he tried to hold on to this season of their life with an open hand, knowing Libby could take her daughter away any time. If he clung too tightly, he feared he would never be able to let go.

Maggie, on the other hand, had embraced this baby as if she

was her own. Heaven help them both if Libby decided to take Heather away.

Sometime soon, they would need to introduce Heather to their friends in the village. No matter what Maggie wanted, they couldn't keep her hidden forever.

As he turned onto their driveway, he heard Heather's cries through an open window and he rushed inside to hold her. But neither she nor Libby nor even Maggie were in the sitting room. He checked inside the kitchen before flicking on the light switch beside the steps and running upstairs.

He found his wife sitting on the carpet outside Libby's bedroom, Heather crying in her arms.

Maggie looked up at him, her face blotched from her own tears. "She's hungry."

He looked into the dark doorway behind her. "Where's Libby?"

Maggie held Heather closer to her chest, crying along with the baby.

He knelt down beside her. "Where is she, Maggie?"

Maggie lowered Heather and looked in the baby's face as if she were searching for answers from the child. "I don't know."

"When did she leave?" he begged.

Her eyes stayed focused on Heather. "I rode by Ladenbrooke this afternoon."

Walter twisted his cap in his hands, confused.

"The gates were open," Maggie continued.

He glanced out the window over Maggie, at the stone wall through the window. "You think she's in the gardens?"

Maggie stood and began gently bouncing Heather to soothe her cries. "I think she's with Oliver."

He dropped his cap to his side. "Oliver Croft?"

Maggie nodded as he stood beside her.

"But why would she be with—" He fell back against the banister, his question suspended between them. "Oliver is the father."

Maggie slowly nodded her head.

"But when did she see Oliver?"

"They were meeting in the gardens," she said, her voice small.

His chest constricted, and he felt as if he might explode. "You knew?"

"I only saw them once, at the folly inside the maze." She refused to meet his gaze. "I told him to leave her alone, and I locked our side of the gate so she couldn't go back."

"Oh, Maggie—" He reached for Heather and held her against his chest. "That's why you told me to check the tower."

"I should have done more."

When would Maggie ever learn that she had to trust him? They were supposed to work together, but after all these years, she still kept secrets from him.

He shuddered. No matter what happened in the past, they had to work together now. If Lord and Lady Croft knew they had a grandchild, they might take Heather away, and it would destroy all they'd built, ripping their family apart from the inside out.

Libby couldn't tell Oliver about the baby.

"She loves Heather, in her own way," Maggie said. "And she loves Oliver."

Walter walked to the window, rubbing Heather's back. "I'm not going to let her ruin this."

"It's too late to find them now."

Walter turned back toward her. "I can try."

"We need to feed Heather first and we're out of powdered milk."

He groaned. "The general store closed an hour ago."

"Daphne will let you borrow some." Maggie rocked back and forth against the wall like the hand of a clock stuck on the wrong time. "He can't take her away."

Walter took her face in one of his hands. "Maggie."

Her eyes found his face, and she stopped rocking.

"I'm not going to let anyone take her."

He handed Heather back to her, and Maggie hugged the baby close, trying to comfort her. Then she reached over and clutched his hand, clinging to it for a moment before turning her attention back to their granddaughter.

Outside he put his cap back on his head and hurried south toward the Westcott home.

Whatever it took—he'd do anything to keep Heather safe.

LIBBY WAITED FOR AN HOUR in the tower. Oliver had said he would come, and Oliver never, ever broke his promises.

Perhaps he'd come earlier and left before she'd arrived. Or perhaps he'd forgotten they were meeting in the folly. He could be sitting beside their gate, wondering where she was.

Through the open window, she watched the last traces of sunlight fold into the darkness, the green maze below turning into dark threads. In the past, she would have wandered in the moonlight, but she had no desire to dance or explore. Tonight her heart ached from missing Oliver and her breasts ached from the milk ballooning inside them.

She must find Oliver and then return home to feed the baby.

Quickly she ran down the steps and wove her way back toward the gardens, wanting to curse the lord from long ago for making his maze so complicated. Instead of taking the stone steps up the hill, she snuck behind bushes and under the lime bower so Henry wouldn't see her.

She must find another way to see Oliver. Tonight.

At the rose garden, she moved toward the stone wall that separated the gardens from her cottage, but stopped at the edge of the bushes. Someone was near the wall, trudging down the slope instead of using the steps.

Her heart leapt again. Was Oliver sneaking down to the folly? Or was Henry returning to insist that she leave?

She mirrored the descent of the other person, taking care to hide in the shadows. It was a man in front of her, much too stout to be Oliver, and he was pushing a wheelbarrow as he descended the hill.

Libby followed him to the edge of the gardens and then through the trees until he reached the river. Curious, she hid behind the branches of a tree, watching him and his wheelbarrow.

A loud splash startled her, and she jumped back. At first, she thought the man had jumped into the river, but a scream rocked the night, as loud as the baby's cries except this sound was angry. Like the roar of the lioness in *Born Free*.

Then his anger turned to sobbing, and in it, Libby heard the pain of a heart ripping in two.

She covered her ears, closed her eyes, trying to block out the sound that tore through her as well, but she couldn't seem to escape the crying—the cry of the baby or the cry of this man before her.

Then she couldn't hear the cries anymore.

Slowly she removed her hands. There was a scraping noise now as the man began to push his wheelbarrow back up the hill.

She waited a moment, to make sure he was gone, then she crept toward the riverbank to see what he'd thrown into the river.

The moon shone down on the inky surface, and she gasped. There was a person in the water. Frozen in the current.

The arms and legs should be flailing, struggling to get out. Instead the legs began to sink in the middle, into the deep place where people drowned.

She clutched her arms around her chest, trying to rub away her fears. She needed to be strong right now. Brave. She needed to wade into the water and bring the man or woman to the bank before he or she was swept away.

But what if the water swept her away too?

The body shifted in the current, and the head began to tilt. In the moonlight, she saw a face. His face.

Oliver.

Terror swallowed up her fears, and she flung herself into the river. This time she didn't feel the cold on her toes nor did she cling to willow branches. She didn't slip on the stones or even think about them hurting her feet. Arms outstretched, she trudged forward in the current, struggling to reach for him.

The hem of her skirt was under the water, but she still wasn't close enough. Another step. A few more inches.

The current raced over her knees as she clenched his shoulders.

"Oliver!" she screamed, shaking him. His eyes were open, but they were focused on the moon above instead of on her.

She curled her fingers under his shoulders and yanked them, trying to pull him toward the shore, but he was stuck on the rocks.

His head—she had to keep his head out of the water so he could breathe.

She swore at the water and whatever snared him beneath it. And she cried out from the pain that ripped through her chest.

The river would not take Oliver away from her.

She pulled harder on his shoulders, fighting against the current as her feet sank deeper in the mud, but she refused to let go of him. Water rushed over her arms, and she tugged again until she freed Oliver from the rocks.

Her arms under his shoulders, she dragged Oliver backward toward the shore, into the shallow pools where the water wouldn't swallow him. Then she knelt beside him, shaking his arms, his shoulders, crying out his name, but he wouldn't wake.

Why wouldn't he wake?

She shook him again until she saw something move in the trees. There was a man near the bank, walking toward her. She reached across Oliver, trying to protect him.

"Libby?" the man whispered as he drew close.

She pulled her arms back and crossed them over her chest. It was Walter. Her father had come to help Oliver.

She didn't move as Walter knelt beside her. His head dropped to Oliver's chest, listening for the beat of life within him. When he looked back up at her, there was sadness in her father's eyes. Sorrow.

She clutched her hands over her heart. "No—"

"Hush, Libby," he said, placing his wet hand on her shoulder, steadying her. "You have to leave."

She shook her head. "I can't leave him."

"There's nothing you can do to help him now."

Her chest bowed over her knees, her hair dangling in the water. She knew Oliver was gone, his wings broken for good, but she couldn't bear to say good-bye.

"You must go home," he said, his voice more urgent now. "At once."

But even as he spoke, the words seemed muffled in her ears. Walter was afraid, and he wasn't supposed to be afraid of anything.

He shook her shoulder. "Libby—"

She tilted her head back up to look at him.

"Do you understand me?" he asked.

"I don't know," she whispered, closing her eyes so she couldn't see the fear in Walter's gaze. Or the emptiness in Oliver's face.

He stood and took her hand. She followed him to the wall; then he lifted her out of the water and carried her, back to the trees on the other side.

This time she wished he would drop her. So the river could take her too.

"I'll meet you at home," he said. "Don't tell your mum or anyone that Oliver is gone."

She nodded slowly. He needn't worry about her telling anyone, but he was wrong about Oliver.

Oliver Croft wasn't gone. Would never be gone.

No matter what happened, Oliver would always be alive in her heart.

32

The sun was fading behind the churchyard outside Bibury, but Heather didn't want to wait until tomorrow to visit the cemetery. Kneeling beside the headstone for Margaret Emerson Doyle, she traced her hand over the epitaph.

Her mum had lied to her about Libby and about Christopher. She must have thought she'd been doing the right thing to protect her, but the ripples from her lies had redirected the course of Heather's life.

She glanced over at her father's new headstone.

Part of her wanted to be angry at both of them for collaborating against her, but more than anger, she understood exactly why they had done it. Years later, she had lied to her daughter as well.

She'd intended to tell Ella the truth about her father—one day—but the untruths grew and became their own reality over the years, until it seemed impossible to untangle it all.

Now was the time to straighten it out, before it was too late. She wanted to stop the deception from filtering again from one generation to the next.

Mrs. Westcott had left her home several hours ago, tears in her eyes. She thought Heather would be angry at her parents—and at her—for keeping this secret, but Heather felt more relief than anger. It explained so much—why her parents had loomed over her as a teenager, why they'd sent her away to a girls-only school when she'd wanted to stay home, and why they'd insisted she attend college.

Her parents had loved her; she knew that without a doubt. And her heart was filled with gratefulness—at the sacrifices they made to raise the child who was technically their granddaughter. It still hurt that her dad had been so distant in his later years, but she knew she'd disappointed him when she'd married Jeffery.

It saddened her as well that Mrs. Westcott—and not her parents—had been the one to tell her the truth about Libby. Perhaps if she'd known about her birth mother, she wouldn't have felt so alone during the years she'd spent as a single mom.

Mrs. Westcott asked her forgiveness for keeping the secrets, and Heather had given it freely. Christopher's mother had helped give her life, and she'd done what she thought best to protect her son. If Heather didn't forgive her, then she had no right to ask the same of Ella.

After their conversation ended, Heather had retreated down to the basement and dug through several more of Libby's boxes, searching instead of sorting this time until she found dozens of envelopes addressed to Oliver Croft, to a house in Woldingham. Inside were hand-drawn pictures of a tower and gardens and the backs of a boy and a girl, sitting hand in hand by a pond—a purple butterfly instead of a signature on every one.

As she sat now on the grass between the gravestones, Heather flipped through the butterfly book in her hands again, trying to grasp understanding from the magical pictures, the unique lines and colors of an artist who captured butterflies on paper.

Libby wasn't her sister, but she couldn't quite process the fact that the couple she'd thought to be her parents were actually her grandparents. Even though the truth of her past might have shifted, her heart had not, could not. In spite of the lies, Walter and Maggie Doyle had sacrificed to send her to a good school, away from the rumors in Bibury. They'd loved and protected her from someone they thought might neglect or even harm her.

Mrs. Westcott said Libby ran away soon after Heather was born. But where did she run?

Heather closed her eyes.

The last time she'd been inside the parish church was for her dad's memorial service. The day was a messy blur in her mind. People from town had filled the sanctuary to pay tribute to the man who'd sorted and delivered their mail for thirty years. The rector asked her to read from the Scriptures during the service and she'd selected Psalm 23. When she'd stepped up to the podium, she scanned the crowd and saw a woman standing at the back. It was impossible to miss her—she wore a pale-blue dress while everyone else wore black, and the copper tones of her long hair glowed in the sunlight that filtered through the stained glass.

After she finished reading from Psalms, Heather had looked again toward the back of the room, but the woman was gone.

She'd thought it strange at the time—and even stranger was the sense of déjà vu she'd felt with the woman's presence, almost as if she'd seen her before in a dream. But like a dream, the memory of the woman faded in the hours after the service.

Was it possible that Libby had come to say good-bye to her father as well?

In the quiet churchyard, sitting among the bluebells, Heather decided she wouldn't leave England until she discovered what happened to Libby. If Mrs. Westcott's story was accurate, forty-five years had passed since she'd left home. It might seem like an impossibility to find her now, especially if she didn't want to be found, but if Libby had loved Oliver, perhaps someone in Oliver's family would have an idea where she'd gone.

A quick text to Brie requested the Crofts' contact info, and seconds later, Heather received a return text with the phone number and address for Lord Croft, the same address from Libby's letters.

But before she contacted the Crofts, she decided it was time to put an end to her own secrets as well. For too long, she'd thought she was protecting Ella, but looking back, it had been cowardly of her to wait twenty-five years to have this talk. The secrets meant to protect her daughter were really shielding Heather from her own shame. A fortress for her pride and a shoddy tourniquet for her wounds.

This time she didn't text Ella. This time she called.

CHRISTOPHER BIKED THE PATH ALONG the placid River Cherwell, passing by a parade of flat-bottomed punts filled with students laughing and singing as they floated in the sunshine. During his first summer as a student at Oxford, he would have gone punting with them, but his gusto for life tanked after Heather's rejection and sent him into a tailspin. It took him years to regain his footing.

He'd thought he and Heather were a sure thing. They'd mapped out a life together, as much as one maps out a life at the ages of eighteen and nineteen. She was going to finish college in London, and then they would marry. He'd planned to pursue a degree in economics and she wanted to teach art.

They'd dreamed about living in London, as a family—Heather wanted four kids but after growing up with three siblings, he opted for two. They'd laughed about their dreams. And in their certainty, their passion, they'd made mistakes.

He thought Heather rejected him because of his foolishness. He'd tried to make amends with her after that summer, to say he was sorry, but he thought she'd rejected him again and again.

All along, she thought he'd rejected her.

No wonder Heather was angry with him. She thought he'd been cheating on her with someone else.

And it was all a lie, propagated by their mothers, out of fear. When his mum called, she told him the truth about what happened the night he and Heather were supposed to go to the dance. And she told him about Libby.

It wasn't that Mrs. Doyle disliked Christopher. His mum said Mrs. Doyle hadn't wanted Heather to make the same choices as Libby, so she concocted a story that would deter her—just until she thought Heather was old enough to marry.

But it was more than that for Christopher's mum. She'd loved Libby and her daughter, but she was afraid as well, fearing Heather would grow up to be as erratic as her mother and hurt Christopher as a result. She cared deeply for the Doyle family, but his mum had a fierce love for her children.

Heather hadn't rejected him or his token of a promise. Mrs. Doyle had returned the ring to his mum.

Something happened when he'd visited Heather last week though. It felt like they were teenagers again, enjoying each other's company as friends. Or even more than friends.

He sighed. He couldn't figure out the state of his own heart.

He'd loved his wife dearly and grieved deeply after he lost her. And he'd tried to move on in his relationships. Some nights, loneliness still seemed to consume him, but he wanted more than companionship from a woman like Adrienne. He wanted to spend the rest of his life with someone he loved.

Perhaps it was time to move past regrets and take an honest look into his future.

Did he want Heather in his life again? The answer inside him was a resounding yes, but he didn't know if she would consider renewing their friendship, even when she found out the truth about what happened.

All he could do was ask.

His mum said she wouldn't meddle, but somehow, inadvertently, she'd texted him Heather's number.

Perhaps he should ring her. Or perhaps these days it was better to start with a text instead.

He stopped pedaling and set his bicycle against the wide trunk of an oak tree. Then he removed his phone from his pocket.

But before he decided whether to text or call, a note popped up on his screen.

It was a simple message. From Heather.

Can I come to Oxford?

He didn't hesitate before texting back.

Yes!

33

JUNE 1970, WILLOW COTTAGE

The knock at half past eight startled Maggie—Daphne had already visited for the night, and no one else ever knocked on their front door in the evening.

Two nights ago, Libby had come through the back door, drenched to her core and trembling like the night last December when they'd discovered she was expecting. Now she was soaking in Epsom salts upstairs while Maggie was in the kitchen, preparing a bottle from formula. Since returning home, Libby no longer seemed to care about feeding her daughter. No longer wanted to do anything at all.

Something had frightened her that night, but just like before, Libby refused to talk about it. Even with Maggie.

She thought it sadly ironic that Libby hadn't caught the influenza when she ran away during their harsh winter, but her escape on a warm summer night sent her to bed in a sort of trance that neither Maggie nor Daphne could break.

When Walter came home two nights ago, he'd been relieved to find Libby there, but after his long search, it seemed as if he contracted an illness too. He'd worked late again last night, then he went straight to bed.

The knock on the front door came again, more persistent this time. Maggie hung her apron on a kitchen hook and rushed out through the sitting room, past Heather asleep in her little cot.

On the stoop was Constable Patrick Garland, Albert and Rebecca's oldest son. She hadn't seen either Albert or Rebecca in years, although she'd heard that Patrick joined the police after serving with the Royal Navy.

Beside Patrick was an officer she didn't recognize, but on the sleeve of his uniform was the double diamond insignia of an inspector.

She put her hand to her throat, her breath constricting in the passageway. Why was an inspector at their door?

Her husband's face flashed in her mind. Walter was twenty minutes late again tonight. Had he been in an accident? She'd been so concerned about losing Libby and then Heather, but heaven help her, if she lost her husband . . .

Patrick tipped his hat, the lines around his eyes deep with concern. "Hello, Mrs. Doyle."

"What's wrong?" she whispered.

"Is Mr. Doyle home?"

She shook her head, taking a deep breath as his question resonated in her mind. If they were asking about Walter, it meant he wasn't injured. "Not yet." She glanced between the two men. "Why do you ask?"

Patrick shifted on his feet, looking quite uncomfortable. "We have some unpleasant business to discuss with both of you."

She stepped outside to join them on the stoop, the door open behind her. "What sort of business?"

"We need to know where you were on Monday night," Patrick said.

She felt as if the floor had shifted under her. "I was right here, caring for my daughter."

Heather began to cry in the sitting room, and she stiffened as his gaze traveled swiftly over her shoulder, to the cot in the room behind her.

"When did you have another child?"

Her mind raced, trying to put together the pieces of their story. In that split second, she decided to claim Heather as her own.

"In December." She stepped back, forcing her voice to be calm. "She was born a bit sickly, but is recovering quite well."

Turning back inside, she lifted Heather from the crib and straightened the collar on her red-and-white-checkered romper. Then she gently rubbed Heather's back to soothe her as she carried her slowly toward the kitchen. The men on the stoop could wait as she tested the temperature of the formula on her wrist. And processed her thoughts.

Something terrible had happened when Libby disappeared on Monday night. Something that sent her daughter back to bed and Walter into a strange stupor. Something that drove these two policemen to her front door.

The second drop of formula still burned against her skin, but she couldn't keep Patrick and the inspector waiting any longer. It was finally time to introduce her granddaughter to their little world. And find out what Walter and Libby were hiding from her.

As she stepped back over the threshold, Patrick looked down at Heather. "I'd offer a toast if the circumstances weren't so dire."

Maggie bounced Heather on her hip. "What are the circumstances, Constable?"

The inspector scribbled something in a notepad, and she prayed Patrick wouldn't ask her about Libby. That he would assume she was still away.

The inspector stepped up beside Patrick. "Where was your husband on Monday?"

She tested the bottle again, and the formula was cool enough now for Heather to drink. She held the bottle up to Heather's lips until she latched onto the nipple.

"Mrs. Doyle?" The inspector persisted. "We need to know where your husband was on Monday night."

Maggie tried to keep the bottle steady. "I suppose it would depend on the time."

"The entire evening."

She pressed her lips together for a moment before she spoke. "After work, he went to Daphne Westcott's home down the hill to borrow some powdered milk."

"Was he gone long?"

"Long enough to get the milk." She took a deep breath. "You can verify with Mrs. Westcott."

"Of course," Patrick said as the inspector made another note on his pad.

She shifted Heather in her arms, her eyes narrowing with her question. "What happened on Monday?"

A glance passed between the men, and she didn't think they were going to tell her. But Patrick began to speak again, his voice somber. "On Tuesday morning, we found Oliver Croft's body on the riverbank in Bibury."

She gasped.

"He went missing the night before."

She felt faint, the doorframe her support as she collapsed back. The baby blanket was draped over her arms, and she prayed neither policeman would notice the trembling under it. "Did someone kill him?"

The inspector clicked his pen. "We're planning to find out precisely what happened."

"That poor family." She pulled Heather closer to her chest. "I should go visit Lady Croft."

"The family left for London this afternoon." Patrick paused, his gaze wandering to the stone wall beside them. "When was the last time you saw the Crofts?"

"I don't know exactly—it's been five or so years, I suppose."

He studied her face. "You used to work for them, didn't you?"

"A long time ago." She forced herself to stand straight even as she prayed that Libby would linger in her bath. And that Walter wouldn't come home yet from work. She had to warn him—

"Did you leave the position on your own accord?" Patrick asked.

"It was a mutual decision between Lady Croft and me."

The inspector lowered his notepad. "One of the house staff said Lady Croft is a difficult employer."

Maggie forced a shrug. "No more difficult than any other I've had."

"The woman said you might hold a grudge against Lady Croft for releasing you from your work there."

She stiffened. "Am I being accused of something?"

"Of course not." Patrick shot a glance at his partner, silencing him. "We're just accumulating the facts. Why did Lady Croft let you go?"

"Their family decided to begin spending most of their year near London instead of staying at Ladenbrooke."

She saw the doubt in the inspector's eyes, but he would not bully her into saying anything that would incriminate her or her family.

"Did you see anything suspicious on Monday?" the inspector asked.

"Not that I can recall, but it's all so shocking. I don't believe I can think straight."

He slipped his notebook back into his pocket. "If you remember anything unusual, please come to the station."

"Of course."

Patrick still didn't ask about Libby, and this time, she was grateful the local police were apathetic about finding her daughter.

She waited by the open door as the men walked down the drive, not wanting to rush to close it. There was no reason to give either man any cause to wonder.

When she finally stepped back inside, she leaned against the wooden panel and slid down to the floor, Heather in her arms. Her recollection of Monday night wasn't nearly as cloudy as she'd tried to portray. But if she was honest . . .

Her mind flashed back to the scene in the alleyway, fifteen years ago. Walter punching Elliot in the face.

Walter might hit Oliver Croft as well, but was he angry enough to kill him?

It was too much to comprehend what might happen when—if—the police began to suspect Walter. Her daughter might be lost to her already. She couldn't lose her husband too.

Walter had been irate over what Oliver had done to Libby—the judge would have to see that. Any father, she hoped, would understand. The judge might have questions about Heather as well and why Maggie had yet to get the required birth certificate. Yet she'd implied—or had she told?—Patrick that she had a baby. If the truth came out about Heather being Libby's child, the police—and the judge—would suspect everything.

For years she'd carefully woven her web, not to trap others so much as to protect herself and Walter and Libby and now Heather. She'd been weaving from that first night she met Elliot in the caves, plaiting a safe cushion around herself and her family, and she wouldn't let anyone unravel it all now.

The door to the steps opened, and her daughter padded into the room. Libby looked down at Maggie and Heather on the floor, her eyes blank. "Who was that?"

Maggie clutched Heather closer to her chest. Did Libby know that Oliver was gone?

She must. And no cure from Daphne, or any doctor for that matter, would take away her pain.

"No one of importance," Maggie said. "Go back to bed now."

Instead of going up the stairs, Libby sat on the bottom step. Her wet hair was tangled, and her cheeks were a bright red. "When will Papa be home?"

"Soon."

"I need him," she whispered.

Maggie lifted the bundle from her lap. "Do you want to hold Heather?"

Libby shook her head.

WALTER COULDN'T SLEEP.

Three months had passed since he'd found Libby and Oliver at the river, but the scene still haunted him. He and Libby hadn't talked about that night. It seemed as if they were two shells living in the same house, both of them empty inside. And both of them needing each other.

In days past, he would retreat with paper and pen to sort through his thoughts, but he couldn't put this in writing.

Sometimes the memory of that night felt like a knife had slashed through his core and ripped out all of his emotions—anger, fear, and even sorrow were all gone. Only his curiosity remained.

He wished he knew what happened that night on the river before he arrived. At first he'd thought Libby had done something to harm Oliver, but as he replayed the scene in his mind, over and over, he couldn't fathom her taking Oliver's life. Libby's grief had sprung from deep inside her, a wellspring of love and loss.

But perhaps there had been some sort of accident. Perhaps Oliver had drunk too much and drowned on his own accord. Still, if the police knew Libby was there, they would suspect she'd done something to injure him.

Maggie had gone to bed an hour ago, but he sat beside the fire, watching the blaze dance as if it longed to break free of the grate casing. With no more coal to feed it, the flames began crumbling into ash.

The police had come twice to their house since they had found Oliver's body, but it seemed they had uncovered nothing to incriminate him or Libby. Walter had lied to them, straight up, saying he hadn't been on the Crofts' property that night. If he told the truth, they would ask why he had gone, and he would have to tell them about Libby.

He could not—would not—tell them that he'd found her in the water with Oliver's body.

After all these years, he finally understood Libby. No matter how hard anyone pressed her to be strong, she'd crumble under an interrogation by the police. And in the courtroom, she'd never be able to defend herself. In her confusion, with a solicitor asking questions, demanding answers, she would break down into a fit of tears. They would pronounce her mentally unfit, and, he feared, guilty.

Since Oliver's death, Libby had disappeared almost completely into herself, wrapped away in the silk threads she'd woven. He wouldn't force her out of the cocoon that kept her heart from being crushed, but he wanted her to thrive inside her shell. And in time, he prayed she would fly again.

He and Maggie had told their friends months ago that Libby's health was fragile. People seemed embarrassed to talk about it, as if they'd known all along she was sick, so they talked about almost anything except what tugged most at Walter's heart.

When the clock chimed midnight, he tried to move quietly upstairs, but the old steps creaked under him. His and Maggie's room was dark, Heather probably asleep beside their bed.

Light crept out from under Libby's closed door, and he hesitated by her bedroom, not sure what to say to her. Still, he knocked.

When she didn't answer, he nudged the door open. Tubes of paint, pencils, and pieces of paper were scattered across the floor, and in the middle of it all, leaning back against her bed, was the girl he'd come to love. For he no longer saw Elliot Bonheur's offspring sitting before him, filling a blank page with color. He saw his daughter, and more than ever before, Libby needed a father to care for her.

She didn't look up, her gaze focused entirely on the paper before her as she drew what looked like a wing. He picked up one of the papers from the floor, and on it was a butterfly, the colors a blending of vibrant yellows and oranges.

He held out the paper. "What's this one called?"

"Golden Shimmer," she said. "She loves the sunlight."

He picked up a picture of a light-purple butterfly with a string of pearls around her neck. "And this one?"

"Lavender Lace. She has the power to heal all sorts of wounds."

He scanned the room, all the pictures on the floor. "Do they each have a name?"

Finally she looked at him, her bright-blue eyes meeting his. "Of course."

And he realized with a pang of sadness that these were Libby's friends for life.

"They are beautiful."

A glint of a smile. "Thank you."

He picked up another butterfly, this one a dark violet shade, a silver streak bleeding across the edge of its wings.

"What is she called?"

"Silver Shadow."

"Does she have a story?"

Libby's smile faded. "She's lost and can't seem to find her way home."

PART FOUR

Maggie and I tried to contain Libby, but we finally resigned ourselves to the fact that we could not cage a butterfly. Our daughter was mesmerized by colors. Light. The Garden of Eden was quite alive in her mind—a place where everything was beautiful again. Where everyone was good.

We tried to shield her wings from sorrow, from the frailties of the human condition, but we couldn't shield her forever. Libby is a wanderer at heart, an artist who doesn't see things like other people. Doctors today might be able to contain her, but back then, we didn't know what to do with a spirit begging to be free.

To cage her would crush her.

To love her, I knew we must set her free.

Maggie was ashamed of her past and—God forgive me—for a long time, I was ashamed of the girl He'd given us as a daughter. Libby made choices I didn't understand. She hurt me and Maggie and many others, but we hurt her as well by trying to mold her into something, someone, she was not.

Some people might think Libby was being selfish for abandoning her baby, and perhaps, in one sense, this is true. But there was also a thread of selflessness through her heart. She knew she couldn't care for a baby so she left her child with two people who could.

The doctors say my days are numbered now. And my mind is beginning to fail.

My one desire is that someday, after I'm gone, Libby and Heather will reconcile. When Libby is ready.

Heather broke Maggie's and my heart when she married a man we didn't know and moved so far away. But I never stopped loving her. I only wanted peace—peace and happiness—for our family, but both were fleeting during my lifetime.

In these final hours, I rely solely on the Scriptures, and I cling to the hope that God has forgiven me of my trespasses. I hope my daughters forgive me as well.

I tried to be a good father to Heather and Libby. Tried to love them both like they were my own. I wish I could have been there to love my great-granddaughter too, but I hope Heather and her daughter will one day know how much I loved them.

The truth, I pray, will bring Libby, Heather, and Ella back together.

Perhaps together the three of them can fly.

34

MAY 1974, WILLOW COTTAGE

Maggie knitted a pair of baby boots while Heather gently set her dolly in the cradle on the back patio. The cottage garden was in full bloom, and the butterflies fluttering around the blossoms reminded her of Libby. She tended the flowers carefully, as if Libby might return to wander among them, but Maggie didn't really expect her daughter to come home. At least not for more than a day or two.

Libby had left again four years ago, in the months after Oliver's death, and only returned once, during a cold spell in the winter of '71. Neither Maggie nor Walter searched for her after that winter, though Maggie suspected that Walter knew exactly where she was. The padlocks between the manor house and their cottage had been removed, and Maggie didn't attempt to find another one since both Libby and the Croft family were gone now.

For the first time in their marriage, she and Walter were focused on their future instead of stuck rummaging around in their past. She was privy to his thoughts, his kind words to both her and Heather. And he finally seemed content as a father to Libby's daughter, for better or worse.

Heather didn't know, would never know, the circumstances that brought her into the world. One hidden blessing in all of the chaos was that Patrick Garland couldn't contain the news about the baby girl he'd discovered at the Doyle's house.

By the time Maggie and Walter went to the courthouse to ask for a birth certificate, it seemed the entire village knew they'd quietly birthed a second daughter. There were whispers, of course, about why they might keep it a secret, but no one seemed to doubt their story.

Some people thought Heather was sickly, like their first daughter, and that Maggie and Walter were trying to hide her like they once had Libby. Others thought Libby might have passed on and Walter and Maggie had spent the winter mourning their loss.

Daphne said she witnessed Heather's birth, and no one questioned her. The only other person who knew the truth was Libby.

Maggie's greatest fear was that one day Libby would change her mind and decide she wanted her baby back. But even before Libby left, it almost seemed as if she no longer recognized the child as hers. Like she would be content, relieved even, if Heather called another woman "Mum."

Heather tugged on the hem of her skirt. "Mummy?"

Maggie lowered her knitting needles. "Yes, love?"

She glanced over the gardens. "Do you want to dance?"

The familiar fear pinged through her, at the worry that Heather might want to dance with the butterflies. "Why don't we sing instead?"

Then Maggie began to sing, her voice low.

Catch a falling star an' put it in your pocket. Never let it fade away.

Heather giggled as Maggie pretended to look in her pockets, searching for the hidden star.

"It's here," Heather said, opening the pocket of her raincoat so Maggie could peak inside. "A pocketful full of starlight."

"Indeed." Maggie shaded her eyes as if the stars might blind her.

"I'll put them back tonight." Heather tilted her head to look up at the sky. "So they won't be lonely."

"They won't be lonely as long as they have you," Maggie said, gently pressing her thumb on Heather's chin to lower her head. "Now off to bed."

"I'm not tired." Heather stretched her arms with her yawn.

"I can see that perfectly well." Maggie patted Heather's pocket. "But the stars are exhausted. It takes a lot of work to shine, and they've been shining for an awfully long time."

Heather looked unconvinced for a moment, but then she smiled. "Can they sleep with me tonight?"

"Hmm, you'd have to be quiet as a mouse."

"I can be quiet," Heather whispered.

"Very good."

Walter stepped out onto the patio, and Heather squealed, rushing toward him. He lifted her, spinning her in his arms, and she flung her head back, her ponytail twirling as she laughed with abandon, as if nothing else in the world mattered to her except being with her daddy.

He set her back down on the patio and knelt beside her. "What have you been doing?"

She opened her pocket. "Catching stars."

Maggie saw the concern in his eyes, at the world of make-believe that seemed to steal away the mind of their older daughter. "Other kids like to catch stars before bed too," she said, trying to reassure him.

"Bedtime, is it?" he asked, checking his watch.

Heather shook her head. "Not for a hundred more hours."

He lifted his hands, curling his fingers into claws. "No one can escape the bedtime bear."

He didn't look the least bit scary, but Heather played their game. Squealing again, she ran into the house this time, her dad growling behind her.

Then she heard Walter and Heather singing through the open window. One of Elvis Presley's songs instead of Perry Como.

Maggie lingered outside. As the stars began to emerge, she wondered again where Libby was tonight. She could wish on one of the stars, but she wasn't sure what to wish—for Libby to come home and join in their fun or for her to stay far away.

Her gaze fell to the stone that lined their property, and she hated this—the feeling of a wall erected between her and Libby. It was a safe wall, to protect Heather, but in her heart, she didn't want anything to separate her and either of her daughters.

A BUTTERFLY FLUTTERED FROM FLOWER to flower in the old garden, gracing the silvery-blue tips of the crocuses and what remained of the icy-white petals of the lady's prized tulips. The yellow strands on the butterfly's wings shimmered in the fading light, and Libby watched the creature in its journey, mesmerized by the graceful rise and fall of its dance.

Her arms outstretched, Libby twirled around like she had as a girl, embracing the last rays of sunlight. Here in this garden, she was as free as the butterfly. Here she didn't have to hide.

The butterfly climbed above the flowers and soared toward the lily pond. Beyond the pond were more flowers, hundreds of them, and then the trees.

Soon the butterfly would curl up under a rock or leaf and

rest for the night, hiding in the darkness, alone and vulnerable until the sun powered her wings again at dawn.

Libby trailed the creature around the pond to see where it would land. If the night stayed warm, she might curl up beside the butterfly to rest, but not now. She no longer had to hide in these gardens.

Soon the moonlight would glaze the paths with gold, and she would explore for hours, enveloped in the shadows and the light.

Near the maze, a patch of larkspur swayed, and Libby stepped closer, curious as to why the leaves danced with no breeze. The butterfly disappeared in the trees beyond the flowers, but she no longer watched the creature. Her eyes were on the little person trying to hide among the stalks.

A girl watched her through the petals and leaves, as if she thought Libby couldn't see her. Her blonde hair was brushed back into two pigtails, and the pastel greens and pinks in her cape blended with the colors of spring. The girl was four, Libby knew that, and already she loved the lady's gardens too.

She leaned down, and the girl's eyes grew wide when she realized the woman had found her hiding place.

"Go home," Libby whispered.

The girl shook her head and then stood, her pigtails inches above the blossoms.

Libby tilted her head, studying the worry in the girl's eyes. "Are you lost?"

This time the girl nodded, and a tear slipped from her eyes, splashing the petals.

"We all get lost," Libby said softly as she reached out her hand. "I can take you back."

The girl studied the outstretched hand for a moment before

she took it. Then Libby guided the child back over the bridge, to the gate in the stone wall.

"Heather?" a woman called on the other side.

"Mummy!" the girl shouted back, pulling her hand away before she rushed home. Libby stepped toward the gate. Her chest ached, but her gaze held steady as she watched the child pass through the cottage gardens, to the woman with the outstretched arms. She'd made her choice. The right choice. Still, sometimes it hurt as badly as the night she delivered the baby.

Turning swiftly, she hurried back through the formal garden and down the terraces, past the maze and old folly until she reached the riverbank.

Libby didn't mind being alone, but she hated the feeling of loneliness that rooted itself in her soul. She hurried through the trees, to the family cemetery on the hill above the riverbank, the old and new tombstones hemmed together by iron stitches on the fence.

She crept through the open gate and collapsed onto the grass below one of the stones. A tear slipped from her eye as her fingers traced the name on the grave.

Oliver

He had understood her. He'd known why she must dance among the flowers and their butterflies. He'd known why she must be free.

But here in the cemetery she never danced.

Sometimes she wondered about that night when she'd found Oliver in the river, wondered if she could have saved his life. Sometimes she thought it was all a terrible nightmare and he would return home one day soon. Sometimes when she was dancing, she even pretended he was still alive.

But here she couldn't pretend.

Pain cramped her chest again. Memories both sweet and

painful spread like wildfire through her. Her heart had been shredded into pieces, and she'd buried the remnants here with Oliver when she'd said good-bye.

No one could make her leave Ladenbrooke during the summers, with her butterflies and her memories.

This is where she belonged.

35

In the few hours Heather had slept, she'd dreamed the haunting dream of her youth, wandering the ruins of an overgrown garden, holding the hand of a woman with copper hair and a pale-blue dress. But when she woke, all she could think about was Christopher.

For too many years, she'd been afraid he would reject Ella, like she thought he'd rejected her, but if Brie and Mrs. Westcott were telling her the truth, he hadn't rejected her at all.

When she finally talked to her daughter, Ella had cried over the phone. Instead of being angry, Ella thanked her for her honesty. Then she'd told her to get herself to Oxford ASAP and have tea with the professor.

She was done keeping this secret. Someone else could restore the cottage, but no one else could restore her relationships for her.

Christopher had invited her to meet him for lunch in Oxford, so she drove east even though everything within her screamed to turn south, back to the airport and Portland, to stability and the safe shell she'd constructed around her heart.

But this was no longer about just her. It was about Christopher and Ella as well.

He met her at a car park near the edge of town, dressed in

jeans, a brown tweed jacket with a tie, and sunglasses. Confidence, kindness even, replaced the frustration she'd seen in his face when she'd surprised him at his mother's house.

"Did my mum tell you about Libby?" he asked.

She nodded.

"Seems like we have a lot to talk about."

He led her past massive stone buildings and formidable iron gates, crowded tearooms and quaint bookshops, fields of bluebells in ancient churchyards. It was a town of fairy tales, he said, of hobbits and wizards, of talking lions and one brave mouse. Stories where good always conquered evil.

As they walked, she almost asked about Adrienne, but his current relationships weren't any of her business. The truth was her business, and she'd withheld it for way too long.

Jeffery had known she was pregnant before they married—and he'd known the baby wasn't his—but he was a gambling man and decided to take a shot at becoming a father and husband at the same time. She'd gambled as well, hoping she could succeed at marriage for the sake of her child, even when her heart belonged to another.

Unfortunately, they both lost their gamble.

She'd justified what she was doing—after all, Christopher had been with another woman—but she had wronged Ella, Jeffery, and Christopher in the process.

As she walked alongside Christopher, better memories flooded back to her. The years that he had been her confidante when she returned from school each summer. He'd loved her and supported her and asked her to marry him so they would never be apart. She remembered being afraid back then that it was all a lie. That he didn't really love her as he said he did. Her mum's deception about seeing him with Britney was simply confirmation.

She prayed it wasn't too late to repair some of the rips and stains in her past after all. With honesty and humility instead of wheat paste and bleach. She prayed Christopher would forgive her like Ella had done.

He directed her through the gates of one of the colleges, past the perfectly trimmed lawn and stone academic buildings, back into a quiet park with periwinkle clematis climbing a medieval wall. In the middle of the lawn was a pool of water with a small fountain, surrounded by tall grasses and creamy coral-tipped tulips.

They sat on a wooden bench, her handbag between them, both of them watching the statue of a boy in the fountain, water trickling over the book in his hands.

"Did you tell Adrienne we were meeting today?"

"No—"

"I don't want to come between you and her."

He crossed his arms. "I'm afraid it's too late for that."

She sighed. "I'm sorry, Christopher."

"Don't be," he said. "Adrienne and I were never meant to be anything more than friends. According to her, I'm terribly dull."

"I don't believe that," she said with a laugh.

"My wife used to tell me that too when I refused to come out of my study."

"I read you were married."

His eyebrows slid up above his sunglasses. "You read it?"

"I—" She stuffed her phone into her handbag. "I looked up your profile on the Oxford website."

He smiled.

"There's something I need to tell you." She fidgeted with the strap of her handbag. "Something I should have told you a long time ago."

He lifted his sunglasses, and the blue in his eyes seemed to swallow her. "We both have a lot to say."

She looked back out at the pool. "I knew you came to visit me once in London, but I couldn't see you."

"Why not?"

She looped the strap around her hand, her eyes on her lap. "I was five months' pregnant."

When she glanced back at him, his eyes were wide. "Jeffery's baby?"

"No." She paused, breathing in courage before she spoke again. "I was pregnant with your daughter."

His mouth dropped open.

She hadn't known what to expect when she looked back up at him. Anger, perhaps. Dismay. Ridicule. Instead there were tears in his eyes.

"Her name is Ella."

He slipped his sunglasses back on, shifting his focus toward the fountain. "I have a daughter?"

"I should have told you both before—"

"Did Jeffery know?"

"He did, and he thought it would be grand to be a father. We married in London, not long after I told him, and he tried to be a good dad. But we were both so young, and he hadn't bargained on having a child with colic and a wife who wasn't nearly as fond of riding motorcycles as he'd hoped." She paused. "And a wife who'd left part of her heart on the other side of the pond."

Christopher looked at her, but she kept talking before he could respond.

"Ella was six when he filed for divorce, and the moment it was final, he disappeared from our lives." She leaned back against the bench. "I should have told her about you when she was a teenager. . . ."

Two mallards landed on the water, and she and Christopher sat in silence, watching them paddle across the pond. She didn't want to pressure Christopher into becoming a father now, only wanted him to know what happened. Still, she had no doubt that Ella would love Christopher, and if he was willing to meet her, he would love her as well.

"What's Ella like?" he asked.

"She's funny and kind and beautiful both inside and out. She's terribly persistent and way too curious—like you used to be."

He flashed a smile. "Still am."

"She got married in February to a man who adores her."

He removed his sunglasses. "For so many years, I wondered what happened to us," he said, his gaze as intense as his voice. "I never cheated on you."

"I know that now. . . ."

"I came by your house that night to pick you up for the dance, but your mum said you had gone without me. I went to the dance, but couldn't find you there either and I wondered then if I had done something wrong.

"I don't know who you saw me with when you came to Oxford, but I wasn't interested in anyone else except you. It wasn't until the next weekend that I found out our relationship was over. When I arrived home, my mum gave me back your ring, saying you'd changed your mind. I took the bus to London that afternoon to find out what happened."

Her stomach rolled as she listened. Without her mum's story, Heather might have married her high school sweetheart and raised Ella in England near both sets of her grandparents.

Of course, her parents didn't discover she was pregnant until after she and Jeffery eloped so her mum didn't know that Christopher was Ella's father. At least, she didn't think her mum knew. Either way, she should have been honest with her parents as well.

Christopher shifted his knees, turning toward her. "I would have married you, Heather. Even sooner if I'd known about the baby."

She'd wondered for years what might have happened if she had told him. "I'm afraid it would have ended badly, just like Jeffery and I. Our mothers may not have handled it well, but they were also right—we weren't ready for marriage."

"I guess it's impossible to say now."

"Please forgive me," she said, looking over at him. "I should have told you I was pregnant, and I—I should have given you the opportunity back then to tell me what happened."

He watched the fountain for another moment before turning back toward her. "I forgive you—on one condition."

"What's that?"

"That you forgive me as well."

A hummingbird flittered above the tulip blossoms, batting tremendous power through its tiny wings. "You didn't know about Ella."

He paused. "I should have kept seeking out the truth until I heard you say it was over."

"It was never over in my heart."

He studied her so intensely that she felt like a giddy teenager again, all wrapped up in silly emotions. Emotions she still didn't know how to process.

"Perhaps it's not too late," he said simply.

A pang echoed through her heart, and she wished she could subdue it. She regretted what she had done in the past, but she wasn't certain she wanted to open up her heart again to the man beside her. Her life in Oregon was stable. As subdued as her heart had been until Christopher reappeared in her life.

The look in his eyes reminded her of their times together so long ago, and for a moment, she thought he might kiss her.

She hopped up from the bench, her nerves frayed. They were supposed to eat lunch together, but she wasn't hungry anymore. "I'm going to London this afternoon."

When he stood beside her, she could feel the warmth from his skin, so terribly close to her.

"Would you mind if I join you?" he asked.

Reluctantly, she agreed.

CHRISTOPHER DRUMMED THE STEERING WHEEL of Heather's rental car as they waited at a stoplight. He'd always wanted to be a father, but most men had eight or nine months to process becoming one. He already had a daughter, alive and well in Arizona, and he wasn't quite certain what to do about it.

How was he supposed to step in as a father to someone who was already twenty-five?

As they drove south, toward the suburbs on the other side of London, Heather told him all about Ella, and then she told him the little she'd found out about Libby. He was just discovering that he was a father while Heather was discovering that she'd been birthed by a woman she'd never met. A woman who disappeared soon after Heather was born.

Heather was determined to find out what happened to Libby, starting with the Croft family, who lived in Woldingham. On their drive south, she telephoned the number Britney had given her, but no one answered it.

She lowered the phone to her lap before speaking to him again. "How long were you and my father friends?"

"About twenty years," he said as the traffic slowed. "Your dad and I had a lot in common. We both loved to research and write and talk about the meaning behind Scripture. We both lost our wives, and we shared a common bond that ran deep."

"What did you share?"

He glanced over. "We both loved you, Heather."

Her gaze skirted toward the window before looking back at him again. "Did he ever talk to you about Libby?"

He shook his head.

"But he wrote a lot—"

"He wrote incessantly in his journals until he had his stroke. The writing was life-giving to him and without it, he declined rapidly."

She mulled over his words. "The retirement home mailed me his things, but they never sent me any journals."

"Perhaps they still have them."

Drizzle dampened the windshield as they drove into the village of Woldingham, and searched for street signs. They found the Croft residence along a row of stately brick homes, each of them dripping with old money and rain. The entrance was carved out of a lofty hedge, and Christopher drove under the hedge, into the gravel courtyard.

He nodded toward concrete steps that led up to a portico. "Do you want me to go up with you?"

She hesitated before agreeing. "I would like that."

As they stepped away from the car, he held out his hand, and she took it.

The man who opened the front door had short, brown hair and looked to be about twenty. His eyes piqued with curiosity when she introduced herself as a neighbor, living in the cottage next to Ladenbrooke Manor.

"Do Lord and Lady Croft still live here?" she asked.

Instead of inviting them inside, the young man joined them on the portico. "My grandmother passed away years ago, but my grandfather is still alive."

"I'm only trying to find—" Heather paused. "My sister and the Croft's son used to be friends. I thought perhaps Lord Croft might have an idea where she went."

"Which son?" the man asked.

"Oliver."

His eyebrows arched. "No one ever talks about Oliver."

"I believe my sister knew Oliver quite well."

"I never heard my grandparents talk about their friends in Bibury, but my grandmother loved the gardens at Ladenbrooke."

"So did my mother," Heather said. "Have you ever been there?"

"Only once," he replied. "My aunt Sarah is responsible for maintaining the house now."

"How many children did Lord and Lady Croft have after Oliver?"

"Two more sons. The oldest one is my father."

She glanced back toward the door. "Could you ask Lord Croft about Libby Doyle?"

"I'm sorry—" He lowered his voice. "Unfortunately my grandfather has turned into a rather grumpy old man."

Christopher wondered if Heather might tell the man she suspected Lord Croft was her grandfather as well, but instead she slipped him a business card. "Please let me know if he'd ever like to talk about her."

He glanced down at the card. "I'll give your information to him, but I don't suspect he'll call."

"Could I get the telephone number for your aunt Sarah?"

He pondered her question for a moment before pulling a mobile phone from his back pocket. Then he glanced down at Heather's business card. "I'll text it to you right now."

She smiled at him. "You should come back to visit Ladenbrooke."

His return smile was courteous, but Christopher guessed the young man preferred the city life much more than the countryside.

"What now?" Christopher asked after they climbed back in the car.

She studied the light in the upstairs window of the house before turning back to him. "I'm calling Sarah Croft on the drive home."

Christopher glanced at the clock. It was seven and they were almost three hours from Oxford with the traffic, but he might never have this opportunity again. "How would you like to have dinner in London?"

"Tonight?"

He nodded.

She eyed the clock as well, a smile returning to her face. "Are you asking me out on a date?"

"I suppose I am."

She tilted her head. "Then I suppose I'll accept your invitation."

36

JUNE 1974, WILLOW COTTAGE

Maggie gently pushed the hair out of Heather's eyes, the copper in the strands hidden among the blonde. Just like Libby's hair.

"Mummy?" Heather asked softly, her head resting back on a nest of feather pillows so she could drift off to her own Neverland.

"What is it?"

"I think I saw a ghost."

Maggie leaned closer, wondering at the new game. "Where, darling?"

"In the gardens, on the other side of the wall."

On the other side of the wall.

The words echoed in Maggie's mind, and she felt faint for a moment. But she fought hard to regain her strength, for Heather's sake. "Are you certain it was a ghost?"

"I don't know—it was a woman and she wore a pretty blue dress."

Relief washed over Maggie that her oldest daughter was safe, but as soon as the wave passed, anger roared within her—anger at Libby on one hand for running away and on the other hand, for not running far enough.

Libby was almost twenty now, and Maggie missed her daughter, desperately at times, the pangs of sorrow acute when she remembered the joy that she'd brought into their lives when she was younger, reflecting color and beauty into this old cottage. And the sorrow was fresh at the thought of her roaming the gardens next door, not coming home to the place where she was loved.

But then again, if she did knock on their back door, Maggie wasn't certain what she would do. Her greatest sorrow was losing her daughter, but it now warred against her greatest fear—losing Heather.

What if Libby returned to reclaim her child?

One day she wanted Libby and Heather to reconcile, when Heather was much older, but if Libby came back now—Maggie feared it would shatter everything they'd built.

Every night, she prayed that God would protect Libby's body, mind, and soul. And she knew now that she would never be able to tame—or contain—her daughter. Her visits, Maggie feared, would be much more painful than her disappearance.

It almost seemed as if Libby wasn't meant to belong in a family, like she was meant to fly alone.

She'd read an article recently about the Monarch butterflies. The Monarchs flew alone during the day, but they roosted in groups at night. Ultimately, when winter was upon them, they sought companionship from other Monarchs, clustering together in a warmer climate. They flew north again in the spring, but only a few had the strength to fly all the way home.

Heather liked to fly, but unlike Libby, she always flew back to their cottage. In fact, Heather seemed to take great pleasure in being their daughter. She held her and Walter's hands and made them laugh, and each night before bed, she kissed Walter on his stubbly cheek.

Contentment wafted through their house now like the subtle, soothing scent of wisteria, rooted deep in the soil of delight. Not only were she and Walter happy together, they were building this common bond to love and care for their granddaughter.

They never talked about the night Oliver died, and it was just as well. Together they seemed to embrace truth in their lives now, staying far away from the make-believe worlds that Libby used to create, worlds that had left their daughter unsatisfied with reality. She and Walter stayed firmly within the pleasant walls of the reality they'd created for themselves.

"Perhaps she wasn't a ghost," Heather said, leaning forward as if she had a grand secret. "Perhaps she was a fairy."

In that moment, Maggie decided it was best to play along. "She could be one of the falling stars from your pocket."

Heather's eyes grew wide. "Really?"

Maggie brushed Heather's hair back over her shoulders. "I think she slid down the moonlight just to visit you."

"Maybe," Heather said, and then she smiled. "Or maybe she's really a butterfly. She said I could fly with her—"

Maggie's heart lurched, and her voice quaked when she spoke again. "You mustn't go back into the gardens."

Her eyes grew wide. Alarmed. "Why not?"

She searched for a reason, any reason, to convince Heather to stay away. She didn't want to frighten her, yet she needed her to be scared. "A boy died at Ladenbrooke, when you were just a baby."

"How did he die?"

She took a deep breath. "He did something he should not have done."

"Maybe she was his angel, coming to look for him."

Maggie shook her head. "There's nothing anyone can do to help him."

Heather seemed to contemplate her words. "But she took care of me when I couldn't find my way back."

Maggie leaned toward her, nudging Heather's chin up so she could look in her eyes. "Angels fly away sometimes," she explained. "And they don't always return."

Heather looked as if she didn't believe her. "But butterflies come home."

Maggie's eyes roamed toward the windows, to the gardens out back. "Not all butterflies," she whispered.

"I won't go again, Mummy."

Maggie kissed her forehead. "I want you to always fly home."

WALTER LIFTED THE HANDLE TO the latch and stepped into the gardens that were becoming overgrown with all manner of weeds. Henry did his best to maintain the manor house along with the gardens in the absence of the Croft family, but last Walter saw the man at the post office, the head gardener said he didn't think Lord or Lady Croft were ever coming back. Walter didn't know if they still officially employed Henry as their gardener, but the man had taken on the role of caretaker in their absence.

It was impossible, though, for one man to maintain all the buildings at Ladenbrooke along with almost a hundred acres of property.

Henry continued to plant vegetables, and Walter suspected that he knew Libby was eating the fruit in the orchards and the vegetables from his garden during the warmer months. He also suspected Henry might be leaving a door unlocked in the vacant manor house so Libby could spend some time indoors.

Maggie didn't know Libby had returned, and while he wasn't as practiced as his wife at keeping secrets, he tried to harbor this one. Maggie still worried that Libby might take Heather, and if she knew Libby had returned—

He set down the brown bag with the bread he'd purchased in town.

During the summer months, he bought extra cheese, bread, and salami from the market at night and set it near the gate. The food always vanished, but he rarely saw Libby until the days grew cold again. Then he bought her a bus ticket down to Kent to stay with his mother.

Walter's stepfather worked for the government, and he often traveled for weeks at a time. Granny Doyle welcomed Libby's company and set up a studio in the basement so she could paint. Every spring, his mother would accompany Libby back to Ladenbrooke and spend a few days playing with Heather at their cottage, though she never told Maggie about her houseguest during the winter months.

Maggie rarely talked about Libby, but he knew she thought about her every day. Her indifference was her way of coping with the loss of the daughter she would have done anything to save.

He circled the gardens once, just in case he might see Libby, but like most of the garden creatures, she remained hidden among the flowers.

37

Christopher took Heather to an Italian restaurant for dinner, an upscale place overlooking the River Thames. The lights of Big Ben flickered in the distance even as the blue lights from the Ferris wheel—the London Eye—circled slowly above the water.

She set her cell phone above her plate, in case Sarah Croft returned her call tonight, but as she sat next to the window, sipping white wine, she wasn't thinking about anything except the man in front of her. Christopher seemed to be a rock, unwavering in the face of her revelation while she was still processing it all.

It was too late to change the past, but perhaps he was right. Perhaps it wasn't too late for their future.

She rotated the wineglass. "Tell me about your wife."

He leaned back in his chair, his gaze traveling to the window before returning to her. "Julianna was a pianist and quite devoted to her talent. I loved hearing her play whether it was at a concert hall or at home. And she loved to laugh often, about everything except her music."

"Did you learn to play an instrument?"

He shook his head. "In my free time, I was either rowing or reading."

"But you loved her."

"Very much."

She looked out the window as well, thinking about what a blessed woman Julianna Westcott was to be loved like that. "I'm sorry you lost her."

He took a sip of his wine. "Did you leave a boyfriend back in Portland?"

Her mind flashed to Nick, and she realized that he hadn't texted her in days, not even to ask about artwork. "Only friends who happen to also be boys."

He smiled. "What will you do if you find Libby?"

"I don't know. Clearly she doesn't want to be a mother."

"Then perhaps you should treat her exactly how your parents intended," he said, setting down his wineglass. "As a sister."

She mulled over his words. If Libby was still alive, would she want a sister?

He cleared his throat. "It's getting late."

She checked her watch and saw it was almost eleven.

"Do you want me to drive you back to Bibury when we finish dinner or should we find a hotel?"

She jolted with the question, wondering what he meant until he held up two fingers. "We'll get two rooms."

She looked back at the city lights. It seemed so surreal to think about spending the night in London with Christopher Westcott, even if they had separate rooms. "Can we leave first thing in the morning?" she asked.

He nodded. "When are you planning to fly back to Portland?"

"In a few weeks—after I find out what happened to Libby. And the cottage is ready to be put on the market."

He leaned closer to her, the strength in his eyes returning. "I think you should stay longer."

Her cell phone pounded with its drumbeat, and she jumped at the interruption, spilling wine from her glass onto the tablecloth. "It's Ella."

He smiled. "I'll pretend not to listen."

"Hi there," she said as she answered the phone, trying to act casual even as her heart raced.

"Did I wake you up?" Ella asked.

"No—" She glanced back over at Christopher.

Ella sighed. "You're sorting through more boxes, aren't you?"

"Not exactly."

"On a hot date?"

She hesitated. "Sort of."

The silence on the other end made her laugh.

"You did it, didn't you?" Ella said, her voice filled with wonder.

"It's a long story."

"Are you having tea together?"

She glanced at Christopher again. "More like a glass of wine."

Ella squealed so loud that Christopher laughed across the table. "And here I was all worried that you would be lonely when I left, but you aren't lonely at all."

"We are—" Heather paused, not altogether certain what they were doing. "We're just getting reacquainted."

"Tell him I approve."

She clutched the phone tighter. "I most definitely will not."

Christopher flashed her a sly look. "Tell her, I'm glad she approves."

Heather glared at him as she continued speaking to Ella. "I have a lot to tell you. Later."

"And I have something to tell both of you," Ella said.

"Both of us?"

"Yes." Ella paused. "Come December, you're going to be grandparents."

Heather emptied her glass.

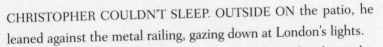

CHRISTOPHER COULDN'T SLEEP. OUTSIDE ON the patio, he leaned against the metal railing, gazing down at London's lights.

The boutique hotel had two rooms available for the night, right next to each other. With a private door connecting them. He'd thought coming here would be a better option than trying to resist temptation at either of their homes, but he felt like a reckless teenager again—one who needed to get control of himself.

Mrs. Doyle had taken matters into her own hands to separate them long ago, before Heather found out she was pregnant, but what would have happened to him and Heather if they had married? He hoped he wouldn't have left like Jeffery had done. Freedom, he'd discovered, was overrated, but back then, he'd craved freedom more than anything.

He'd gladly given up his freedom when he married Julianna. Then he bitterly gave it up when she became sick—not angry with her but furious at the brain tumor that first stole away her ability to play her piano and then stole her life. Julianna had said she wanted him to marry again one day, but even though he'd dated, he couldn't imagine marrying anyone else except—

There was a knock on the door between their rooms, and he hesitated before inching it open.

Heather was on the other side, dressed in the T-shirt and shorts they'd bought at a tourist shop. Her hair was pulled back in a ponytail; her makeup, washed away; and she looked beautiful.

She didn't try to step into his room. "Ella just sent me a text. She wishes she hadn't told you about the baby."

He leaned against the dresser. "Why shouldn't she tell me?"

"She's afraid you're freaking out."

He laughed. "Tell her I'm not freaking out nor will I."

At least not about her baby.

"It's a lot at once, isn't it?" she asked.

"I don't know how to be a father, much less a grandfather, but I'd sure like to learn."

The city lights flickered across her face as she smiled, and his heart did that strange flip-flop thing it used to do when he was young. When all reasoning began to drain away. "You should have slipped me a note under the door," he said.

"Were you asleep?"

He shook his head.

She leaned against the doorpost. "I can't sleep either."

He ached to take her into his arms, to love her like he had long ago. But if he was going to do this, he wanted to do it right this time. "You're killing me, Heather."

She smiled up at him, and he saw a hint of teasing in her eyes. "Weapons of the heart?"

He waved her away, inching the door closed again. "Go back from where you came."

She held up her phone. "Maybe we should text?"

He groaned. "I don't think we should do anything until morning." Then he propped the door back open a few inches so she could hear him. "If you knock again, I'm not answering."

"And if you knock, I won't answer either," she said before closing—and locking—the door.

HEATHER HUMMED AS SHE DRESSED. The sun wasn't quite up, but she couldn't remain in bed another moment. Something had shifted in her during the night. She was going to be a grandmother, and it seemed as if Christopher wanted to step into Ella's life as well as into the life of their grandbaby.

She was no longer alone.

Gone was all the bitterness, her fears dissipating as she embraced this new day. Whatever it held for her.

She'd been up until late, long after she'd locked the door between her and Christopher. He'd been the quintessential gentleman, and she was glad he remained strong because she didn't feel as if she had any strength left within her.

Christopher met her at eight thirty in the lobby for eggs, sausage, and grilled mushrooms. She smiled as she poured English breakfast tea from the pot. Finally she and Christopher were having tea together—Ella's heart might fail if she knew they were having it over breakfast. In London.

They didn't talk about last night, focusing instead on their day ahead. "I have a lunch meeting in Oxford," he said. "If you want to drive to Bibury, I can take a bus home."

She shook her head. "I'm going to Oaken Holt Care Home this morning to check on my dad's journals."

They stuffed their few things into plastic bags and checked out of the hotel to walk down the block, toward the lot where he'd parked her car. When they rounded the corner, she saw a sign for *Bridget's Bookshop*, the window display filled with teddy bears and colorful children's books.

Christopher pointed up at the sign. "I want to buy something special for Matthew and Ella's baby."

"Baby won't be arriving for another seven months."

"But it's good to read to babies, isn't it?" he asked. "While they're still in the womb."

She smiled at his enthusiasm. "I've heard that."

"Then my grandchild needs a good book, from a British author."

"What's wrong with American authors?"

He rolled his eyes, as if she should know. "I can't send her a book written by a Yankee."

Heather laughed. "I'm sure Ella would love a British book, especially if it's from you."

Standing at the bookstore counter was a young woman with bright-purple streaks through her black hair, the name *Bridget* on her nametag. Christopher walked up to her. "Do you have a copy of *Autumn Dancer*?" he asked.

Heather stopped walking, and everything within her seemed to freeze at his question.

For a moment she couldn't say anything at all.

"I just received ten copies," Bridget said, waving them toward the children's section. "But half of them will be gone by the end of the day."

Heather reached for Christopher's arm to stop him. "What did you say?"

"I want to buy a special book—"

"The name of the book," she prodded. "What was the title?"

"*Autumn Dancer*," he repeated as he turned to follow Bridget. "It's my niece's favorite book and I think the writing is quite brilliant as well."

The woman guided them past another display, this one with farm animals, then by an entire wall devoted to *Fancy Nancy*. If she'd been thinking clearly, Heather would have pointed out that

Fancy Nancy came to London via New York, but her mind was all jumbled as she stared at a section with sparkly butterflies hanging on the wall.

Bridget walked her fingers along a row of brightly colored spines until she reached a red one and plucked it off the shelf. "Here you go," she said as she held out the book to Christopher.

As he took it, Heather reached over and traced the glittery orange and reds that were splashed on the hardcover, the shimmering butterfly in the center that looked like it might indeed dance off the confines of the page. At the bottom was the name of the author.

L.D. Walters

The name tumbled in her mind. L.D.—Libby. *Libby Doyle.* And Walters—perhaps for her father's name?

Libby's Book of Butterflies

"Who is L.D. Walters?" she whispered.

Bridget tilted her head, a quizzical look in her eyes.

"She's not from England," Christopher explained to the woman.

"No one seems to know who the author is," Bridget answered her question with a shrug. She pulled two more books off the shelf—*Moonlit Fairy* and *Lavender Lace*. "The publisher says it's a British woman, but they won't say anything else about her. There have been rumors that the books are really written by a man, and that's why the author is incognito.

"Others say she's really an American, pretending to be British—not that there is anything wrong with being American—but in the country known for Harry Potter and Peter Rabbit, we pride ourselves on our children's authors." She took a quick breath. "Quite honestly, it doesn't matter one whit to me who's writing about the butterflies. All the books in the series sell like crazy here."

Christopher handed her the book and Heather held it lightly, reverently. “How many are in the series?” she asked.

“Twelve of them,” Bridget explained. “Each one about a different daughter of the Butterfly King.”

Heather opened the cover and began to read the story of the Autumn Dancer—the places she visited in her garden, the friends she met. The playful dancer was free from the cares of life until a motley gang of bees imprisoned her for stealing their nectar, and she couldn’t dance anymore. The king and his army had to rescue her before the winter snow.

Heather put the book down on a table and the room felt as if it had wings as well, tilting and looping in circles around her.

Mrs. Westcott said that Libby couldn’t write, but at one time, Walter Doyle had loved to put stories on paper. And according to Christopher, her father wrote a lot in his last years.

Perhaps Libby was not only alive. Perhaps she was doing quite well.

38

MARCH 1992, WILLOW COTTAGE

Broken bones he could fix, but the doctor said it was too late to stop the internal bleeding in Maggie's vital organs. Walter had found her in the ditch going down into the village, after their car had slid on the ice, and she'd been conscious enough to tell him that she didn't want to go to the hospital.

But he hadn't listened. He borrowed the Westcotts' estate car and drove her straight into Cirencester. When the doctors said there was nothing they could do to save her life, Walter had brought her home, and in Maggie's final hours, Daphne labored alongside him to care for her.

Walter sat by Maggie's bed that last night, holding her hand and wiping the sweat off her brow. "I need to know something," she said, her breathing labored.

"Ask anything you want."

"Did you kill Oliver Croft?"

He shook his head.

She struggled to take another breath, the pain almost paralyzing her. "Libby cared about him."

"I know." He stroked her hand, hoping to settle her heart.

"And I know you were caring for Libby."

He dipped the rag back into the cool water and dabbed her forehead.

"I've done too many things wrong, Walter." She stopped again for a breath. "I need to make it right."

"It's okay—"

"With you and Libby," she continued. "And with Heather and Christopher. They belonged together, but I was afraid. I—I would have done anything to keep her heart from being broken."

"I know you would have." He carefully brushed her hair. "Heather made her own choices, just like Libby made hers."

"Do you know where Libby is?"

He shook his head. He couldn't tell her now that Libby left after his mother passed away and never returned.

"Please find her. Tell her how much I loved her."

"I will," he said, though he wasn't certain how he'd find her.

"You cared for me, even when I wasn't the woman you needed me to be."

He kissed her forehead. "Quiet, darling."

"Thank you for rescuing me . . . and for rescuing our girls."

This time he gently squeezed her hand, tears welling in his eyes. "I need to thank you, Maggie."

"I didn't do anything—"

"Thank you for loving me even when I was hard to love."

She seemed to search for her breath, and when she found it, she spoke again. "Walter?"

He kissed her cheek.

"You need to find Libby," she said, "and you need to do something else."

There was nothing else he wanted to do, but still he listened.

"I want you to start writing again."

"I don't have anything to write about."

She smiled at him one last time. "You should write about butterflies."

HEATHER HAD BROUGHT ELLA HOME for Maggie's memorial service. It was too late for Heather to say good-bye to her mother, and Walter thought it was for the best. She was happily married, living in the state of Oregon with her husband and beautiful daughter. There was no reason to muddle her happiness with the truth about Libby and much too late for Maggie to make amends.

He hadn't told his wife, even in her last hours, that he knew the storm back in Clevedon hadn't tried to blow her away. She'd planned to go willingly with the wind. He was glad, so very glad, she'd lived, and that she chose to give Libby life as well.

It was quiet in the house now without Maggie or their girls. Too quiet.

He padded down into the basement and began sorting through the boxes that Maggie piled together after Libby had left, to make room for Heather and her things.

For the first time in years, his desire to write was returning, welling within him. The words swarmed together, all jumbled. Order is what they needed. On paper.

But the words inside him weren't like the stories he'd written back in Clevedon. He wanted—needed—to tell a different kind of story.

Inside Maggie's boxes, he found exactly what he was looking for: the many pictures of Libby's friends.

He sat on the step and pulled out the empty tablet from his front pocket, the notebook he'd been carrying for years in case inspiration struck. Then he picked up the first picture, studying it for a moment before he began to write.

This butterfly likes to explore in the gardens before the sun sets, in the hour when no one can see her dance.

He scratched out his words and tried again.

Autumn Dancer flies in the cool of the evening, in the minutes before the trailing sunlight disappears into darkness.

Better, but that still wasn't quite right. Underneath he tried one more time.

Autumn Dancer flutters among the flowers, chasing the last rays of sunlight until her haven is swallowed up by the night.

Smiling, he began to scribble more words in the notebook, staying up all night to tell the story of Libby's friend.

39

Heather slid her passport to the attendant across the front desk of Oaken Holt Care Home, and then she signed a form saying she was indeed the daughter of Walter Doyle. The attendant typed her information into Walter's file before scanning the record on his screen.

"This says we mailed his belongings to you in Oregon. Six boxes that contained all the personal things left in his room."

Heather fidgeted in her chair. "I received all the boxes, but there was only clothing and books inside." Dozens of books.

"Were you expecting something else?" the man asked.

She nodded. "His journals."

He glanced down the list of items they'd mailed. "There's nothing here about journals."

"A friend said he kept them on the bookshelf by his bed."

"Let me talk to his nurse."

The attendant stood and stepped back into a room behind the desk. When he returned, he typed something else on his keyboard before facing her.

"The nurse said the journals were gone before he passed away. Apparently, he asked her to mail them to a relative here in Oxford."

Heather's heart pumped faster. "Do you have the address?"

He scanned his computer screen again. Then he wrote something onto a piece of paper and slipped it back across the desk. She glanced down at the street address in Oxford along with an apartment number.

"There's no name of the recipient in our records," he said.

She picked up the paper. "This is perfect."

Christopher said his meeting would be finished by one o'clock, but she didn't wait for him. This was something she needed to do alone.

Instead of driving, Heather walked two miles to what she hoped was Libby's flat, tucked away from the busy shopping and academic districts. Tilting her head back, she looked up at the closed curtains on the second floor.

Was it possible that the woman who'd birthed her lived here in Oxford? If so, what was Heather going to say to her? And what if Libby, like Lord Croft's grandson, turned her away? She'd learned with Jeffery that there was nothing—at least nothing healthy—she could do to control those around her, but she hoped Libby would at least talk with her.

She knocked twice on the door of #16. When no one answered the knock, she turned, disappointed, to descend the steps until she saw a woman emerge from a taxi, onto the sidewalk below the landing. It was the woman she'd seen at the memorial service.

Libby had long, auburn hair that flowed over her shoulders. Instead of blue, she wore an orange sundress today with a floppy straw hat and sandals that laced high up her ankles.

Heather drummed her fingers together as she waited for her birth mother to climb the stairs.

When she finally stepped onto the landing, Libby pressed her lips together, quietly studying Heather's face. "You have Oliver's eyes," she said simply.

"You know who I am?"

Libby took her keys out of the beaded purse looped over her shoulder. "You're my sister."

Heather nodded.

"We used to play together in the gardens, when you were little."

"I remember," Heather said.

"You loved the butterflies." Libby unlocked the door and waved her inside.

Heather followed her through a narrow hallway, to an area meant to be a living space except there were no couches or even a chair on the wooden floor. Instead there was a carpet of splattered paint, a dozen milk crates stuffed with art supplies, a cardboard box topped with paintbrushes, and three easels near the window, each one displaying a painting in various stages of production.

Libby opened up the curtain along the window and natural light poured into the room. Then she picked up a paintbrush and turned toward one of the canvases, staring at the cloth as she spoke. "How did you find me?"

"Dad's retirement home gave me your address."

"Because of his books?" Libby asked.

She nodded. "The nurse said she sent them here."

Libby mixed several colors together on her palette. "Do you want to read them?"

"Yes—but I'd like to know more about Oliver first."

"I loved Oliver," Libby said as she began to dab navy-blue specks of paint at the top of her canvas. "With all my heart."

As if there was nothing else Heather needed to know.

"Can you tell me what happened to him?"

Libby didn't answer her question. "Walter wanted you and I to meet."

"He never told me—" Heather hesitated, not wanting to explain that she'd thought Libby had passed away. "He never told me you lived in Oxford."

She rinsed off her brush and began adding a pale-red color to her picture. "I asked him not to."

"Why didn't you want to meet me?"

When Libby turned toward her, her gaze didn't quite meet Heather's, traveling instead over her shoulder. "Do you still like butterflies?"

Heather blinked. "I suppose."

She unclipped one of the paintings from an easel and replaced it with an empty canvas. Then she handed Heather a brush.

Heather stared at the brush for a moment before dipping it into the paint.

LIBBY CHANGED FROM HER DRESS into a turquoise satin robe with a thin cord belted around her waist, and the two women spent the afternoon painting. The hours reminded Heather of the times she and Ella used to spend together, immersed in their own schoolwork.

Heather quickly realized that painting was Libby's way of keeping herself present in one sense. With her hands busy, Libby's mind seemed to find clarity, slipping back and forth between fantasy and reality, present and the past.

Whenever she stopped, Libby struggled to find herself again.

As they worked together, Heather understood even more why her parents chose to harbor the secret of her birth mother and also why they didn't encourage her own love of art. They were probably terrified she would lose herself as well.

When she finished her painting, Heather inched back to look

at the gray stone of the manor house before her, overlooking a bed of flowers. Libby stepped up behind her, her brush in hand, and Heather moved away as Libby painted the backs of two girls, hand-in-hand, exploring the flower beds together.

"Thank you," she said softly before turning to look at Libby's canvas. She'd painted a young man, standing beside what looked like the ruins of a castle, his brown hair blowing in the wind. His green eyes seemed to pierce through her.

Heather touched the edge of the easel. "He's quite handsome."

Libby stepped forward and ripped down the picture. Then she began to tear it into tiny pieces, scattering the memory of Oliver Croft across the floor.

She looked at Heather, her eyes desperate. "I can't remember what he looked like."

"Perhaps it's more important to remember what he was like on the inside."

Libby sat down on the hardwood, the satin of her robe circling around her. "The lady said he didn't love me, but I know he did. He loved me as much as I loved him."

"Who said Oliver didn't love you?"

"His mother."

Libby picked up the pieces from the floor, holding them to her chest. Heather wanted to ask again what happened the night Oliver died, but she feared if she pried too much, Libby would retreat into the hollows of her mind.

Instead Heather sat down on the paint-splattered wood beside her. "I saw your butterfly books at a bookstore in London. It seems as if all the children in Great Britain love them."

She looked distressed again. "I can't make books anymore."

"Did Dad—" She stopped herself. "Did Walter write the stories for you?"

She nodded. "He was worried about me—he wanted me to have money after he was gone."

"So he found a publisher for them?"

Libby nodded.

"He took good care of you."

"I left home, for a long time." Libby stood up and walked toward the kitchen. She opened a cupboard, but instead of dishes inside, Heather saw the black-and-brown spines of four books. "He found me in London."

Libby lifted the journals out one at a time, stacking them up on the granite counter. Then she carried them across the room to Heather, setting them on the floor beside her. "Walter wrote a lot."

"Did you read them?" Heather asked.

"I can't—" She looked flustered again, and Heather remembered that Mrs. Westcott said Libby sometimes struggled with words.

"It's okay," Heather said, pulling the stack to her chest.

"I saved them—just for you."

"Thank you."

Libby clipped another piece of canvas onto her easel and hummed quietly as she began painting. Heather opened the first journal, her heart racing again. Her father might be gone, but part of him lived on in his words.

The papers liked to call it "the storm of the century."

A sense of foreboding swept over her as she read the first pages in his journals, the words about his regrets.

Had she been one of his regrets?

The story of his life unfolded from the pages, Walter's journey from the time he began caring for Maggie and her daughter, the child that wasn't his.

His words were gut-wrenchingly honest—the struggles he'd had raising a daughter who was so different. Yet once he decided to love her, it was relentless. He'd rescued Libby over and over through the years, from the moment on the promenade when Maggie leaned into the storm to when Libby was an adult, living with a man in London who didn't love her.

He'd found Libby again after Maggie died, searching for her artwork in studios across London until he located the "butterfly artist" who signed her pictures L.D. The studio didn't know her full name, but they knew the man who brokered her work, and when Walter found her that time, he'd refused to let her go again.

Tears slipped out of Heather's eyes, and she wiped them away before they smeared her dad's words. Libby wasn't Walter's birth daughter and yet he had rescued a broken woman, offering her healing and hope, and in his offering, he poured himself out.

She'd thought of her father as a man who'd lost his words, but the truth was Walter Doyle was a man of both words and action. In his journals, he focused on his faults more than his successes, but she knew the whole story. He'd sacrificed many of his dreams to care for Maggie and Libby and for her.

After Heather left for America he had mourned the loss. Deeply. Heather never knew he'd missed her like this. Nor did she know about the conflict in his heart after he found Libby, torn between caring for Libby and loving Heather from afar.

In hindsight, Heather had rejected him as well when she stopped trying to communicate after Mum died, her own pride and shame keeping her away. He might have been disappointed that she'd become pregnant before she married, but he would have forgiven her, like he had both Maggie and Libby. Dad had loved Libby in spite of all that happened and he'd loved Heather as well. And in his love, he'd tried to protect them both.

When she looked up again, she realized the sun was beginning to set. In the dimming light, she saw a new butterfly on Libby's canvas: this one the deep-green color of a stormy sea with silver tints to carry her wings.

"She's beautiful," Heather said. "What's her name?"

Libby studied her painting for a moment. "I was thinking Morning Glory—or perhaps—" Libby looked back at her, meeting her gaze this time, apprehension seeded on her face. "What do you think about Emerald Dawn?"

Heather stood. "I think it's perfect."

Libby turned back to her picture. "She searches for jewels early in the morning."

"Emerald Dawn," Heather repeated as she stepped forward, studying the picture beside her. "I think your princess needs her own book."

When Libby looked back, her eyes were sad again. "Walter is gone."

Heather paused for only a moment. "We'll find someone else to write her story."

40

Lady Sarah Croft Wyndham returned the telephone call while Heather and Libby were eating takeaway salad rolls on top of milk crates. Heather explained that she'd found Libby in Oxford and began to ask Sarah about her brother's death. Sarah politely stopped her, requesting instead that the three of them meet tomorrow at Ladenbrooke.

Heather glanced over at Libby and readily agreed.

Libby dug a blanket and two pillows out of a closet, and after texting Christopher about her plans, Heather slept remarkably well on the hardwood floor. The next morning she woke Libby up early and the two of them drove over to Bibury.

Libby refused to go through Ladenbrooke's main gate, choosing instead to walk up the pathway from the cottage, so Heather met Lady Wyndham by herself at the front entrance.

"Welcome to Ladenbrooke," Lady Wyndham said, holding out her gloved hand to shake Heather's hand. She was an elegant woman, approaching the age of seventy, and with her proper black-and-white linen dress, a fashionable black hat, and matching handbag, she looked as if she'd stepped away from a royal event for the day.

Wisteria climbed wild up the gray stone towers before the women. Several of the upper windows were cracked, birds roosting in the eaves above. The house looked rather lonely, as if it longed for the days when its rooms were filled with dances and teas and the feet of young Oliver, perhaps, pounding through the formal rooms while his parents were away.

When Libby joined them at the front of the house, Lady Wyndham stared at her for a moment, at the bright colors in her flowing, sleeveless dress, her bare feet. Then she extended her hand again.

Libby shook it.

Lady Wyndham stepped up to the door, but Libby didn't move.

"I've always gone through the servants' door," she explained.

"You're my guest now."

Libby hesitated. "I only want to know about Oliver."

Lady Wyndham removed a keychain from her handbag and unlocked the front door. "I'll tell you about him inside."

Light filtered through the front windows, casting shadows over the grand staircase that framed the front hall. Lady Wyndham directed them to the right, leading them along a corridor with worn red carpeting plastered with dust. There were bare spaces between the portraits on the wall, empty pedestals.

They passed a large hall with a piano, preserved under a sheath of white cloth, and Heather imagined the room once filled with clusters of elegant couches and chairs, people singing and dancing and sipping on glasses of champagne.

"My parents sold most of the furniture in the seventies," Lady Wyndham explained as they walked. "They didn't want to return, but they didn't want to sell the house either."

"What is your father planning to do with the property?" Heather asked.

"He doesn't want to do anything with it, but after his death, it will pass down to my brother, who will probably sell it."

They stepped into a dining room with tall windows and faded blue-and-gold wallpaper. Strips of the ceiling hung in shreds above a long table that was still centered in the room, eighteen upholstered chairs tucked in around it.

Outside the windows, Heather could see the terraces of old flower beds and empty pools. The ruined gardens in her dreams.

When she turned back, Lady Wyndham pointed at a space between two of the windows. "A giant oak sideboard used to stand right here, with an antique sculpted vase displayed on it. My mother loved all her valuables, but this one in particular was one of her favorite pieces."

Libby didn't seem to hear her. Her eyes were focused on a dusty portrait that hung over the vacant space. It was a picture of a young man, dressed in a black suit jacket and tie. His thick hair was parted on the left and combed neatly back, his smile stiff.

"Why didn't your parents take Oliver's portrait with them?" Heather asked.

"My dad thought Oliver needed to stay right here," Lady Wyndham replied, her voice sad.

"It's not right," Libby said, touching the edge of the canvas. "Oliver isn't smiling."

"Oliver rarely smiled," Lady Wyndham said. "Except, perhaps, when he was with you."

"He always smiled with me."

Lady Wyndham nodded. "That's because he loved you."

Both she and Libby turned toward Lady Wyndham, surprised by her words. Heather hadn't doubted Libby's story, but she didn't realize Oliver's family had known about their relationship.

Lady Wyndham opened a window, the fresh air mingling with

the dust, and pulled out one of the chairs. She sat down on it, seemingly unconcerned about the dirt ruining her attire as she stared up again at the portrait of her brother.

"We were all in this room the night Oliver died, eating lemon sole. He had just returned home from school, and he told my parents over dinner that he'd decided not to marry Judith Perdue. My father was irate, telling him that he had no choice . . ." She took a deep breath. "Then my mother dismissed the servants."

Heather glanced over at Libby. Her gaze was fixed on the gardens outside the window.

"I did a foolish thing next, not knowing of course what would transpire." Lady Wyndham paused again, sorting through her memories of the night. "I dared to ask Oliver whom he intended to marry, and he stopped for a moment, contemplating his words. Then he told my parents he planned to marry the girl next door."

A noise escaped from Libby's lips, a messy mixture of a gasp and cry.

Lady Wyndham was whispering now, and Heather stepped closer to hear her words. "Oliver said they couldn't stop him from marrying you, Libby, and my mother, she wasn't thinking—she grabbed the bronze vase from the hutch and said she could stop him. I think she intended to throw the vase, to scare him, but instead she lifted it up and brought it down over his head. The sound . . ." Her whisper trailed into silence as she turned again to look at the painting of her brother.

"My father should have called for an ambulance right then, but we were all so shocked. My mother was on the floor with Oliver, trying to revive him, and I remember thinking, There's no blood; he'll be okay as long as he isn't bleeding . . . but he wasn't okay."

Lady Wyndham stepped up to the portrait, her fingers grazing the edge of the canvas like Libby had done. "After that night, my parents and I plunged into despair. We all felt guilty for our part in what happened, and my father and I spent decades trying to protect Mother and ourselves, I suppose."

Libby moved away from the window. "There was a man that night in the gardens. He left Oliver in the river."

"My father took Oliver's body away that night," Lady Wyndham said. "I didn't know where he went at the time, but apparently he tried to make it look like Oliver drowned. I think the local police suspected that my parents were hiding something, because they dropped the case rather quickly. No one wanted to accuse Lord or Lady Croft of killing their son."

"All these years—" Libby said. "I thought if I'd tried harder, I could have rescued him from the river."

Lady Wyndham shook her head. "He was already gone."

The sadness of the room seemed to overcome all of them, the bitter secret that bound their families together.

"He loved me," Libby recited softly.

"Very much." Lady Wyndham's gaze wandered one more time to the somber-looking young man in the picture. "And he would have liked knowing you were here remembering him."

"I still miss him," Libby said.

"I miss him too." Lady Wyndham reached for Libby's hand, and for a moment, Heather felt like an outlier. Then Libby took her hand as well.

The three of them walked outside onto the patio and traversed down through the terraces together, under overgrown lime bowers and grape arbors, past acres of weedy flower beds, sleepy fountains, parched pools.

They walked through a copse of trees until they reached the riverbank where Libby told Lady Wyndham her story, to the best of her ability, of that night she'd found Oliver in the water.

Together they continued their walk, back to the cemetery tucked into the trees. There was a stack of old bouquets on Oliver's grave, and next to him was the headstone of Lady Croft, the mother who'd accidently taken the life of her son.

The people of Bibury might think the Croft family never returned to Ladenbrooke, but it appeared they came back in the shadows.

LIBBY STARED AT THE ENTRANCE to the overgrown maze, her heart stirring within her, and for a moment, it felt as if it might explode.

The memories of Oliver were everywhere: Along the riverbank. Among the trees. And most of all, in the folly that loomed before her. She once thought she could be closer to Oliver here, when she'd thought she needed him to be whole.

Decades she'd spent running away from her memories, the ghosts that taunted her with their whispers saying she could have saved Oliver if she'd pulled him out of the water before Walter arrived.

If only she'd been stronger. Smarter.

But Sarah said there had been nothing she could do. The lady killed him. Not Libby.

She had loved Oliver and Oliver loved her. He'd told his entire family that he wanted to marry her.

When Sarah left this afternoon, she said that as long as the Crofts owned these gardens, Libby was welcome to roam freely wherever she liked. There'd be no lock on the wrought-iron gate anymore.

The last time she'd been in these gardens her heart had

yearned to be free, but it was strange—this time, the familiar yearning was gone. Instead of wanting to run, Libby wanted to please the child she'd left behind. Help her understand why she'd had to go.

Still, she was afraid—afraid that Heather would be disappointed in her like so many other people had been. Except Walter. He'd stopped being disappointed in her that night they'd tried to save Oliver. And she'd stopped being disappointed in him.

On the days Walter came to her apartment, to write down the stories of her butterflies, he always prayed with her, that in their weaknesses—both his and hers—God would be strong. That she would rely on the Creator more than her own creation.

She needed that strength now to face her demons. To remember the good things about Oliver without so many of the regrets.

Before he went away, Walter said he was proud of her because she'd learned to be honest with him. Perhaps now she could make Heather proud as well.

She turned back and found Heather by the lily pond. "Do you want to see my—my special place?"

Heather hopped up from the bench. "Of course."

Libby motioned toward the aging yew bushes. "It's back here."

She guided her through the narrow path that remained between the bushes, like she'd guided Heather home when she was a child, the path as familiar to her feet as her paintbrushes were to her fingers.

The old tower stood strong above the yews. Several of the shutters were broken, but the window glass was intact. Heather opened the door, and they climbed the steps together.

Animal droppings covered the wooden floor and it looked as if rodents had picked through the old clothing and blankets. Libby stared at the floor for a moment, and then began to back away. She'd wanted Heather to see this place, where her memories of Oliver were once clear, but the memories of him here had faded.

Heather walked among the rubbish as if she was looking for something, pushing aside the blankets and old sketchbooks, the pages mildewed and torn. Then she reached down and flipped back the lid of a picnic basket.

Libby remembered Oliver bringing the basket, filled with sweet fruit from the orchard. She'd used it years later to collect pears and apples during the summers she'd pretended Oliver was still coming back to her.

Heather lifted one of Libby's sketchbooks out of the basket, and when she opened the cover, a soft gasp escaped from her lips. Stepping forward, Libby looked down at the first page in the book and then took it in her hands. It was wrinkled from moisture, and stained, but on it was a picture she'd sketched of Oliver, long ago.

When she saw his smiling face, distorted by the damage, her thoughts began to blur again, and her fingers twitched, longing to try to draw him one more time.

Heather reached out and took the picture from her. "I'll clean it up," she said simply as she placed it back in the basket.

Libby shook her head, fighting to regain clarity. "It's ruined . . ."

This time when Heather spoke, confidence bolstered her voice. "I can still fix his smile."

And in that moment, Libby realized that perhaps Heather could help her fix a lot of things. Perhaps, when God created her daughter, He'd created a pillar to help her stand.

They left the folly and maze behind and wandered up the pathway, to the sunlight in the rose garden.

"Do you know how to dance?" Libby asked.

"I haven't danced in years."

A butterfly flew past them, a vibrant indigo coloring its wings.

"I don't want this to be a place of sadness anymore," Libby said, watching the butterfly dip and then soar again.

Heather took her hand. "Then let's dance."

41

Before the sun rose, Heather took a quick shower and drank a cup of strong breakfast tea before hauling her old light table up from the basement. After replacing the bulb, she flipped on the switch.

Light illuminated the picture of Oliver, and she studied the wrinkles and stains on his face. He might have fathered her in the technical sense, but she'd never think of him as her dad. And in her heart, Libby would always be her sister.

Walter and Maggie Doyle had loved her as their daughter. They'd cared for her and protected her. They'd parented her in every sense of the word.

Last night, she and Libby laughed in the gardens over at Ladenbrooke as the moon chased away the sunlight. They'd laughed and they'd danced in the shadows. When the light was gone, Libby hadn't wanted to go back through the gate. She'd wanted to wade through the river.

And so they had done it. Holding hands in the same river where Libby had found Oliver, they gained back some of what they had lost.

Then Libby had stayed up late, painting more pictures of Emerald Dawn before falling asleep in her old bedroom upstairs.

Heather was glad she'd agreed to spend the night. In a way, Libby reminded her of Ella—sometimes scattered but full of love and laughter. This old cottage needed a good dose of both.

While Libby slept, Heather examined the picture of Oliver. It would take some work to fix it—like all good artwork took time to restore.

Oliver and Libby's love could never be restored in this life, nor could Heather tell her father how much she loved him. But perhaps it wasn't too late to restore all the broken relationships along with Oliver's smile.

It wasn't too late for Christopher and Ella.

Or Christopher and her.

Someone knocked on the door, and she slipped off her stool. Pushing back the curtain, she saw Daphne Westcott on the stoop and her heart somersaulted when she saw Mrs. Westcott's son standing behind her.

Quickly she twisted her wet hair back into a knot before opening the door, but with all the emotions churning inside her, she didn't dare look up at Christopher.

Mrs. Westcott's eyes were swollen, as if she'd been crying, and her hands were clutched to her chest. "I'm sorry we're so early," the woman said, though she didn't sound sorry at all. "We waited until the sun came up."

"I've been up for awhile," Heather said, her gaze fixed on Christopher's mother.

"Did you really bring Libby home?"

"I did."

"Maggie would be so glad." Tears sprang fresh in Mrs. Westcott's eyes, and she dabbed at them with her handkerchief. "Is she awake?"

"I don't know."

Mrs. Westcott glanced over at the doorway that led to the stairs. "When we were younger, I used to come play with Libby while Maggie worked. I'd have to wake her up in the morning."

"Would you like to wake her up now?" Heather asked.

"I suppose I do," Mrs. Westcott said as she scooted around her, though she paused before she walked upstairs. "My son needs to speak with you while Libby and I are visiting."

"Mum—"

"He has something important to say."

Christopher crossed his arms. "You told me you weren't going to meddle anymore."

"It's not meddling if you're speaking the truth."

Heather finally glanced up and saw him smiling back her.

THE MORNING SKY WAS STREAKED with a hundred shades of pink and yellow, the morning grass glimmering with dew. They were the colors of renewal. New life.

Libby's Emerald Dawn.

Christopher took Heather's hand and led her back into the garden where he'd proposed all those years ago. Instead of sitting on the bench, he sat on a rock across from her. "Heather, I . . ." His voice drifted off.

"What is it?"

Standing up, he paced to the edge of the garden, his hands in his pockets. Then he turned back to her. "I was hoping you might want to stay in England."

Heather didn't reply, not quite knowing what to say. She'd been living in the United States for more than twenty years now, and while Ella no longer lived in Oregon, she had a solid job in Portland and the city was laden with memories of Ella's childhood.

But then again, Ella seemed to love England, and there was plenty of art to be restored here.

And possibly art for her to create as well.

Perhaps it was time for her to put the memories behind her, from both Oregon and England. Perhaps it was time to embrace the next season of life as a sister to Libby and grandmother to Matthew and Ella's child and even—dare she hope—as a wife to the man before her.

"It might take me longer than I expected . . ." she said. "To prepare the cottage."

He sat down next to her on the bench. "Are you certain you want to sell it?"

"Yes."

He inched a bit closer to her, smiling. "You know what I think."

She wasn't completely certain she wanted to know, but he kept talking.

"I think my mum should buy the cottage from you. Libby can live with her here, and you can come to Oxford with me."

"Christopher—"

"Please, Heather," he begged. "I want to do it right this time."

Then he knelt on one knee in the grass, just like he'd done when they were younger and didn't have a clue what life would offer them. Now they were all too aware about the realities of life as they'd both stumbled and fallen. And got back up again.

But there was hope even in their failings. New beginnings.

He dug into his pocket and pulled out a brass ring with an opal, the same one he'd given her in 1988.

She smiled at him. "You kept it?"

"It was lost and then found up in our attic."

"I'm glad you found it."

"I'm going to buy you a diamond ring."

"I don't want a diamond," she said as she slowly held out her hand. "I want this one."

"You'll marry me?" he asked as if he'd almost forgotten his question.

"I will."

His kiss traversed deep through her veins, into the corners of her heart that needed to be restored, a kiss to heal the tears and stains.

And he didn't stop kissing her until her cell phone rang out, the loud drumbeat from Ella's call pulsing through the garden. Still, she didn't want him to let her go.

Christopher moved away from her, his smile warm. "Good timing, I think."

She sighed. "Welcome to parenthood," she said before she answered the phone.

EPILOGUE

A long line began forming outside *Bridget's Bookshop* before dawn, little noses smudging the window as a host of girls tried to glimpse inside. The line wrapped its way around the city block as hundreds of kids and their bedraggled parents waited on a Saturday morning to get one of the first copies of *Emerald Dawn*, personally signed by the elusive L.D. Walters.

Heather sat beside Libby at a table decorated with a bright blue cloth and dozens of butterflies.

Libby finally acknowledged illustrating all of the *Butterfly Princess* books, but she refused to reveal the wordsmith behind the stories. She told the reporter from *The Telegraph* last month that she wanted to honor an author who wished to remain anonymous—and Libby honestly didn't know, nor did she seem to care, who had taken over Walter's role.

Behind the table, Christopher bounced their grandson Oliver on his knee in the children's section. Oliver was barely a year old, but Christopher kept insisting that he was ready to read.

Heather thought their grandson was much more interested in the pictures.

Ella shuffled into the room with a cardboard box filled with coffee cups and lids, a vibrant-red scarf knotted around her neck.

She was far too chipper for the hour as she delivered an orange mocha to Libby and black tea to everyone else.

"Do you need anything else, Aunt Libby?" she asked.

Libby took a long sip of her drink. "Wings."

Ella winked at her. "You're not allowed to fly away until after lunch."

Libby smiled up at Ella, and Heather loved how her daughter seemed to lift Libby's anxiety away with her laughter.

"All you need to do is sign your name," Ella instructed. "My mum will do all the talking."

"Mom—" Heather muttered, but Ella was off through the back door to distribute hot tea to those who'd been waiting for hours. Ever since Ella had discovered both of her birth parents were British, she'd been calling Heather "Mum" and reading all sorts of British-born literature to Oliver.

Before her and Christopher's wedding last year, Heather had told her daughter the entire story—about Libby and Oliver, and Maggie and Elliot. About the courage and compassion of Walter Doyle.

Ella was thrilled to discover Libby was not only alive but also wanted to be an aunt to her. Others might think Libby was different, but Ella didn't seem to think she was the least bit odd. The first time they met, Ella told Libby that she'd researched her name and discovered it meant "God's Promise." After that, they'd quickly knitted together a friendship, and Libby even seemed to enjoy playing with little Oliver.

Somehow Mrs. Westcott—Heather's newly installed mother-in-law—had convinced Libby to live in Willow Cottage with her. The two of them seemed content in their new rhythm, Libby in her wandering and Mrs. Westcott in her renewed work escorting life into the world.

Libby eyed the front door again. "I still want to fly away."

"Where would you go?" Heather asked.

Conflict reigned in her eyes. "I don't know."

Heather glanced back at Christopher and Oliver then nodded at the window. "Because there are a whole lot of people who want you right here."

Libby nodded, her fingers twitching until Heather pulled a sketchbook out of her handbag. As Libby began to draw, her shoulders relaxed, and she started humming.

Heather opened the book on top of the stack to be signed, reading the first lines one more time, her heart full.

Heather turned back to smile at her husband, but he was much too enthralled with his grandson to see the throngs of children waiting to read his story about the real treasures in life.

Bridget pulled back the curtain on the front window before turning toward her guest. "Are you ready?"

At Libby's slow nod, Bridget unlocked the door, and Ella helped her prop it open. In seconds, the room flooded with wide-eyed girls wanting to meet the artist of the butterfly stories.

Stories about healing and redemption. Love and friendship.

Stories about shifting shadows and an armory full of color to drive the darkness away.

Emerald Dawn rises early before her sisters wake. With her smile, she charms the sun and chases clouds away. Diamonds hide among the silvery dew. Rubies shimmer in the roses. And she tiptoes through the castle garden to find their hiding spaces.

AUTHOR'S NOTE

Every shadow needs light, and this novel was my own exploration of God's light shining through the shadows of life along with the beauty and power of His restoration through generations.

Libby Doyle was a character that emerged deep from within my heart as a mom of two beautiful girls who love beautiful things. Libby isn't diagnosed in this story, but if she were born today, I believe her diagnosis would fall someplace under the umbrella of the "autism spectrum." In the 1950s and '60s, many doctors and psychologists believed autism was caused by emotionally distant mothers whose children then struggled socially as a result. Even if she loved her children, a mother of an autistic child was often condemned as a "refrigerator mom."

Heartbreaking for both mother and child.

Our family has both friends and loved ones on this spectrum, and we are grateful for the medical advances and education about autism today. However, even with more understanding, children with autism, Asperger's, or sensory processing issues are still sometimes rejected by adults and other children. The children on this spectrum are often incredibly bright and creative kids who look "normal" but struggle to communicate well or become easily frustrated or awkward in social settings.

Even with a diagnosis, guilt haunts many parents who are raising a child like Libby, and my desire through this story is to encourage moms and dads who are doing everything they can to love and instruct their children.

One of my favorite verses is 2 Corinthians 12:9: "My grace is all you need. My power works best in weakness."

If you are a mom or dad of a struggling child, I pray God's grace and peace would saturate every moment you spend with your son or daughter. That His strength would prevail in weakness.

There is an overwhelming amount of information about the autism spectrum online. If you are searching for more information or resources for your child, I recommend starting with these two websites:

www.autismspeaks.org

www.myasdf.org

To research this book, I spent a week touring England and fell in love with the English countryside and all the old manor homes, the wisteria growing on gray stone walls, the rambling lanes through brilliant yellow fields, and all the kind people who collaborated to help me with directions and bus schedules and finding a proper pot of English tea. I loved all the history in Oxford and was completely enchanted by the quaint villages and elegant gardens in the Cotswolds—everywhere I turned, I could see the beauty that inspired Libby's butterflies.

If you'd like to send me an e-mail or read more about my story, please visit my website at www.melaniedobson.com. I will have book club questions and pictures from my trip here as well.

Thank you for taking this journey with me.

ACKNOWLEDGMENTS

Long before the concept for this story began to develop, a host of people surrounded my husband and me with prayers and insight for our family's unique journey. Some people simply encouraged us while other professionals and friends educated us on the challenges of sensory processing. When a parent risks sharing his or her story of successes and failures, it gives others the strength to be vulnerable—and in that vulnerability, to find hope and healing.

In my own questions and doubts, as I begged God for wisdom in my life, Libby's story began to burn inside me. I'm grateful for each person who helped me put it onto paper.

Thank you first of all to my agent Natasha Kern for continuing to challenge, inspire, and encourage me as I wrote this story. You are an amazing mom and a blessing to each one of your clients.

Thank you to two other amazing moms—my editors Beth Adams and Jenny Baumgartner—for helping me weave together this novel. And to a wonderful group of moms who read my first drafts and gave me feedback as I wrote what I hoped would be a redemptive story—Janet Ainsworth, Kimberly Felton, Michele Heath, Ann Menke, and Jodi Stilp. I feel so blessed to have each one of you as a friend! Thank you for sharing your stories as you read mine.

To everyone who helped me plan or hosted me on my "whistle-stop" tour of England—a huge thank-you to Caroline Watts, Dominic Done, Kerstin Jeapes at Wycliffe Hall, and Bridget Baxter at The Old House in Calmsden, who went out of her way to help me find exactly what I needed in the Cotswolds. Paul and Sheila Herbert for your help before I left the States and then for traveling down to the Cotswolds to take me out for "bubble and squeak." It was such a pleasure to spend time with both of you. And Sheila—I so appreciate your answering my many "English" questions.

A special thanks to Evelyn Hamilton, who spent an entire day showing me the Cotswolds. Evelyn helped shape this book by graciously sharing her life and stories about growing up in a manor home in the 1950s and then becoming a special education teacher in England. We ended our day at Bibury Court, ordering a pot of tea along the River Coln. She said she thought Ladenbrooke should be set in this village, and she was exactly right!

Thank you to the entire staff at Howard Books including Becky Nesbitt, Amanda Desmastus, Chris McCarthy, Brandi Lewis, and Bruce Gore for designing the gorgeous cover to depict Ladenbrooke Manor. Shannon Geddes-Keene for your help understanding the process of art restoration, Jonathan Kiernan for sharing your memories about growing up in a village along England's coast, and occupational therapist extraordinaire Melissa Goodwin for educating me about the autism spectrum. Jodi Stilp for volunteering to photograph my dad and me for the dedication—it's a picture I will treasure for life. And to the ladies in my writer's group—Nicole Miller, Leslie Gould, Dawn Shipman, and Kelly Chang—thank you for all your encouragement and insight as I wrote this story.

Dobby and Carolyn Dobson—thank you for traveling across the country to help care for my family while I was in England. I am incredibly blessed to have you as my dad- and mom-in-law. To my parents, Jim and Lyn Beroth, for your consistent love and support and continuing to cheer me on as I pursue the dreams God has placed in my heart. Love you so much . . .

To my husband, Jon, and our daughters, Karlyn and Kinzel, for pouring yourself into every new book alongside me. I'm so grateful for each of your prayers and encouragement and the sacrifices you made so I could put this story about Libby onto paper.

And to my Lord and Savior Jesus Christ who remains the same yesterday and today and forever. I'm confident that He is weaving together a beautiful story in the lives of all who love Him—a story of hope, redemption, and ultimately transformation.

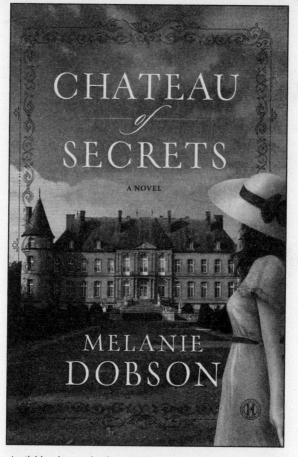